SPECIAL MESSAGE TO READERS

This book is published under the auspices of

THE ULVERSCROFT FOUNDATION

(registered charity No. 264873 UK)

Established in 1972 to provide funds for research, diagnosis and treatment of eye diseases. Examples of contributions made are: —

A Children's Assessment Unit at Moorfield's Hospital, London.

•

Twin operating theatres at the Western Ophthalmic Hospital, London.

•

A Chair of Ophthalmology at the Royal Australian College of Ophthalmologists.

•

The Ulverscroft Children's Eye Unit at the Great Ormond Street Hospital For Sick Children, London.

You can help further the work of the Foundation by making a donation or leaving a legacy. Every contribution, no matter how small, is received with gratitude. Please write for details to:

THE ULVERSCROFT FOUNDATION,
The Green, Bradgate Road, Anstey,
Leicester LE7 7FU, England.
Telephone: (0116) 236 4325

In Australia write to:
THE ULVERSCROFT FOUNDATION,
c/o The Royal Australian College of Ophthalmologists,
27, Commonwealth Street, Sydney, N.S.W. 2010.

Ann Barker was born in Bedfordshire. She is a part-time music teacher, and in her spare time she enjoys reading, cooking, and taking breaks in the family holiday home in Norfolk. She lives in Berkshire.

HIS LORDSHIP'S GARDENER

Arriving home after three years' absence, Lord Lyddington discovers that his sister is having his garden remodelled. The Earl is pleased to discover a roistering companion in his gardener's nephew, 'Master' Sutcliffe. However, young Sutcliffe is not all he seems, and soon the Earl is obliged to reassess his previous ideas concerning appropriate female behaviour and attire. Meanwhile, someone seeks to sabotage the garden alterations, viciously attacks Sutcliffe senior and even assaults the Earl himself. Who could be responsible? The Earl's happiness depends on a swift resolution of this matter.

ANN BARKER

HIS LORDSHIP'S GARDENER

Complete and Unabridged

ULVERSCROFT
Leicester

First published in Great Britain in 1999 by
Robert Hale Limited
London

First Large Print Edition
published 2001
by arrangement with
Robert Hale Limited
London

British Library CIP Data

Barker, Ann
His lordship's gardener.—Large print ed.—
Ulverscroft large print series: romance
1. Detective and mystery stories
2. Large type books
I. Title
823.9′14 [F]

ISBN 0–7089–4328–4

Published by
F. A. Thorpe (Publishing)
Anstey, Leicestershire

Set by Words & Graphics Ltd.
Anstey, Leicestershire
Printed and bound in Great Britain by
T. J. International Ltd., Padstow, Cornwall

This book is printed on acid-free paper

For my parents

Prologue – 1811

'Hell's teeth!' swore his lordship, reining in his horse and looking about him. 'Where the devil has it gone?'

It was a perfectly pardonable question. For as long as anyone could remember, this spot had been if not adorned, at least occupied, by the village of Lyddington Over. True, it had been small, unremarkable, and rather unattractive for the most part. Nevertheless, it had certainly been there. Now it wasn't.

This put his lordship into something of a quandary. Rising a little in the saddle, he glanced around him. Ampthill hill rose over to his left in the gathering dusk, at precisely the distance that it should from the village and, much closer at hand, he could make out the dim outline of his own park gates; but of the village itself there was no sign. Only the church loomed, looking large and threatening in its solitude.

'What the devil do I do now? Go home, I suppose.'

He had already sent his groom, Ruddles, back to Lyddington Court to prepare for his return. Now, reluctantly, he turned his horse in its direction, and in so doing, he noticed a few twinkling lights towards his right in the near distance. He could not understand why he had only just noticed them, and put it down to his preoccupation in thinking about reaching Lyddington Over, and more particularly, the Lyddington Arms, for it must be understood that the earl was a convivial soul, and had always rather been inclined to prefer a cosy night at the local hostelry to a solitary evening with a fine bottle of brandy and a book. His sister and his late wife had both frequently remonstrated with him concerning his plebeian tastes, but never to any avail.

There had never been any kind of habitation there that he could remember. He hesitated, half wanting to go home, now that he had almost made the decision to do so. Then curiosity, one of his besetting sins, got the better of him, and he nudged his mount with his heels, urging it forward. They were both tired, so his lordship contented himself with an easy walking pace. In any case, he was not so sure of the surface underfoot, and it was too dark to see properly.

As they drew nearer to the lights, it became clear that it was a small village of some kind.

'Odd,' murmured the earl. 'There's never been one here before. Well, I hope there's an inn.'

It was an extremely neat, modern village, with a remarkably classical look to it. Clearly it had not been in existence long, for some houses were still being worked on, but it was the inn that caused him to rein in, or rather the inn sign, which was immediately the object of his wrathful astonishment.

The Lyddington Arms, it proudly proclaimed itself to be; and there was his very own coat of arms to prove it.

'The devil it is,' declared his lordship forcefully, as he dismounted. 'Take this,' he snapped at the ostler, and made his way to the entrance of the inn, flinging the door open. 'Landlord!' he roared with all the force his voice could muster — and that was not inconsiderable. A hush fell upon the assembled locals and the landlord hurried out from the tap room.

'My Lord!' he exclaimed, grinning from one fat ear to the other. 'Lord Lyddington! Well, this is a happy day and no mistake. Mary!' he called to the girl who was serving. 'A tankard of home-brewed for His Lordship!'

Lord Lyddington stood stock still, his firm, square jaw looking uncommonly as if it might drop at any moment, his dark eyes full of surprise. Then he laughed ruefully, and came forward to grip the landlord warmly by the shoulders.

'Sam! Stap me if it isn't good to see you! But how comes this about? Where is the old Lyddington Arms? And what happened to the village, come to that?'

'Come and sit by the fire will you, My Lord, and I'll tell you the whole story.'

They moved over to the fireplace, and those who had been occupying places there needed no prompting to move, most of them already getting up with a touching of forelocks, and comments like 'Good health to Your Lordship,' or 'It's good to see Your Lordship back home.'

The earl was a popular master. In the opinion of his tenantry, he raged and stormed and swore and drank just as a gentleman should, and they adored him for it — a fact which would have surprised him considerably.

It must be said, however, that this adoration stemmed to a large degree from the fact that those who knew him were well aware that beneath the bluster was an honourable gentleman with a very kind heart. No tenant farmer needed to hesitate to ask him for more time to pay if the reason was just; no servant was ever afraid of him and no maidservant at the Court had ever had to return to her family in disgrace because of his lordship's familiarities.

During the earl's absence, his estate had been ruled over by his sister, a competent and just woman. But there was not a man present in the inn that evening who was not heartily glad to see the 'real' master back.

The earl now took time to look about him and realized that the homely touches given to the inside of this inn very closely resembled those of the old one, and also that he recognized many of the faces of those greeting him. He drew his heavy dark brows together.

'Come now, Sam. Explain everything to me — but draw one for yourself first.'

The two men settled by the fire, and when they had both taken a mouthful of home-brewed, and Lyddington had sighed with satisfaction, Sam spoke.

'Well now, My Lord, I take it that you know there've been a few alterations up at the Court,' he enquired carefully.

'Yes, I know — put about by m'sister. She's written to me about them. Many times.' Lyddington thought a little guiltily of the letters that he had received and often stuffed into the capacious pockets of his coat, not even bothering to read them until later, and then sometimes not in their entirety. 'Go on.'

'Well, it seems that some of these folk that

make big changes to their houses like to move the village. Get it out of the way, if you take my meaning.'

'Out of the way? Devil if I do. You know, this is even better than I remember it, Sam. Pull me some more — and something to chase it down.'

'Right you are, M'Lord.' Sam signalled to the girl then went on, 'Well it seems that landowning people such as yourself like to have a pleasant view from their property — and who's to blame them? And they like their guests to see pleasant things when they arrive. And you can't deny, M'Lord that Wal Seekings's place was anything but pleasant so . . .'

'God in Heaven!' exclaimed his lordship. 'You mean, m'sister had the whole village knocked down and moved — lock stock and barrel — without a word to me? So she wouldn't have to see Wal Seekings's cottage?'

Again he thought of those letters, but reflected that he had generally managed to read the first half of most of them, and that such an important piece of news would surely be in the first half of any letter, and that if it wasn't it damn well ought to be.

'That's about the size of it, M'Lord. Without a word to anyone, as far as I know. Very sudden, it was. She's a formidable woman, is Her Ladyship.'

'Bossy old bitch, you mean,' muttered his lordship into his tankard. Sam, quite understandably, had no comment to make on that head, but simply made sure that the wherewithal was at hand to fill his lordship's tankard whenever required.

'Not that it hasn't been an improvement for the most part,' said Sam thoughtfully. 'None of the roofs leak, and we're a mite closer to Bedford. Took the carrier's wagon a time or two to find us, though. And no one's sure what to do about the church as yet.'

'But hell and devil confound it,' declared his lordship, thumping the table at which he sat. 'I shall have twice as far to travel in order to come here!'

This was such a distressing consideration to him, that it took Sam a considerable amount of liquid refreshment to accustom his lordship to the idea. So grateful was the earl that before his departure, he paid handsomely for what he had drunk, and also for drinks for the locals, which largesse was very much appreciated.

Having bade Sam a polite goodnight, he made his way carefully to the door, and went out to where the ostler was waiting with his horse.

* * *

Miss Marigold Stevenson checked in the mirror to make sure that her braids were precisely the same length. Yes; most satisfactory. Noticing a small fly mark on the mirror, she frowned slightly. She looked around her immaculately tidy room, but there was nothing she could use with which to wipe off the mark. It could, of course, wait until the morning, but she might not be able to sleep, knowing that the mark was there.

She sighed. What a shame that maids had to be so careless! Her slippers were set side by side, their heels lining up to part of the pattern on the carpet. She put them on her feet and fastened her dressing-gown, beginning at the middle button and working upwards, then working down to the bottom.

She took up her candle, opened the bedroom door, and walked down the stairs, taking great pleasure in their neatness and regularity. She had not been sorry to move to this house. Of course, the upheaval of actually moving had been dreadful. But she had rather enjoyed the business of finding places for everything; and certainly the classical regularity of this house was infinitely preferable to the rather untidy design of the one she had inhabited before.

She made her way to the kitchen and opened the drawer where dusters were kept. She took one out carefully, so as not to disturb the others. She was about to leave the kitchen, when she heard a scratching noise outside.

'Oh no, not a fox!' she exclaimed. 'All those paw marks across the flower beds.'

She put her candle down on the table, and cupped her hand to the window. The moon was full and she could see quite well. There was no fox in sight, so perhaps it had just been a night bird. Heaven forbid that it might be a mole!

She was striving to make her garden as perfect as her house. Nature often seemed to be against her, but she was gradually beating it down.

She could not quite make out her carnations, but she knew exactly where they were — in a neat row, about a foot away from her white wooden fence. They would soon attain perfection. Then, everyone would see who would win the Daughters of Flora carnation competition. In her imagination, she could almost see Lady Valeria smiling approvingly as she examined the exquisite blooms.

She was about to practise her curtsy when suddenly the fence appeared to shudder

— no, not just shudder, but to wobble and then to fall — horror of horrors — onto those precious blooms!

Without a second thought, Miss Stevenson hurriedly unbolted the door and ran outside, seizing the first thing that came to hand, which happened to be a small hoe, standing just outside.

Closer to the disaster, the reason for its occurrence became all too apparent. Next to the fence, cropping the grass and anything else it could get its jaws round was a strong-looking thoroughbred horse. Seated on the broken-down fence was a large, dark and rather drunken gentleman.

'Damnation! I think I've broke my ankle!' he exclaimed. 'And what the devil is this pile of firewood doing here?'

'That, sir, is my fence!' said Miss Stevenson, her voice trembling. 'And those were my carnations!' and so saying, she advanced upon him, her hoe raised.

1

Lyddington Court would never have figured as a fashionable place to visit, but those who knew it, loved it. In an age when taste was everything, it was a tribute to no one's taste, precisely because everyone who had lived there had added something to give themselves pleasure, but had knocked nothing down.

In life, there are people who hoard; people who never give anything away, either because they love it, or because 'one never knows when it might come in handy'.

The Sarrell family were in the main mostly hoarders by nature, and none had yet wanted to tear down any part of what had been built and was always seen as a family home. There had been Sarrells living there in the fifteenth century, but at that time, the castle where they lived had been up on Ampthill hill, looking out not towards Bedford, but in the direction of Woburn and Dunstable, and taking in the little village of Lidlington. It was from that village that the first earl had taken his title, when it was bestowed upon him by Queen Elizabeth I.

In the days when there was a castle there,

there was also a castle at Bedford, which took precedence. It was this, as much as anything, that caused the second earl, perhaps the most ruthless of the family historically, to decide that the days of castles were done. He tore down most of the castle, leaving an interesting ruin on the hill, and built a manor house nestling in a more sheltered position at its foot.

Around the gates of the new house, a village grew to serve its inhabitants — in fact, the self-same village which had just recently been demolished. This was named Lidlington Over, in order to distinguish it from the original village of Lidlington. Visitors interested in historical detail were apt to ask for the significance of the word 'over'. They were generally disappointed to have explained to them that the word was used to signify the Lidlington 'over there' as opposed to the original one.

Time went by and words changed their pronunciation, until eventually, by the time of Charles II, the village's name, and the earl's title, were both settled as Lyddington.

It was the second earl who had built the main central area of the house, with its hall, adjoining kitchen area and parlour, and great chamber with other chambers above, together with a chapel. Thankfully for the solvency of the Sarrells, he offended the queen by marrying against her will — not greatly, but enough to ensure that she never paid him one of those royal visits, so cripplingly expensive for the host.

A succeeding Sarrell added the gatehouse, long after such fortified entrances were necessary. However, no later Sarrell ever had the heart to tear it down; and anyway, it was useful for housing visitors. A later, Palladian-minded Sarrell, tried to make the house symmetrical, but with very little success, as his sentimental nature would not allow him to demolish anything that was already there. The result of all this activity over the generations was a real hotchpotch of styles which pleased no one of an artistic bent, but which felt like home to those who inhabited it.

The present Earl of Lyddington — the ninth — had gone away leaving his sister *carte blanche*, for he had had every confidence in her ability to handle all matters of business. Of course, it had not occurred to him that she might demolish an entire village, or he would almost certainly have prohibited it. However, the villagers seemed perfectly happy, as far as he could tell.

As for his own house, other than redecoration, the building of an orangery and the total reorganization of his garden, she had not touched the fabric of the place, and that was what mattered to him. He had never had any real fear that she would change his home in any essentials. She was too much of a Sarrell for that.

The parlour in the oldest part of the house was where the earl took most of his meals when he was not entertaining. It was a cosy room, with a low ceiling, exposed beams, and wood panelling. Instead of the original flagstones, the floor had been lined with wood and carpeted, and on winter days, it was one of the warmest rooms in the house.

It was in this room that Lady Valeria Cardingholme found her brother, Spencer Stephen Sarrell, Lord Lyddington, seated in a chair by the fire — for although it was June, the weather was unseasonably chilly — enjoying a hearty breakfast, his bandaged foot resting on a stool.

'Good morning, Spencer,' she said briskly, helping herself to scrambled eggs and toast from the chafing dish. 'You have always wanted an excuse not to rise when I enter the room, and now you have found it.'

'Damnation, Valeria, have a little sympathy,' responded his lordship with a wry grin. 'I spent the whole of yesterday in bed, remember. Pour me some more ale, there's a good girl.'

'I'm sure I don't know why I should,' replied her ladyship, obliging nevertheless. 'After all, you brought this entirely upon yourself.'

'Brought it . . . ' His lordship's voice faded away in wrathful astonishment.

'Yes, brought it upon yourself. And do not try to tell me that you were not as drunk as a . . . a . . . '

'Skunk? Newt? Wheelbarrow?' suggested the earl helpfully.

'Yes, any of those! Because I should not believe it.'

'Well, and what of it? If an Englishman ain't entitled to get roaring drunk on his own land, then it's the first I've heard of it. And if it hadn't been for this leg, I would have been up on my feet, as polite as any dashed courtier.'

Lyddington forked up a mouthful of cold beef from the tray set on the table at his right hand, followed it with a piece of bread and butter, and washed the whole down with a draught of ale. Her ladyship turned away disdainfully.

'I might have guessed you would find an excuse for not sitting at the table as well.'

'If you can find a means whereby I can get

this under the table then I shall be happy to join you,' said he, pointing to his bandaged foot.

'I presume the doctor will be returning to look at it again,' remarked his sister.

'Mmm,' replied the earl, failing for some reason to look her in the eye. Her ladyship regarded him intently, instantly mistrustful of his change in manner.

'Spencer, the doctor has been, hasn't he? Did he come when I was over at the home farm?' she asked.

'It's not broken,' said the earl blithely. 'It's just a severe strain. I've got to keep off it for a few days.'

'Spencer, who saw it?' asked his sister suspiciously.

'Ruddles looked at it for me,' said his lordship, again not looking at her.

'Ruddles!' exclaimed Lady Valeria almost in a shriek. 'You asked your groom to look at your ankle?'

'Well, you know, when Bessy strained a fetlock . . . '

'Spencer, you are not a horse with a strained fetlock, you are a peer of the realm!'

'Yes, I am!' replied the earl vigorously. 'And I'm damned if some managing female — '

'Who happens to be your sister — '

' . . . whoever she is, is going to dictate to

me what I do with my health. When my leg drops off, then you can send for the doctor. Will that suit you?'

'You know perfectly well that will not suit me at all!' retorted her ladyship, 'for despite your excessive obstinacy, I am disposed to be fond of you. You are, after all, the only brother I have.'

Lyddington smiled.

'My dear sister, such an admission deserves a reward, so allow me to say that I like the new colour scheme in the dining-room. It's a vast improvement, I find.'

Lady Valeria coloured slightly with pleasure. She had put a great deal of thought into the decorations that she had chosen, and always at the back of her mind had been the consideration that the previous Lady Lyddington — the earl's late wife — had been responsible for the choosing of them.

She had never really understood the relationship that had existed between Spencer and Alfreda Comberley. Certainly, he had courted and married the well-dowered beauty within a very short space of time, and the match between the season's greatest toast and London's greatest care-for-naught had been the talk of the town. Such was the speed of the courtship that it was rumoured to be a love match. Despite such rumours, however, once wed, they had gone their own ways, as did many fashionable couples.

When six months with child, the Countess of Lyddington had travelled home from London, making a diversion to her parents' home in Cambridgeshire, and leaving her husband behind in town; it was to be her last visit to them before her lying in. Indeed, it had proved to be a last visit altogether, for the night before she was due to leave them, a raging fire had all but destroyed Comberley Hall, taking with it many lives, including that of the countess, her parents, and her unborn child.

Upon his bereavement, the earl had conducted himself with all the solemnity and dignity that might have been expected of one in his situation. But he did not remain in England long, and indeed during the fifteen years since his wife's death, he had been out of the country for longer than he had been in it, and the latest absence had been for three unbroken years.

Her mind dwelling on these facts, her ladyship found herself saying, 'For how long are you staying this time?'

'I'm not at all sure,' he replied, passing his tankard for more ale. 'Long enough to inspect all the changes, at any rate. Which reminds me, why the devil did you move

Lyddington Over?'

'It was no longer fashionably situated,' said Lady Valeria defensively. 'And besides, you did say that I might do what I pleased.'

'Did I really? I must have been demented. And in any case, I was referring to my own home. I didn't say you could do what you pleased with anyone else's. Did you ask them?'

'Ask them? Certainly not,' retorted her ladyship haughtily. 'It is your village, after all.'

'Yes, I know. But it's their home. Only the circumstances of most of them seeming to feel that they like it better now reconciles me to the idea.'

Lady Valeria looked a little offended.

'I only wanted to help, after all . . . ' she began.

'Stuff and nonsense,' retorted his lordship good humouredly. 'What you wanted was to be in charge. You've nobody to boss about at your house in Bath, and Charlotte's husband would soon send you packing if you tried it at Sunnings, so my house is ideal. Well, I don't mind, in fact, I think you've done a fine job; I've just said so. But there are limits; and I think that in moving Lyddington Over without my express approval, you crossed those limits. That's all.'

Lady Valeria stood up, utterly speechless,

and absolutely furious. Then at last, her bosom swelling, she managed to give voice to an outraged 'Ooh!' whereupon she swept majestically from the room, leaving the earl chuckling to himself.

* * *

The unpleasant atmosphere between brother and sister did not last long; it never did. The earl had always been able to wheedle his way around his sister. While she was seated in the newly decorated drawing-room, totally ignoring the fine view of the terrace, and instead stabbing her needle viciously into a piece of embroidery that would never be the same again, he came upon her, grinning ruefully and assisted by two impassive footmen. Her temper was no more resentful than was her brother's, and she found herself returning his grin with one so alike that no one seeing them at that moment could possibly have failed to recognize them as brother and sister.

She put down her embroidery, but knew better than to try and help him to his chair.

'I'm glad you approve of some of the things I've done,' she remarked.

'Of all of them, to be honest,' he replied, after a word of thanks to the footmen who then effaced themselves. 'Even the village;

although I have to say that it is the apparent improvement in the condition of the houses themselves that I approve; not the moving of the village.'

'Only because it means you will have to ride further in order to get drunk at the Lyddington Arms.'

'There have been worse reasons for leaving something where it is. Now tell me about the gardens.'

Her ladyship immediately became animated.

'Ah yes, the gardens. I have put a great deal of time and thought into what to do about them, and at length I have decided to employ one Thomas Sutcliffe.'

Lyddington drew his brows together.

'Sutcliffe? I don't believe I've heard of him.'

'No, perhaps not, but he comes very highly recommended, and he worked under Repton for a time. His plans are very impressive.'

'I should like to meet him, and also to see these plans.'

'I believe that they are laid out in the steward's room,' she replied.

'Then I had better go there,' replied the earl, making as though to stand, and realizing again his incapacity. 'Damn!' he declared forthrightly, then lifting his voice, he bellowed, 'James! Frederick!'

'Spencer, really,' murmured his sister, in the long-suffering tones of one who has said a thing many times and never been heeded. 'There are such things as bells, you know.'

The footmen hurried in, and helped his lordship to his feet, for which service he thanked them politely, but with gritted teeth. He was a vigorous, active man, and hated to be so dependent upon another for the smallest thing.

On arrival in the steward's room, he found to his consternation, a completely empty table and no steward visible.

'Confound it,' he declared irritably, once settled in a highbacked wooden chair with arms. 'Frederick, go and see if you can find the steward. And James, make sure that m'sister meant the steward's room and not the book-room, will you?'

Both of the footmen departed on their different errands, and the earl sat impatiently, drumming his fingers on the table top. Eventually, the door opened, but to the earl's surprise it did so to admit a complete stranger. It was a young man dressed neatly and with propriety and wearing a close brown wig. He was slightly built, but there was in his step a resilience that hinted at wiry strength. At sight of his lordship, he bowed politely, whilst the earl knit his thick dark brows.

'Who the devil are you?' he asked.

'I am Masters, My Lord,' said the young man with wary respect, as he moved forward into the room.

'I'm none the wiser,' retorted the earl. 'Perhaps I should rather have said, 'what the devil are you doing in my house'?'

'I . . . I am your agent, My Lord,' replied the young man, rapidly losing any self-assurance that he might have had to start with.

For several long moments, the earl stared at him in silence, then, in tones of fury, he exclaimed, 'God in heaven, am I to be treated like a child at every turn? Upon my honour, it appears that I had best never leave again, for fear of what might occur! Whole villages are destroyed, my house is altered beyond recognition, plans that I have a perfect right to peruse are not available to me, and the management of my estate is given over to a . . . a babe in arms. What is the meaning of this, and where the devil is Bobkiss?'

'Spencer, you would try the patience of a saint,' said his sister, who had come in behind him. 'You know perfectly well that you have been pleased to approve the changes that I have made to the Court, whilst the business of the village has been settled. There is absolutely no need for you to rip up at Masters in that dreadful style.'

Masters looked apprehensively from brother to sister. Such a speech would surely only incense the earl further, were that possible. However, after a moment or two, the earl responded in a far more moderate tone.

'You are right as always, Valeria. Your pardon, Masters; but I would still like to know how you come to be here.'

'What I should like to know,' interposed Lady Valeria, giving Masters no chance to speak, 'is what has happened to all the letters that I have sent you, Spencer? I have informed you in writing of every decision that I have taken, but you disclaim knowledge of any of them. I wrote to you some months ago, telling you that Bobkiss has had to retire because of ill health, and that I was taking on Masters who comes strongly recommended by my friend, Rosemary Ferrier. You, however — '

'Thank you, Valeria,' said his lordship firmly. 'You have now very thoroughly put me in my place and can have nothing more to say! Don't be afraid on Masters' account; I shan't bully him any more.'

'Women,' said the earl in accents of loathing as the door closed. 'Take my advice,

Masters, and never marry. Women are the very devil.' He smiled quizzically at the young man as he spoke. Masters inclined his head slightly in acknowledgement that his lordship had spoken; but in his eyes there remained a slight wariness, and not a flicker of humour. Leaving the subject, therefore, the earl continued in a businesslike manner, 'Now, two things I want to be satisfied about straight away: what provision has been made for Bobkiss and his wife?'

'They have been given a cottage on the estate, My Lord,' said Masters, still feeling nervous. 'They have already moved in. And Lady Valeria arranged for them to have a pension.'

The earl nodded his approval of these arrangements.

'I shall require you to show me where they are as soon as I can get about again. I shall want to visit them. The other thing I want to know is, why you come so strongly recommended when you are so young, and whether you can give me evidence that you can actually do the job?'

'My father is agent to Mr Cuthbert Ferrier,' explained Masters, feeling a little more confident now that he was on more certain ground. 'I grew up learning about land management. When I left school, my father sent me to the North of England to gain experience on another estate. I then felt myself to be competent to take on the job of agent in my own right. It was just a question of waiting for the right opportunity. Mrs Ferrier heard that an agent was needed here, and she recommended me for the post.'

'Very strongly, according to my sister,' added the earl, not quite liking the way the young man's explanation had seemed to come out pat, but not really sure why. 'Well, time will tell. I'm fussy about my people and how they're treated, and when I'm here you'll find that I take a very close interest in what's mine. That's why I'm here to look at these garden plans, and yet I see no sign of them. Where are they?'

'My Lord, I confess that I am at a loss,' replied Masters, scratching his forehead and coming perilously close to dislodging his wig. 'Strictly speaking, of course — '

'They are not your responsibility, yes, I know that, Masters. But when I am informed that the plans have been laid out in the estate office — your domain, you will agree — and after I have found two footmen to transport me here at a cost of no little discomfort, I am sure that you will also agree that I am entitled to feel aggrieved when confronted with an empty table.'

'Yes ... yes, of course, My Lord,' murmured Masters, looking under the table, behind it, and on any other surface that might conceivably have housed them. 'I cannot imagine where ... perhaps one of the gardeners ... '

His voice faded away as he met the ironic gaze of his lordship, seated in a chair at the side of the table.

'Or maybe a housemaid has lit a fire with them,' he suggested. 'Oh, enough, man. It seems to me that everything is prone to disappear these days, from villages to agents, to new garden designs. In their absence, I'll take a look at the alterations themselves, as far as they've gone, before they too disappear like morning mist. James! Frederick!' he roared in a sudden change of tone that made Masters start visibly. The two footmen returned hurriedly. 'Fetch the sedan chair. I'm going outside.'

* * *

When Lady Valeria had decided to employ Thomas Sutcliffe as her garden expert, it had seemed obvious that the gatehouse would be a good lodging for him. It was very near to his work, and it also meant that it would be very convenient to consult him in case of need. Without lodging him in the house, it also acknowledged that he was a gentleman by birth.

For his part, Thomas Sutcliffe found the situation very acceptable. There had been occasions when he had been lodged at an inconvenient distance away from his work, and that had caused all kinds of problems. Here, the only problem was that of being under rather close scrutiny from the inhabitants of the Court; but this had not proved to be a difficulty so far.

The gatehouse was very comfortable, once one got used to the way in which things were arranged. It straddled the drive just as it drew close to the house, so there were two entrances to it, one on either side of the roadway on the side facing the great house. On the left, was the formal entrance, leading into a small hall, and it was through this entrance that most visitors came; on the right, there was an office, with a kitchen leading off it.

At one time, the kitchens of the Court itself had served the gatehouse. Then, about a hundred years previously, a member of the family had caught smallpox, and had been isolated in the gatehouse. It had been perceived then what an advantage it would be to have the ability to isolate the gatehouse completely.

The gatehouse kitchens were still under the authority of the cook at the Court, and food there was prepared by one of her pupils. Foodstuffs were provided by the main kitchens; so it would often happen that the Sutcliffes would have the same food as was being eaten at the Court, but not always prepared with the same skill.

Above the archway which passed over the drive, were situated a dining-room, a small sitting-room, and a book-room. Above these rooms were the bedrooms in which Thomas and his daughter, Frances, slept. Ruby, who had been Frances' nursemaid and then her maid for many years, had a room next to her mistress, and Thomas's valet, who also acted as footman, slept next door to him. There were further rooms in the attics which were not used at present.

On the same morning when his lordship had angered his sister by not rising from the table, Thomas Sutcliffe and his daughter were also having breakfast, though somewhat earlier than the earl and his sister's repast. Any onlooker would have been forgiven for thinking that two men were sitting at the table, for Frances was dressed in serviceable coat and breeches, and a dark tie wig.

'Have you heard yet when you are to meet

the earl?' asked Frances, pouring herself more coffee. Limited as they were in their numbers of staff, they always waited upon themselves at table.

'I believe that he wishes to see me later today, after he has examined the plans,' replied her father. 'I must admit to feeling a little apprehensive about that meeting.'

'Why is that? You know that your work is satisfactory — more than satisfactory! It has been commended by all your past clients — after all, that is why you received the commission. You have nothing to be anxious about.'

'No,' agreed her father doubtfully. 'But the commission was given not by the earl but by his sister. They may have widely differing views on what is pleasing in a garden.'

'Perhaps,' agreed his daughter. 'But nevertheless, if anyone is at fault, it is not you.' Deciding that a change of subject might put the worry out of his mind, she went on quickly, 'What are your plans today?'

'I think that I ought to get on with some of the tree-moving that we agreed upon, in order to make the wilderness a little more substantial, and clear some of the area where we want the new beds to be. What of you?'

'If you do not need my help, then I think I will get on with the water garden.'

She got up from the table. At 5′ 6″ she was tall for a woman, and fortunately not built so generously that she was unable to get away with male attire.

'In any case, since he did not give you the commission he may take no more than a cursory interest,' she said. 'He is probably only asking to see the plans for form's sake.'

She went up to her room where Ruby, a small dark woman in her late thirties was mending a shirt with every evidence of distaste. She had come into the Sutcliffe household as a nursery maid when Frances was a little girl. Frances' mother had died giving birth to her, and Nanny Grigson, who took care of the little motherless girl soon found the work too much for her, as she had been nanny to the deceased Mrs Sutcliffe in years gone by. Soon, all of the nursery work fell onto Ruby's shoulders and, as Frances grew up, Ruby became her dresser, mother, and companion. She had never liked Frances' masquerade, and time had not reconciled her to it, but not for anything would she have been parted from her mistress.

'I've a bad feeling about this one,' she said without round-aboutation as Frances came in. Frances crossed the room in easy strides, for all the world as if she were really the youth that she pretended to be, and kissed her on the forehead.

'Dear Ruby, you always say that,' she said smiling, 'and there has never been a problem so far.'

'Yes, but you've never been so close to the great house,' Ruby pointed out. 'Right under his eye, you'll be. And don't tell me that a man of the world like his lordship is said to be won't see through your disguise in the twinkling of an eye.'

'He won't notice me,' said Frances reassuringly as she picked up her notebook. 'I'll probably be far below his well-bred nose. Anyway, most people only see what they expect to see. Once the earl has seen the plans he'll be off on his travels again and we'll see no more of him.'

'Well, he who lives the longest'll see the most,' replied Ruby sagely, just before Frances closed the door.

* * *

Once in the gardens, Lyddington directed the footmen to carry his chair across the area that had once been the parterre, and was soon to be sweeping lawns, divided by a broad gravel path and a fountain. The day was pleasant enough; cool for June, but warmer than it had been inside.

'Take me to that seat yonder,' growled his lordship, angry that such a brief journey should mean his making such a spectacle of himself. The footmen staggered up the steps onto a path overlooking the area over which they had just passed. When they had reached the seat, the earl said, 'Now help me out of this blasted thing, then take it to where I can't see it, will you? Then get back to the house, there's good fellows. I shan't want you for an hour.'

The footmen did as they were bid, and returned to the house. His lordship looked round at his domain. There was very little to be seen as yet. It was rather odd to look down and to see the pattern of the parterre, but without the hedges that had used to be an essential part of it. As for the rest, the fountain was dug out, and the base was there, but not the top, and the lawns were looking rather mangled.

Behind him, there was some evidence of planting, but no clear design had emerged as yet. He was exceedingly annoyed that the plans had disappeared. He would have liked to have asked someone some questions, but no one was visible just now.

There was another reason why he would have liked to see a stalwart gardener at present. It was being borne in upon him that an hour was rather a long time to stay seated upon a cold bench. There was a blanket in the sedan chair that he might sit upon, but that was out of reach, thanks to his orders. Furthermore, he was starting to realize that the pleasure of consuming an English breakfast once again in his own home had made him rather over-enthusiastic in the amount of ale that he had drunk that morning. The memory of that consumption was beginning to make him rather uncomfortable, and he would have welcomed someone who would lend him a supporting arm so that he would be able to make use of the vegetation.

Eventually, however, he was considerably relieved to see over to his left and walking in his direction, a young, respectable-looking lad dressed in leather waistcoat and old-fashioned tricorne hat.

'Hey you! Young feller! Over here!'

The youth hesitated for a moment.

'Yes, you!' called his lordship. 'Come here, will you?'

The youth hesitated again, then walked over to the earl. He was a slightly built lad, not over tall, with a dark wig that went ill with his fair complexion. He looked a trifle wary.

'One of Sutcliffe's men, are you?' asked his lordship.

'Yes, sir. I'm Francis Sutcliffe, Mr Sutcliffe's nephew.'

'Nephew, eh? Excellent, get the whole family on the job. I'm Lyddington, by the way, and I need you to do a couple of small favours for me, if you'd be so good.'

'Yes, of course, My Lord,' said young Sutcliffe, touching his hat.

'No doubt you'll have seen a sedan chair as you passed. Would you mind getting me the blanket that's inside it?'

'Of course not, My Lord.' Frances sighed as she hurried back to the sedan chair. As luck would have it, she had never been so close to an employer as this before, as all business dealings were conducted through Thomas Sutcliffe. Oh well, her disguise had survived close inspection so far. There was no reason why it should not continue to do so.

She returned quickly with the blanket, and made as if to spread it over the earl's knees.

'No, no,' said Lyddington impatiently. 'I'm not a blasted invalid. I need you to put it under me; this bench is damnably cold on one's backside. But first, I want you to help me up, then keep me balanced whilst I piss in those bushes.'

Frances turned scarlet, and her jaw

dropped. The earl struggled to his feet. He was taller than she had expected, with broad shoulders; and somehow, she had not imagined that shock of chestnut hair. She found herself having to take hold of his arm, or allow him to fall to the ground.

Once balanced upright, his lordship took his arm from her grip, and put it around her shoulders, leaning heavily upon her.

'Now help me over there,' he said, pointing to a clump of bushes a few steps behind them. Once there, he instructed her to take hold of his arm once more. So preoccupied was she with the novelty of the situation that she did not take in immediately what he was saying. She was still flushed, this time with exertion as well as embarrassment.

'Been livin' so long in gardens that you think you're in Arcadia, do you?' said Lyddington ironically, as he began to unfasten his breeches. 'I'm not asking you to hold my cock — just to help me stay upright. Take my arm, I said.'

Frances could not think of a way out of this situation that would not destroy her disguise and therefore disgrace her father. There was no one visible to ask for help. Fainting would be too absurd. Fatalistically she did as she was bid, resolutely turning her face away until the horrid splashing noise had ceased, and his lordship had said, 'All right, I'm decent. Bit squeamish ain't you, young shaver?' He looked at her with an ironically amused expression, which for no accountable reason caused her heart to skip a beat.

'I . . . that is, I . . . it is a fault, I confess it,' she said at last, thankful that the return trip to the bench was sufficient for her remaining blushes to subside. Once there, she busied herself with placing the blanket for his lordship to sit down, which he did with a sigh of satisfaction.

'Comfort restored,' he said with a smile. 'Now tell me, young Sutcliffe — by the way, what is your given name?'

'Francis, My Lord,' said Frances. When she had begun this masquerade several years ago, she had decided that one of the best ways of avoiding detection would be to use the masculine equivalent of her own name, so that it would never surprise her when she heard it on someone else's lips.

'Very well then, young Frank,' said the earl, thereby confounding all her careful reasoning, 'what do you intend to accomplish here?'

'I could show Your Lordship best with reference to the plans,' replied Frances.

'I've no doubt you could,' answered the earl, 'but the damn' things have disappeared.'

'Disappeared, My Lord? That is very strange.'

'Bloody annoying,' returned the earl, who, like many a robust gentleman of his time, saw fit to sprinkle his conversation with copious oaths, especially when, as he thought, there were no ladies present. 'That'll cause problems for you, I suspect.'

'No doubt it would, My Lord, had there not been copies taken.'

'Copies? Thank God for that.'

'Yes, My Lord. The original is locked away safely, and the one that you had was a copy. There is another copy too, the one we are working from.'

'Good. No doubt the blasted thing'll turn up. It's probably been used to line drawers or something. But tell me about what you're doing.'

Frances gestured towards the area in front of the house.

'Well, My Lord, as you see, the parterre has been removed, thus enabling us to develop a style of garden in which nature is no longer restricted, but is allowed to show its full beauty.'

'How are my gardeners taking it?' asked Lyddington. 'Some of them don't know how to do anything but clip hedges, I'll wager.'

'Higgins, your head gardener, is very

enthusiastic,' replied Frances. 'His brother works for Sir Charles Cockerell, and has been writing to him about some of the things that have been achieved at Sezincote. Now he's keen to get started on some new ideas here.'

'Cockerell? Never heard of him. What a name though!' said the earl with an amused grin.

'Yes, My Lord,' replied Frances, unsure whether or not it would be appropriate to agree. 'My uncle was involved with some small commissions for him a few years ago and found him to be a knowledgeable and helpful employer.'

'Whereas you'll find me an ignorant and devilish bad-tempered one. What about Rance? How has he taken it?'

Frances' face darkened a little. She had come across Peter Rance soon after they had arrived at Lyddington in order to begin work. A simple-minded fellow, he had been against the changes from the start. Everyone, from the head gardener, to the cook, to the Sutcliffes, right to Lady Valeria herself had tried to explain to him that he would still have a role after the alterations were done; but it was of no avail. He looked upon the changes almost as a personal slight.

'Badly, I fear, My Lord,' answered Frances at last. 'When the parterre was removed, I almost feared for his reason. Thankfully, Higgins has had the happy notion of placing him in the kitchen gardens, where there are to be no changes, and that seems to have settled him a little.'

The earl looked at her for a long moment, then nodded in approval.

'You were telling me about the changes,' he said eventually. 'Please go on.'

'Well, the parterre will be replaced by a lawn with a fountain in the centre with a path around it. A statue is on order for the fountain which will be arriving soon.'

'And what does this statue represent?' asked the earl, adding hopefully, 'Venus? Aphrodite?'

'A river god, My Lord.'

'Damn Valeria. Go on.'

'You may recall, My Lord, that up in this area, the gardens continued with another parterre and more formal gardens. That was the area that is now behind you.'

Lyddington glanced round.

'Quite a contrast,' he remarked. 'I trust, young Frank, that there is going to be more to it than this.'

The site was in quite possibly the worst imaginable state for its owner to see it. The ancient parterre had disappeared, but had, to his lordship's eye, been replaced by little more than roughly turned over earth, some sticks here and there with string between them, piles of stones and trenches.

'Oh yes, of course,' exclaimed Frances, quite forgetting in her excitement to say 'My Lord' this time. 'Behind the seat there will be a path — that is partly made as you see. Behind, there will be hedges with paths in between.'

'Sounds remarkably like a parterre to me,' grunted his lordship.

'Oh no, indeed it will not be!' she responded eagerly. 'The paths will be winding, with different kinds of beds between them, some on different levels. Each hedge will hide a contrast; and at the end of the paths will be seen prospects of interest; a temple, a statue, a fountain, or an ornamental pond.'

'I see. It sounds very romantic, young Frank. Just the place to bring a lady of one's choice, eh?' remarked the earl with a wink.

'Just so, My Lord,' murmured Frances, hurrying on to say, 'The work itself will not take too long; but what will require patience will be the waiting for the plants to grow to maturity.'

'So no doubt I'll be dead before this garden is worth looking at.'

'We must trust that you will be spared to us

a little longer,' replied Frances impishly, then wondered if she had gone too far.

The earl gave a crack of laughter.

'Impudent young shaver,' he said with a grin. 'Now give me a straight answer.'

'I would think that in say five years, you might see a very good result,' she replied, relieved that he had taken her remark so well.

'Well, that sounds promising. I might just take myself off to the Continent for another long visit, and by the time I come back, it'll be at its best. Unless, of course, by that time m'sister has ripped it all up and changed it.'

They were silent for a time. Frances knew that she ought to get away for all kinds of reasons, but she was rather enjoying his company and she wanted to stay.

'I trust my longing for conversation is not keeping you from your work?' asked Lyddington, providing her with the perfect reason for making her excuses. Nevertheless, she found it impossible to voice them. Sitting there, his injured leg stretched out and propped on a convenient stone, he looked every inch the master of all that he surveyed. It was quite beyond her to answer in the affirmative.

'I . . . there is always plenty to do, My Lord,' she replied, compromising.

'So there is, but I doubt a few minutes will make any difference. It's devilish quiet round here; nothing to see. Don't any of the men work?'

'Some are collecting plants from Bedford, and my uncle is supervising the moving of some trees. There is also some work going on behind the west wing. Indeed, I should be there to supervise it. We are installing a water garden. That is my special project,' she concluded, with a certain amount of pride.

'I should like to see some of that work in progress. What are you using for the lining? Clay?'

'Yes, My Lord. Clay and stone.'

'Plenty of that in Bedfordshire. You look very young for this work, Sutcliffe,' said the earl, suddenly changing tack. 'Why are you not at school? Surely you're not more than sixteen or so?'

'I'm nearly nineteen, My Lord,' said Frances, wanting to drop her naturally deep voice even more, but not daring to do so for fear of sounding unrealistic. She did not risk giving her real age of twenty-four.

'Mmm. You're very slight for your age; especially considering you do manual work. Mind you, Masters is a slightly built fellow as well — and young, too. Have you met my agent?'

'Only briefly, My Lord. He has much to do with the estate. Apparently, the previous man was ill, and things had been neglected a little.'

'Indeed?' murmured his lordship, raising his brows. 'And from whom did you get this story of neglect? Masters himself?'

'Well, yes, My Lord,' said Frances hesitantly. 'Or perhaps I misunderstood,' she went on quickly, 'or simply surmised it . . .' Her voice faded away.

'Well, I've no objections to the young fellow trying to make his mark,' said the earl fair-mindedly. 'And I like you for trying to save another fellow from trouble. But Bobkiss was a fine agent and nothing was neglected three years ago. I'll not have his name blackened just to enhance young Masters' reputation.' He turned his head and looked Frances up and down again. She did not care for this kind of scrutiny; it was far too dangerous.

'Yes, you are slight,' began the earl, reverting to the previous topic of conversation. 'Not sickly, are you?'

'Not now, My Lord, but I was as a child,' lied Frances. 'I had to spend much of my infancy abed. My mother always believed that that was what kept me small.'

'You've still a year or two to grow. And at least you've escaped the smallpox.'

It was true that Frances' fair complexion was completely free of scars, whereas his lordship's face was pitted here and there with the tell-tale pock-marks. On a face that had had a pure natural beauty this would have been a tragedy, but the earl's looks had always been more in the rugged style, and the additional scars — among them one interestingly placed near the corner of his mouth just where a childhood dimple had been, and another just at the outer corner of his eye, where in days gone by some might have placed a patch — were even held by some admirers to be an enhancement of his manly charms.

Very conscious of his eyes upon her, Frances judged it wise to attempt a retreat.

'My Lord, may I be about my duties? I am very anxious that everything should be in order for the Daughters of Flora.'

'The Daughters of who?' asked his lordship, uncomprehendingly and ungrammatically. 'And who the devil may they be?'

'The Daughters of Flora, My Lord. They're a horticultural society of ladies. I understand that they will be making a visit here soon.'

'A visit? Here? At whose behest?' He made as if to rise, remembered, for the second time that he could not do so, and swore, his face the picture of fury. 'No, don't tell me: it'll be all down to my blasted sister — hell and devil confound the bitch!'

At that moment, James and Frederick could be seen emerging from the house in order to collect his lordship. Seeing them, Lyddington bellowed at the top of his voice, 'Confound you, you scoundrels! Run, dammit! Can't you see I'm waiting?'

It was Frances' first exposure to the 'Lyddington roar' and she looked at him in rather a startled manner.

'My Lord, pray do not shout at them,' she said, indignant on their behalf, and speaking before she had given herself chance to think. 'They were not to know that you were in a hurry.'

'Mind your own business,' snapped Lyddington. 'Confound you, boy, this is none of your concern. Anyway, that's what I pay them for.'

'To be mind-readers, My Lord?' she asked incredulously, then began to tremble in her shoes at her temerity. His easy relaxed manner had made her forget that he was her employer, and that it lay in his power to send her and her father packing.

The earl stared at her in astonishment for a moment, then gave a crack of laughter. The footmen hurried up to where they were and the earl said briskly, but with good humour, 'Get that confounded chair thing, and quickly. I want to speak to my sister.'

Quickly but calmly, the footmen collected the sedan chair.

'I like you, young Frank,' said Lyddington unexpectedly while they were doing so. 'You square up to me — and not many do.'

Frances blushed in confusion.

The footmen helped him into the sedan chair, which assistance he accepted with a grunt of thanks. Seeing her heightened colour and thinking that she must be distressed at the earl's display of temper, one of the footmen whispered, 'Never you mind him, young sir. He wouldn't be His Lordship if he didn't put himself in a passion now and then.'

'Get me back to the house unless you want to see me in a passion the like of which you've never seen before,' came a testy voice from inside the sedan chair.

'Aye, My Lord,' said the footman with a wink to Frances, and they were gone.

2

'Daughters of Flora? What the devil do you mean by it?' demanded his lordship, confronting his sister, this time in the book-room.

'I am sure I do not know why you should have any objection,' replied his sister, trying not to sound defensive.

'And I don't know why you should think that I would have none to a parcel of tro — women descending upon me in my own house,' retorted the earl. 'A man's home is his castle — not his sister's!'

'But Spencer, until you arrived this week I had no idea that you would be returning . . . '

'I beg your pardon, you had every idea, Valeria, for I wrote to you informing you of the fact. You are not the only person who can write letters,' he added with heavy sarcasm.

At this, Lady Valeria did look rather uncomfortable. She stood up and began to walk about a little, her purple gown with the violet petticoat swishing majestically behind her, her eyes never quite meeting those of her brother.

'Yes, well, you have often written saying a

number of things which you never intend to do at all, so . . . '

'So you decided to assume that this would be one of those occasions; and even if it wasn't the deed would be done, the guests invited, and there would be nothing I could do.'

'Spencer, this is hardly fair! You have been gone from your home for nigh on three years and you have left the place in my hands. Have you seen signs of neglect?'

'No, I admit that . . . '

'Have you noticed any changes made in your own personal accommodation?'

'No, but I . . . '

'Then upon my soul, Spencer, I think that if you expect me to remain here year after year in solitary state, never entertaining any of my friends, you are being even more unreasonable than I thought you were!'

Lyddington looked at his sister for a moment with his brows drawn together in a hideous frown, and then laughed abruptly almost despite himself.

'Agreed, Valeria. But the Daughters of Flora! You know how I detest these all-female gatherings. It will be utterly devilish.'

'Then no doubt in that case, my dear brother, you will feel entirely at home,' responded his sister blandly.

* * *

His lordship was an active man and being leg-tied did not suit him — nor did it suit anyone who was obliged to associate with him, for he was a very bad patient — so the entire population of Lyddington Court were almost as glad as the earl himself when his ankle improved sufficiently for him to be able to get about on his own feet again.

Apart from anything else, he was very pleased to be able to top Valeria with his usual six foot stature. It made him feel that at least he now had a fair chance of being master in his own house.

It had not taken long for the staff to get used to him again. Half the house had heard him bellow at his valet on one of his first mornings home, and all those within earshot had smiled contentedly at one another, relieved that his lordship was back, and just the same as ever.

Lyddington was still absolutely determined to avoid his lady guests as much as possible, and was trying to work out ways and means. Although the Court was a fair-sized house, it was not so very big that one could lose oneself in it; and his favourite retreat — the library — was sure to be invaded by botany-mad females in search of learned tomes on the flora of the British Isles.

In Lyddington's experience, at least two or three would be more interested in his person and his title than in his plants; and Valeria's friends had seldom in the past been congenial to him, as they were generally as domineering as she was herself, or else utterly subservient to her. If neither of these qualities had applied to them then, worst of all, they had been especially selected by his sister because she thought that one or other of them would be acceptable as the future Countess of Lyddington, and unfortunately, Lyddington's taste in women seldom coincided with his sister's ideas of what was suitable.

One morning, only three days before his sister's guests were due to arrive, the earl was standing in the hall, frowning across at the gatehouse, before entering the parlour for breakfast. He had been for his usual morning exercise. Sometimes he rode, but more frequently, as on this occasion, he took himself and his dogs, two great mastiffs, for a long walk. It was as he stood gazing across, that an idea, so simple and so brilliant occurred to him, that he struck himself across the forehead for not having thought of it before.

* * *

In the gatehouse in the small dining-room in which Thomas and Frances ate all their meals, breakfast was in progress; but it has to be said that, most unusually, Frances had very little appetite.

'It's no good,' she said, laying down her fork and giving up on her scrambled egg at last. 'I am so afraid that I will be discovered this time.'

'Why this time particularly?' asked her father, eating his breakfast with perfect equanimity.

Physically they were not at all alike. Frances was quite tall for a woman, and slender. Underneath the wig that she wore to help her disguise, her hair was blonde and straight, and her complexion, although slightly tanned because she worked outdoors, was also fair.

Dressed in women's clothes, she would have passed anywhere for a pretty girl, if not a beautiful one. Dressed as a man, her delicate-seeming appearance sometimes encouraged people to think that they could get the better of her. To counteract this, she had developed an air of confident authority, and this, coupled with her undoubted understanding of the sphere in which she worked, generally gained her the respect that she wanted.

Thomas Sutcliffe, needing no disguise, wore his own pepper-and-salt hair in a severe queue. That was, however, the only severe thing about him, for he was a stout, good-humoured man, rather on the short side, and only an inch or two taller than his daughter. His weatherbeaten face was covered in creases, partly from good humour, and partly from exposure to the wind and weather. Nevertheless, beneath the good-humoured exterior was a determined will, coupled with a real love for the soil and for nature, and a great capacity to capture a vision within a landscape.

Six years ago, Frances, having her father's love of and flair for gardening, had begged him to allow her to work with him. He had refused categorically, pointing out that ladies never worked in such a way. She had bowed to his dictates, even though she had resented them because she knew that in her cousin Edmund, her father had a very able assistant. But then, tragedy struck. Edmund caught a severe chill and despite advice to the contrary, he had neglected it. A week later, he died of inflammation of the lungs, sinking with frightening rapidity for such a robust young man.

At that time, Thomas Sutcliffe was on the point of starting an important and very demanding commission, and did not have time to look about him for a new partner. Taking rather unfair advantage of him at this critical moment, Frances had persuaded him to allow her to masquerade as his 'other' nephew on a temporary basis. She had succeeded so well in what he had given her to do that he had agreed to keep her on, on condition that she kept her real identity a secret, and that she always resumed her true identity when at their home in Plymouth.

Frances had never doubted her ability to work; her ability to remain undetected had concerned her a little, until she had realized that most people are quite unobservant, and tend to see only what they expect to see. This, added to the fact that they always took with them their own servants — Ruby and Edward — and that Thomas was always the one to have direct dealings with employers, meant that so far her disguise had been fool-proof.

Now, six years after the commencement of their deception, it seemed to Frances that her father almost accepted her as the boy the world imagined her to be; whereas for her part, she had found that she was beginning to find in herself a weariness for the male role that she had originally embraced so eagerly; she had started to long for the pretty things worn by those in the great houses at which they worked. Most of the time she was able to suppress that longing, but over the past few days, it had come upon her afresh, together with an apprehension about discovery that was proving hard to shake off.

'I don't know,' she said in answer to her father's question. 'Seeing the earl for the first time at such close quarters unnerved me, I suppose.' She put up a hand to her black wig, hating the feel of it.

'Don't let it distress you, my dear,' said her father taking another piece of toast. 'As he is newly back in England, he will probably be taking himself off to visit his friends, and will very soon be far away from here.'

'Yes, that was my view,' replied Frances, 'but he has not gone yet, has he? In fact, according to local report, he has been seen riding around his estate and talking to tenants. That doesn't sound much as if he means to leave, does it?'

At that moment, there was an imperious knock on the door. Looking at one another in puzzlement, they waited to see what it could mean, for it was far too early for calls, even supposing that they might ever receive any.

Moments later, their manservant opened the door, but before he could say anything, Lord Lyddington strolled in. Both the Sutcliffes rose and bowed.

'Morning,' said the earl, bowing in a way that would have been insultingly casual, had it not obviously been entirely natural. He looked interestedly at the table, then glanced towards the chafing dishes on the side. 'Any bacon?' he asked.

'Why . . . why of course, My Lord,' said Thomas turning to the manservant. 'Edward, lay for His Lordship.'

Thomas had met the earl several days before as arranged, when Lyddington had sent for him to explain the new set of plans that had been delivered to the Court. Contrary to his misgivings, Sutcliffe had found the earl to be an intelligent and shrewd listener. He was clearly not as interested in his ornamental gardens as he was in his home farm, but he had given the matter his time and full attention, and had been courteous and helpful; and, what was most important, had shown himself ready to lay out his money in order to achieve the completion of the scheme.

The earl helped himself to bacon, eggs and toast, and sat down at the place laid for him.

'Forgive my intruding upon your meal,' he said a little belatedly between mouthfuls. 'The fact of the matter is that I was on the point of going in to breakfast at the Court when I had a devilish good idea, and came straight across to put it to you.' He paused and glanced round at the contents of the table. 'May I trouble you to send for some ale?'

Thomas immediately rang for some. The earl, glancing across at Frances, saw her flush slightly, and with a twinkle in his eye, he leaned across the table to say reassuringly, 'Never fear, my lad, I can manage my own personal arrangements today, so I can have as much ale as I please!'

Seeing Thomas's mystified air, the earl explained, with much laughter, the service that 'young Frank' had performed for him at their first meeting, and the extent of the 'lad's' modesty at the time.

Feeling herself blush, Frances buried her nose in her coffee. Luckily, because Thomas did not know how to react to this story, the ale arrived at this point, and the earl was diverted.

'Splendid!' he said when he had drunk deeply. 'Nothing like an English breakfast. Now, sir, you can be of great service to me if you will.'

'Anything, My Lord,' said Thomas, still somewhat flustered. 'If it is in my power.'

'It certainly is in your power to save my damned sanity,' said Lyddington bluntly. 'These devilish women are arriving the day after tomorrow and I don't think I can endure it. I've been racking my brains to think how I can avoid them, and I think I've come up with the very idea.'

'And what is that, My Lord?' asked Thomas blankly. Frances got up from the table and walked over to the fireplace. A nasty, creeping apprehension was suddenly starting to come over her.

'I'd like to stay here, if you'll have me,' said the earl, belching discreetly and leaning back in his chair with great satisfaction. Thomas, who had just taken a mouthful of coffee, began to choke, and Frances came over to thump him on the back.

When the paroxysm was over, the earl looked across at the two of them, Thomas mopping his streaming eyes, and Frances looking at him warily. He smiled a little ruefully, the warmth not reaching his eyes.

'It seems my idea is less than appealing to you,' he said, trying not to sound hurt. 'Well, of course, this is your home while you remain here. Far be it from me to thrust myself upon you.'

Frances suddenly thought of him arriving home after three years, and not being able to call his home his own, because of alterations and visitors. Quickly, at the same time as the idea formed in her mind and before she could have second thoughts, she said, 'It is not that, indeed, My Lord. We would be more than happy to entertain you. We are only concerned that we will be unable to offer you the kind of accommodation and attentions to which you are accustomed. You must think of us as . . . as working men, you see.'

Lyddington smiled a little more warmly.

'Don't concern yourselves,' he said in something approaching his usually hearty tone. 'I'm not so niffy-naffy that I have to be waited on hand and foot all the time. And a maid can come over from the Court to cope with any extra work. Well? Can I come?'

Thomas had by now recovered his equanimity, and had recollected the folly of offending an employer, however apparently genial.

'Of course, My Lord,' he said as enthusiastically as he could manage. 'You are very welcome.'

'Excellent!' said the earl, rising from the table. 'I'm looking forward to this. I'm fond of women — devilish fond of them, to be honest! — but there's nothing like a group of men round a table for good company. I'm damned glad you've come.'

So saying, he bowed slightly and left them. Thomas and Frances looked at one another in consternation.

'Far away from here!' said Frances, striking the table with her fist. 'You said that he would be far from here! He couldn't very well be much closer, could he? Now what am I going to do?'

3

'Go to the gatehouse and stay?' exclaimed Lady Valeria in outraged tones, her dark brows looking nearly as thick and threatening as her brother's in her fury. 'But this is preposterous, Spencer!'

'Preposterous? How so?' The earl had strolled into the saloon where his sister was sitting, sketchbook and pencil in hand, a pot of pansies before her. She now laid down her drawing with something less than her usual care, and stood up, drawing herself up to her full height, which was tall for a female, but still, to her everlasting regret, nowhere near her brother's inches.

'You will have guests,' she declared. 'To absent yourself in this way — and to so short a distance — would be a terrible slight!'

'*I* have guests? *I*?' exclaimed the earl in dreadfully exaggerated accents of surprise. 'Forgive me, Valeria, but I understood you to say not many days ago that you wanted to entertain your friends. I have not instructed you, as a less reasonable man . . . ' — here Lady Valeria snorted with disdain — 'I repeat, a less reasonable man might have done, to write to these people cancelling your arrangements — and you cannot deny that as master of this house, I would be perfectly within my rights to do so. But,' he concluded, his voice rising to something near the Lyddington roar, 'I'm damned if I'm going to be caught in the middle of this blasted floral dance!'

On hearing that note in the earl's voice, most people usually left the matter at that. Not so his sister.

'But Spencer, to leave the company of ladies of your own station — some of them old acquaintances of yours — to stay in company with — well, I feel one must say a . . . a servant and his family — it's positively indecent!'

Suddenly realizing that she had said too much, Lady Valeria abruptly turned away to look out of the window which gave onto the fountain above which the earl had sat during his first visit to the gardens.

'Sutcliffe ain't a servant, he's an employee, and what's more he's a gentleman so . . . ' He broke off, realizing at last what else his sister had said. 'Acquaintances?' he questioned wrathfully. 'Acquaintances? Hell and devil confound it, woman, you're trying to marry me off again! Confess it!'

'Certainly not!' replied his sister defensively.

'I should hope not, because perhaps you've forgotten that was what drove me abroad last time. What in Heaven's name do I have to do to convince you that I have no wish to marry again? Enter a monastery?'

'I doubt they'd have you, Spencer,' retorted her ladyship ironically.

The earl laughed.

'Even if I came penitently with all my worldly goods for the church's disposal? Don't you believe it! But don't try to get off the point. Are you planning a marriage for me? Because I tell you now, I'll have none of it.'

'No, not planning,' said Lady Valeria somewhat wearily, as she came away from the window to lay a hand on her brother's arm. 'Just hoping.'

'Blessed if I know why. After all, if I don't marry, your boy will get all this when I kick up my heels, so . . . '

'So I am supposed to be so avaricious as to want your property for my children? Well, I don't. Richard has his career in the army, and everything that Cedric left him, and that is plenty for him; and Charlotte's husband is very well to pass. But it is the title that concerns me. Only you can secure that for future generations.'

'Yes, so you've said before,' replied the earl, as he rang the bell for wine. 'But so have I told you my views before.'

'Three years ago, Spencer. No, no wine for me, thank you. But you have been gone for three years, and three years can change a person greatly.'

'Agreed; and I have spent a very enjoyable three years, partly in France, partly in Italy, where I made a number of agreeable acquaintances, none of whom ever mentioned marriage to me at all!'

'I can well believe it,' replied Lady Valeria grimly. 'But that won't secure the succession.'

'Perhaps not. But leave be, will you, Valeria? I'm not staying here and that's final. I'm going to the Sutcliffes. As I told you before, Sutcliffe is certainly a gentleman, and his nephew is as quiet-spoken, polite and delicate in his ways as you could wish.'

'Well, if you are going to stay in the same house as him, perhaps he may pass some of those qualities on to you,' said Lady Valeria, waspishly.

* * *

That night, Frances sat before her dressing-table mirror, whilst Ruby brushed out her hair. It was very dark blonde and thick, and fell to just below her shoulders.

'I wonder if I should cut it all off,' she said casually. 'It would be much easier to wear under a wig if it were really short.'

'Over my dead body,' replied Ruby forthrightly.

Ruby had always disapproved of Frances' disguise, but she had now become accustomed to it, and looked upon herself not only as the fierce protector of her mistress's honour, but also as the guardian of any scraps of femininity that could be preserved. The discussion about the hair was a perennial one. So often had the subject been aired, that Ruby would have been deeply disappointed had it not taken place. According to tradition, Frances should now have defended herself by saying that her hair grew very quickly. Instead, she remained silent, looking thoughtfully into the mirror.

'What is it, my chick?' asked Ruby in a very different tone, as she laid down the brush. 'Something's troubling you, and we both know that — '

'A trouble shared is a trouble halved,' smiled Frances, as she completed the saying. 'Yes, I know. But not in this case.' She thought for a moment, then said anxiously;

'Ruby, how am I going to maintain my disguise?'

Ruby looked a little nonplussed.

'Well, why ask me after all this time? You know I've never approved, but you seem to have managed to fool everyone so far.'

'Yes, but never at such close quarters as this,' explained Frances. 'On every other occasion, we have had lodgings at some distance from the house. Here, we are right on the doorstep.'

'We were on the doorstep yesterday,' said Ruby bluntly. 'Didn't seem to bother you then.'

'But you know that the earl is going to stay. I shall be meeting him at close quarters at all hours of the day and night.' Frances could feel herself blushing, but although Ruby glanced at her mistress quite sharply for a moment, she did not comment upon it.

'You could plead a headache,' she suggested.

'Once, perhaps, but not at every evening meal when he is here, and every breakfast. Oh Ruby, I . . . '

'Well?'

Frances was silent for a few moments, then she went on, 'I like to think that when we are home and we close the door, I can relax a little, and at least be myself for a short time.

Now, even that is denied me.'

'You could've said no. By all accounts, His Lordship wouldn't have insisted.'

'But I couldn't have done that,' answered Frances, choosing the book she wanted from her small selection. 'He would have been so hurt.'

Ruby made no comment on that subject, saying instead, 'Well, the whole problem would never have arisen if only we'd stayed in Plymouth; but you know my opinion on that,' and she bustled round tidying up whilst Frances got into bed.

'Yes I do, and you know my opinion. Why should I sit at home and do nothing, when at the cost of a little harmless deception, I can do a job that satisfies me?'

'There you are then,' stated Ruby, as she finished her task and stood at the side of the bed, her hands folded over her apron. 'You're just as you always were. You want to — '

'Have my cake and eat it. Perhaps so. Goodnight, Ruby dear.'

'Goodnight, Miss Frances. But just remember,' she added, as she got to the door, 'harmless it may seem to you — but those who are deceived aren't always apt to be so understanding.'

After she had gone, Frances sat up in bed, thinking about her problem. Working in the garden she could do with confidence; that was her milieu, and she was on certain ground; besides, she had grown into the role by now. But aping the boy at social occasions — that was entirely beyond her experience. She had no evening clothes, for a start! The earl, with his easy manners, might expect her and her father to dine at the Court at times, and then where would she be?

Worst of all, she could just imagine the earl's idea of a convivial evening with other men. He would of course be a hard drinker himself, and would expect the same of everyone else around the table. And what of the conversation? Ribald stories and romantic encounters, perhaps! She started to laugh, but it came out more like a sob.

As she lay in bed, however, her thoughts began to take a more cheerful turn. After all, the likelihood was that the earl would be obliged to dine on many occasions at the Court, and she would thus manage to avoid meeting him very much in the evenings. With any luck, their rising times might differ too, and with a little ingenuity, she would easily be able to avoid him at the breakfast-table. But to have him near her in the house, sleeping just along the corridor . . . Sternly, she repressed such thoughts, and went through all the Latin names of plants that she could think of until she fell asleep.

The following morning she rose early, as was her custom, and set out at once for the gardens. She found herself heading for the kitchen area, paused for a moment, deciding whether to walk the other way, then went resolutely on. She was becoming increasingly reluctant to risk meeting Peter Rance, with his threatening stare and his inability to listen to reason.

She walked from one walled area to another, noticing the glass frames, and the fruit trees grown against the serpentine walls in order to give them maximum protection. All areas of gardening fascinated her, and she was sometimes regretful that her work in ornamental gardens prevented her from becoming more involved in food growing.

At the far side of the kitchen area, she could see that there was smoke rising. It was the place where the garden fire was generally lit, if such a thing was necessary, and it had been necessary with the uprooting and destroying of the parterre. Such destruction never left her unaffected. It had been easier here, if anything, because the parterre had not been a particularly fine example, and had been allowed to become a little out of hand. However, the job was done now, and there was none of it left to burn. Of course, there might be a hundred other reasons why a fire might be necessary; but Frances resolved to go and make sure that it was under control.

Walking beyond the walled area and into the space allotted to the fire, Frances thought at first that it was unattended, and looked round to see who was responsible. Then she saw Peter Rance. Muttering to himself, he was carrying what appeared to be a pile of rubbish, which he then placed onto the flames, and pushed in savagely with a long-handled fork.

Uncertain as to whether he should be entrusted with the fire, Frances stood for a moment, undecided as to what to do. It was then that Rance saw her. He left his task and lumbered towards her, fork in hand, a fragment of something caught upon its prongs. His expression was anything but welcoming. He was a big, dark, spare man, with shaggy unkempt hair, heavy brows, and a stooping, shambling gait.

'You're here to spoil it,' he said accusingly. 'You said you'd not come here.'

'No, I only came to look at the fire,' said Frances, trying to sound placating.

'Came to see the fire, did you?' said Rance grinning suddenly, and showing his stubby, discoloured teeth. 'Then come a bit closer,' and seizing hold of her arm, he began to pull her towards the flames. Rather alarmed, but sure that resistance would enrage him further, she went, but reluctantly. Moreover, his grip was convulsively tight, and she was sure that she would not be able to pull herself free. She laid her hand on her belt, and touched the hilt of her gardener's knife. She was thankful that she had remembered it, but hoped that she would not have to resort to using it.

She was just wondering what should be her next move, when there was the sound of a dog barking and, moments later, one of the earl's great mastiffs came bounding over to her, to be followed shortly after by his lordship, looking fit and vigorous after his early morning walk, the skirts of his coat swinging about him, and his other dog at his heels.

'Good morning, Sutcliffe, Rance,' he said. Frances bowed as well as she could, for Rance was still holding her upper arm very tightly; Rance himself stood looking at his master as if he did not know what to do next.

'Tending that fire must be hot work, Rance,' said the earl briskly with an eye to Frances, whose look of apprehension had not escaped him. 'Go and get yourself a drink.'

For a few moments, the issue hung in the balance, then the habit of a lifetime asserted itself, and Rance touched his forelock.

'Aye, My Lord,' he said, putting down the fork and walking away.

Very unnerved by the encounter, Frances rubbed her arm vigorously. The earl put an arm affectionately around her shoulders, thus flustering her further.

'You mustn't allow Rance to discompose you,' he said kindly. 'He's always been simple, and all these changes are difficult for him to understand. Once everything is completed he'll soon settle down again. But I would advise you to avoid this area if you can, especially if you are alone. You're only a slight fellow, you know, and he's quite big.'

'You . . . you are very kind, My Lord,' said Frances, feeling weak and vulnerable in a way that surprised her, because it was very unlike her. If the earl had shouted at her for being in the wrong place, or for wasting time, she would have found it easier to keep her countenance. 'This fire must be tended,' she went on, bending to pick up the fork.

'Indeed it must,' said the earl, 'but not by you.' Spotting a gardener in the distance, he summoned him by means of the Lyddington bellow. Frances was still looking at the object that had been caught on the tines of the fork.

'My Lord,' she said in an arrested tone. Lyddington walked back to her side.

'Yes, what is it?'

'This paper. It is part of the garden plan. I am sure of it.'

'Perhaps an earlier draft that you discarded?' suggested Lyddington, as he looked at the paper with her. Frances shook her head.

'No, My Lord. We destroy all earlier drafts ourselves, so that there is no possibility of error. This is part of the plan that we are using.' There was a brief silence.

'The one that disappeared from the steward's room has never been discovered,' said the earl slowly.

'But that was over a week ago. If someone wanted to destroy the plans, would not he do so immediately?'

'Not necessarily. He might want to delay doing so until the fuss over the disappearance was over. And even if he did destroy them immediately, it has been very dry. A fragment like that could be blown away amongst other rubbish and remain undetected for some days.'

'Perhaps there might be some more pieces somewhere?' suggested Frances. They looked round the whole area, but nothing more came to light. Leaving the new man in charge of the fire, they walked slowly away through the kitchen gardens. The earl thrust the fragment into the pocket of his full-skirted coat.

When they were out of earshot, Frances said, 'Do you suppose that Peter Rance burned the plans, My Lord?'

The earl frowned thoughtfully. 'Perhaps. But I do not think that he took them.'

'Why not, My Lord?'

'He does not have access to the house — except for the kitchens. He could not have made his way to the steward's room without being seen; and besides, he cannot read, and would not have known what they were if he saw them — he hasn't enough wit to work out what they were. No, he may have burned them, but I don't think that he knew what he was burning when he did so.'

'Then who can have taken them — and with such malicious intent?'

'The Lord knows; and I can't think with an empty stomach. I've had no breakfast yet and I'm devilish sharp set. Come with me, young Frank, and I'll show you one of the most important places in the house.'

So saying, he clapped a heavy hand on Frances' shoulder, almost causing her to wince, and kept his arm around her shoulders in a style of friendly camaraderie until they reached the kitchens.

This was one of the oldest parts of the house, retaining its lofty ceiling to carry away the smoke, its huge fireplace with the spits big enough to roast a whole pig, should his lordship desire it, and the great scrubbed tables, kept scrupulously clean under the command of Mrs Bartlett.

As soon as the arrival of the earl became apparent, that lady came forward, plump, red-faced, smiling and curtsying, a few dark-brown curls escaping from beneath her cap.

'Well, My Lord, and this is a pleasure indeed! And young Master Sutcliffe! How can I oblige you, My Lord?'

Lyddington, who had released Frances as they entered the kitchens, slid an arm around the cook's plump waist, and said plaintively, 'Barty, I've been walking for miles and I'm hungry!'

'Now go on, My Lord, do!' said Mrs Bartlett, firmly removing his hand, but still smiling. 'As if there isn't always a good breakfast laid for you in the house whenever you want it!'

The earl said nothing, but went on smiling in a manner that was somewhat reminiscent of a half-starved schoolboy. At length, Mrs Bartlett relented, saying, 'Oh very well then, My Lord, just sit down and I'll bring you something in a trice. And young Master Sutcliffe'll be glad of something, no doubt.'

Frances began to protest but the earl would have none of it.

'Of course he'll have something. Can't you see what a slight thing he is? He needs building up. More of your excellent cooking will soon make a man of him, Barty!'

It'll take more than a few extra breakfasts to do that, thought Frances to herself, but she made no further protest, instead contenting herself with observing what was going on.

They were very soon served with thick slices of home-cured ham and newly baked bread, still warm from the oven, together with ale, the earl's favourite breakfast drink, which Frances forced herself to swallow down. She would really have preferred coffee, but she knew that being allowed to interrupt the kitchen routine was a privilege accorded to very few, and so she matched her requirements to the earl's accordingly.

A number of the servants were in the kitchen area, going about their duties, and it was quite plain that the sight of the earl eating at the kitchen-table was by no means a new one to them. He spoke to any who passed him, not always remembering their names immediately, but always recalling their family connections when prompted. Nowhere was there evidence of over-familiarity from any of them, but neither was there any fear.

Eventually, his repast finished, Lyddington got to his feet.

'Well, young Frank,' he said, with another of those hearty claps on the shoulder with which Frances' frame was becoming quite familiar. 'Here our ways must part. I have an appointment with Masters, so I'll bid you good day and see you later.'

'Very well, My Lord,' said Frances, rising and bowing. As she did so, she noticed that as his lordship left the room, every servant stopped what he or she was doing and made a reverence.

* * *

Lyddington had decided that he would dine with his sister that day. He owed her that much, at least, until the unwanted guests arrived. His manservant had supervised the bringing over of his belongings earlier in the day, and was to stay at the gatehouse with his master. Yet another complication, thought Frances to herself. Owing to the smallness of the accommodation, Soames, the Earl's valet was to share with Edward.

Determined to please, the earl had made a special effort in dressing, and knowing his sister's preference for old-fashioned courtly styles, he had even allowed his valet to powder his hair. Feeling a boyish desire to show off, he casually walked into the dining-room of the gatehouse, where his hosts had already begun their meal, in order to display himself to them before going over to the Court.

Both rose, Frances in a state of stunned amazement. To see his lordship striding about his property in breeches, boots and coat, with his hat clapped carelessly upon his chestnut locks, had become a common sight. Seeing him now, in a coat of dull gold with cream breeches and cream waistcoat embroidered with gold thread, she felt as if her breath had all been taken away.

'My Lord, you look . . . ' she was about to say 'magnificent', then stopped for fear that she might sound too feminine.

'Devilish, ain't it?' said his lordship ruefully, misunderstanding her hesitation. 'Still, it'll please m'sister. Don't expect me to act the fool for you, though, when we dine together. Damned if I know why the women like it, but they seem to.'

Frances could have enlightened him. She would be glad when he had gone. Seeing him standing there in all his glory somehow made her feel rather weak at the knees.

Lyddington turned to go, but then bethought him of something else.

'Y'know, young Frank, it's time somebody educated you in manly pursuits. I'll take you into Bedford one evening to find some congenial company. How does that sound?'

Thankfully, he did not wait for Frances' reply before closing the door.

4

The earl was certainly right in believing that his sister would be pleased with his efforts. She had herself donned an apricot gown with a cream petticoat embroidered with tiny flowers, which became her admirably and, like her brother, she was wearing powder.

'Demme if we don't both look fine enough for court,' said the earl as he handed his sister into her chair, very much in the grand manner. Then he rather spoilt the moment by adding, 'Glad we ain't there, though. Devilish place.'

He took his own seat at the head of the table, next to her. The dining-room looked magnificent. Lady Valeria had had the walls decorated in blue, and with curtains of a slightly darker hue, the room certainly looked better now that the previous rather dingy brown colour scheme had been replaced. The dining-table was easily large enough for twenty persons, so it was just as well that brother and sister had decided not to be seated at opposite ends of the table.

The conversation proceeded along conventional and fairly predictable lines, ranging as it did over problems with the estate, the new gardens and Lady Valeria's son and daughter.

Lady Valeria's marriage had been arranged for her. It might be supposed that such a strong-minded female would have fought strenuously for her own way in such a matter — and won. However, Lady Valeria had a very strong sense of duty, and at the time when she had married, the Sarrell family had been in dire financial circumstances, owing to the late earl's fatal gaming tendency. Mr Cardingholme had had his roots in commerce, but he was an extremely wealthy man, and it was this attribute that had made his suit acceptable to the impoverished earl.

Shortly after his marriage to Lady Valeria Sarrell, he had bought an estate in Berkshire, and it was there that Richard and Charlotte had been born.

Lady Valeria had never talked about her marriage very much, and Lyddington had never pried, but the fact was that no sooner had Cecil Cardingholme died ten years ago, than Lady Valeria sold up the estate that her husband had bought fourteen years before, and went to live in Bath, where she exercised enormous influence, inspired the Master of Ceremonies with great respect, and terrified everyone else. There she had remained, only leaving to take up the reins of government at

Lyddington Court when needed.

'So, Valeria,' said the earl at length, after they had reached the second remove. 'Who are these people that you are inflicting upon me?'

'The Daughters of Flora,' replied her ladyship calmly as she continued to enjoy the excellent meal that had been set before them.

'I want names, woman,' demanded the earl. 'I want to know whether I can risk making an appearance, or whether I should simply have some rampantly infectious disease and stay within doors at the Sutcliffes. Stay, though! I've had a splendid idea! You could pretend that I haven't yet returned from the Continent!'

'Impossible,' replied his sister. 'Too many people know that you are here. Don't forget, for example, that only two days ago, Bedford came to see you on his way to Woburn. You are the kind of man whom it is somewhat difficult to miss, once you are there!'

The earl grinned and raised his glass to his lips, but the next instant he coughed, spluttered, and hastily put it down, slopping wine onto the table as he did so.

'Scrivens!' he uttered, in as much of the Lyddington roar as he could summon in his present condition. 'What the devil is this muck? Water from the pond?'

Scrivens hastened to his master's side, attempting to help him dab splashes of wine from the sleeve of his coat.

'Oh get off, man, do,' said the earl testily, doing the job himself. 'But tell me where this comes from. Not from my cellars, I'll swear — or I've been away too long.'

'No, My Lord,' began Scrivens soothingly, then Lady Valeria stepped in.

'It is not from the cellars, Spencer. It was a gift.'

'A gift?' exclaimed his lordship in horrified tones, raising his glass gingerly between finger and thumb, and looking at the contents in disbelief. 'From whom? Beelzebub?'

'Thank you, Scrivens,' said her ladyship meaningfully. 'Please have this cleared up.'

While the table was being wiped and the offending wine was removed, Lady Valeria said, 'Yes, a gift; from Miss Marigold Stevenson, and very kind indeed I thought it of her.'

'Marigold . . ?' began his lordship, then noticed Scrivens hovering at his elbow with more wine. 'Thank you, Scrivens,' he said taking it gratefully, then hesitated. 'This is from my own cellar?'

'Indeed, My Lord,' replied Scrivens reassuringly.

Lyddington took a hearty mouthful, then sighed with relief.

'Thank God for that,' he uttered. 'And for the future, Scrivens, nothing is to come to my table unless it is either from my own cellar or from a reliable source. Good God, man, do you want to poison me?'

'I shouldn't be surprised if he did, the way you shout at him,' remarked Lady Valeria matter-of-factly.

'You don't mind, Scrivens, do you?' said Lyddington coaxingly.

'It is expected, My Lord,' said Scrivens with a bow, before withdrawing.

'You were telling me who gave me that devil's brew,' remarked the earl to his sister as soon as Scrivens had gone.

'Yes. Surely you remember demolishing Miss Stevenson's fence on your way home?'

'Thunder and turf! And she actually sent me some wine?'

'Not sent! Brought it herself. The day after your return, when you kept abed. Apparently, she felt rather guilty about trying to hit you with the hoe. Personally, I think that she should only have felt guilty about missing her target, but there we are. And she also wanted to thank you for sending the estate carpenter so quickly to measure up for repairs to the fence.'

The earl, who had grinned and silently toasted his sister when she had insulted him, replied, 'It was the least I could do. I call it devilish good of her to bring me a gift — even if it was utterly unpalatable.' Then after a pause he added, 'What does she think of your alterations, Valeria?'

'She doesn't care for them, but I have to say that I don't know her very well,' she replied. 'We don't really speak very much. She's a strange woman — very difficult to talk to. She likes everything in order and in its place — well, that was why she was so angry when you demolished her fence. She likes things to be neat and tidy . . . '

'Like the parterre, in fact.'

'I suppose so.'

'So she must see me as a destroyer of all that is ordered and, in her eyes, beautiful.'

There was a short silence.

'Spencer, this is absurd,' said her ladyship in an urgent undertone, unnecessary as the servants had long since left them to their dessert. 'Surely you are not suggesting that Miss Stevenson brought you poisoned wine because you destroyed her fence and dug up the parterre?'

'Poisoned wine? No, certainly not. But think, Valeria, where did you receive her?'

'Well, in . . . in the saloon, I think. Yes, it

was, because we looked out of the windows at the changes, and she appeared to be quite stricken. I assured her that all was well in hand, that the gardeners who had made the plans had come highly recommended . . . '

'So you told her about the plans.'

'Well, yes I wanted her to understand that all these changes are being made with the greatest of thought and skill. I certainly assured her that she and all the ladies in the Daughters of Flora group would be able to examine them, to see what was being done. But it made no difference to her. All she could do was stare out of the window and talk about how there had been so many deaths — for all the world as if you were killing off your servants, rather than digging up your plants!'

The earl smiled perfunctorily at the pleasantry, but said merely, 'Do you think you might have told her where the plans were to be found?'

'Perhaps. I don't recall. Well, there was so much to do,' she went on defensively. 'You had only just returned home, and you were roaring about like a wounded bear, and I believe I even had to leave the room without bidding the woman a proper farewell because you were making such a commotion . . . ' Her voice faded, then she added slowly, 'Spencer, do you think she took the plans?'

* * *

By the time the earl and his sister were starting their meal, Thomas Sutcliffe and his daugher, sometime nephew, were just finishing theirs. Although neither of them were in evening clothes, they had both washed and changed, for Thomas did not believe in sitting down to a meal in all his dirt.

As they ate, Frances felt very disinclined to conversation. Normally of an evening, the two of them would discuss the work that had been done during the day, but tonight, Frances found her mind wandering to other things. She found herself thinking about the earl and about how splendid he had looked when he had come into the dining-room.

Perhaps at court, or at a great ball, his appearance would be nothing special; but here, in their little dining-room, his magnificence had been quite overwhelming. His height and the breadth of his shoulders always made him a dominating figure. Even in the far more casual attire of a country gentleman that he more usually favoured, he was impossible to ignore.

She gave herself a little shake. This was

sheer foolishness, and it was getting her nowhere at all. Deliberately, she wrenched her thoughts away from him, and began to think about her father, watching him as he ate.

He was such a sensitive man when it came to gardens and plants. He had the immensely valuable gift of being able to see the whole wood without losing his appreciation of each tree as well. He was quite capable of setting in train and carrying out a massive garden transformation, even greater than that which he was undertaking for the Earl of Lyddington.

Only the previous year, they had completed work on transforming the Duke of Broughton's gardens, and they had been warmly commended as well as handsomely paid. But Frances well remembered how at their final viewing of the finished triumph, Thomas had suddenly sprung forward and kneeling, had cradled the leaves of a primula plant with his short, stubby, capable hands. Chuckling, he had turned to look at Frances.

'Look at that!' he had exclaimed. 'How hardy they are! Now this one at the end I had hardly expected to survive. It must have been trodden on countless times, and transplanted nearly as often, but look at it! New leaves already!'

Frances had smiled in agreement. She could appreciate the beauty of individual plants, but the grand design and the total effect were much more important to her.

She was very grateful that she was able to work in an area that appealed to her so much. She would never have enjoyed being a governess. She liked music, but had never found any aptitude in herself for performing on any instrument, or for singing, and embroidery had never held any pleasures for her. Drawing she enjoyed — if it involved making plans. Her father was the one who whiled away any spare time he had with drawing floral specimens he had collected, and writing about them.

Yes, she was grateful that all this was permitted to her, and for the most part she was content to live for the moment.

Sometimes her mind strayed to what might happen in years to come. What if anything happened to her father? Would she want to sustain her masquerade indefinitely? How would she feel when she was thirty? Forty?

These kind of thoughts had very seldom troubled her until now. But since coming to Lyddington Court — no, that was not true — since the earl had come home, she had found herself more and more questioning the rightness of what she was doing.

Sometimes, she pictured herself accepting a dinner invitation from him, and going there dressed in one of the very few gowns she had with her, with her own blonde hair dressed high, and dazzling him. Only, of course, she would not dazzle him, she reflected, looking down at her work-worn hands, and thinking of her wind-blown complexion. Seeing her beside those ladies whom he affected so to despise, he would probably laugh in her face, and then recommend her to go back to what she had been before, to what suited her most. She could hardly bear the thought. Better by far to stay as a boy, and to enjoy his friendship.

So absorbed was she in her thoughts that she missed what her father had said, and had to ask him to repeat his words.

'My dear Frances, you are wool-gathering tonight! I was just saying that I shall have to leave you in charge here for a few days. The sample of plants that I have received from the nursery are not at all satisfactory, as you know. I have written to the nurseryman, but no response has been forthcoming. I shall have to go myself and see what is toward if we are not to become hopelessly behind. Hopefully, I shall discover that there has simply been a misunderstanding.'

By now, they had finished eating, and

Thomas sat sipping his wine, blithely unconscious of the havoc that he was creating with his daughter's peace of mind.

'But surely, sir, you cannot go and leave me in this way,' she said, in tones that carried as much anxiety as surprise. 'Allow me to go in your place, please!'

'I can't do that, I'm afraid,' he replied, putting down his glass. 'If someone has to be dealt with severely — and I suspect that might be the case — then I do not think that commands from a mere stripling would carry enough weight.'

'No, but . . . oh surely, sir, some way can be found around this? I cannot be left alone!'

'But why not? It won't be the first time that I have left you in sole charge in this way. Why, when we were working for that fellow in Suffolk, I was abed with a putrid sore throat for well-nigh a fortnight, and was delirious for several days, and you carried the full weight of everything.'

Frances got up, paced the room under her father's puzzled gaze, then returned to grip the back of her chair.

'Think of our situation here. Papa, you cannot leave me like this!'

Only in moments of great stress did Frances ever call her father 'Papa' nowadays. Recognizing from this that she was seriously disturbed, Sutcliffe arose from his place, took hold of her arm, steered her into their small drawing-room and guided her to a chair by the fire, then took his place opposite her, and commanded her to say what was troubling her. But this she found it hard to do without revealing her feelings for the earl which, to tell the truth, she still did not fully understand herself.

'I just feel that my . . . my disguise is far more liable to discovery here than in any other place. Never before has an employer accorded me more than a passing interest, if even that. I have simply been your deputy, and clients have dealt with you, and ignored me for the most part. Here it is very different. Lyddington seems disposed to make a kind of . . . of protégé of me . . . '

Here her father could not hide a smile. Frances smiled ruefully herself, but went on, 'Yes, I know it is diverting; I would find it so were anyone else involved. But I am finding it harder to avoid his . . . his overtures of friendship — I cannot snub such a man! And with him here in the house, and you away . . . '

Her father patted her reassuringly on the knee.

'I am sure that you are worrying needlessly,' he said. 'If I am away, there will be all the more valid reasons for you to stay close to your work; and as far as the social outings are concerned, well, I am sure that his sister will keep him far too busy for him to take an interest in you.'

There was a long silence; then at last, Frances said in small voice, 'Papa, it may not have occurred to you, but with you away, I shall be completely unchaperoned.'

Sutcliffe looked at her in frank astonishment.

'Since when have you bothered about that?' he asked her. 'I thought that when you donned boys' clothes, you put aside all those anxieties.'

'Yes, so did I,' agreed Frances mournfully.

Sutcliffe looked at his daughter in puzzlement. When his wife had died, he had viewed the prospect of bringing up a girl with consternation. When she had, of her own free will, decided to transform herself into a boy, he had, after a certain amount of struggling, accepted her decision almost with relief. Now, 'feminine' concerns appeared to be arising again, and he thought that he had done with all that. Nevertheless, he could see that she was really anxious, so he did his best to speak words of comfort.

'My dear,' he said, bringing her a glass of wine. 'You are feeling tired, and that is why all these worries are rising to the surface. Remember, too, that you will not be totally on your own. Ruby is here to look after you and Edward is loyal. In any case, I really do not think that there is the smallest chance that your secret will be discovered. And moreover,' he went on thoughtfully, pouring himself a glass, 'I cannot suppose that you would be in the smallest danger even if it were. I understand that there is quite fierce competition among local girls if ever a vacancy for a maid occurs at the Court, because Lyddington is known never to foul his own nest, nor to allow others to do so.'

Frances stood up and put her glass down on the table, the wine untouched.

'Thank you, Papa,' she said drearily, as she bent to kiss him on the top of his head. 'I think I shall retire now.'

'Very well,' replied Sutcliffe, satisfied that the whole matter had been resolved. 'Sleep well, my dear and don't worry any more. I shall possibly be gone by the time you rise. The sooner I'm gone, the sooner I shall be back.'

'Goodbye, then,' replied Frances. 'Travel safely, and please return as soon as you can.'

She went slowly up to her room, reflecting that for a man with such sensitivity towards plants and gardens, her father had shown an amazing lack of that quality in his approach to her situation. He had shown absolutely no comprehension of her difficulties at anything more than a very superficial level.

Perhaps it was her fault. She had never treated him to tantrums, hysterics, the sullens, or any of the other displays of mood that were thought to be essential elements of a woman's temperament. Consequently, he had failed to realize that she had any woman's feelings at all; for which she could not really blame him she reflected, as she dressed in her one habitual female garment — her night-gown — and waited for Ruby to brush out her hair.

Her father, confident that he had answered all her doubts to both their satisfaction, soon followed her up the stairs and once he had gained his bed, was very quickly asleep.

5

Frances was busy supervising the arrangements for the water garden the following morning when she heard the bark of a dog, and soon afterwards spotted the earl, the picture of a vigorous man in his prime, beaver hat on his head, coat tails flying and cane in hand.

As always, Frances found her emotions very mixed. Something inside her flickered to exuberant life at the sight of him, but fear of discovery made her bend suddenly to check the stone and clay lining for the pond, hoping to escape notice.

The earl, however, always an easy mixer, strolled over to see what was happening, and at his appearance, all the men straightened to touch their forelocks so Frances could not very well remain doubled up.

'Good morning,' said his lordship in a general way, and then added, 'Good morning, young Frank! Is this work something that you cannot leave, or may I have a little of your time?'

After a brief word with the most senior workman, Frances went with Lyddington. He was such a man of surprises. He roared and bellowed and stamped around as much as, if not more than, any gentleman of the day, and yet he had requested, not demanded her attendance, with great courtesy. She was becoming more interested in him by the minute.

'Do you know Marigold Stevenson?' asked the earl at length, when they were out of earshot.

'Not really. Doesn't she live in the village?' Then remembering the story of the earl's arrival, she said, 'Oh.'

'Precisely, my dear Frank,' said Lyddington grinning. He never minded stories being told against himself. A fine horseman, he never blamed his mounts for his own mistakes, and laughed as heartily about the tosses he had taken as the next man.

As they walked, he threw an arm around her shoulders, as was now his usual custom, and again Frances found herself feeling very torn. She had begun to find a sweetness in his proximity that she had never felt with any other man; and yet there was always her masquerade between them. Who was to say what his reaction would be if he discovered her to be a woman? He found her a congenial companion at present, almost in an avuncular way, but if she were to appear as a woman, he might not find her in any way interesting or unusual.

'She was here the day the plans disappeared,' Lyddington continued. 'My sister left her alone in the saloon, so perhaps she might have gone to the steward's room, taken them, and left by the French windows in the saloon.'

'Do you think it was indeed she, My Lord?'

'I can think of no one else with the motive and the opportunity.'

'And after she had taken them, she could have walked round by the kitchen gardens, and put them amongst the things to be burned . . . '

'Where Peter Rance found them and burned them, having no idea what he was destroying.'

'It's an interesting theory, My Lord, but where does it leave you? I mean, how are you going to make use of this information?'

'Devil if I know. Watch them both very carefully, I suppose. I don't think there's the smallest chance that they are working together, but it don't do to be complacent. A woman who's capable of giving wine like the stuff I drank last night is surely capable of anything.'

'Wine, My Lord?' asked Frances, puzzled.

'Forgot you didn't know. Yes, the dratted

woman brought some to the house the day after I arrived. M'sister brought it out last night. Gave me a very nasty turn, I can tell you.'

Frances suddenly felt an icy touch of fear.

'My Lord, surely it was not poisoned!'

'Poisoned?' laughed the earl. 'Good grief, no. You're beginning to sound like Valeria! D'you think I don't know the difference between poison and bad wine? But I'll tell you something, Frank: it's been a grim lesson to me; never drink anything unless you know where it's come from.'

The earl laughed again, and Frances forced herself to join in, but after he had gone inside, having clapped her on the back again in his usual vigorous style, she was left with a vague uneasiness that not all her concentrated application to her work could quite dispel.

* * *

The following day brought the visitors that Lady Valeria had invited, and whose advent Lyddington so much dreaded.

The first to arrive was Miss Gertrude Renshaw. She was an old school friend of Lady Valeria from coming-out days, and it was never very long before the two of them came to cuffs, because they were both made of the same strong metal.

Unlike Lady Valeria, Miss Renshaw had come from an extremely wealthy family, and her mother, very indolent at the best of times, had never found the strength of mind to insist that her daughter should marry. Indeed, the forceful Gertrude had come as rather a shock to her easy-going and rather timid parents, and they had found it simpler to let her get her own way.

To have described Miss Renshaw as hatchet-faced would have been unkind. She had never been a beauty, but she was wise enough to avoid frills and elaborate jewellery and ornamentation of any kind, and succeeded, in her maturity, in looking so distinguished, that she had in fact received more offers of marriage over the past ten years than she had ever received as a girl; all of which she had refused with the greatest equanimity.

She had always been interested in botany, and had been commended by her governess for her scrapbooks of pressed flowers, her painstaking drawing of garden specimens, and her neat floral needlework. Now, her garden was her pride and joy, and the most sunny smile that ever adorned her features was elicited by a complimentary remark about her choice of plants, careful arrangement of flower beds, and so on.

The second visitor to arrive was Mrs Felicia Cranborne, a guest whom Lady Valeria had included rather guiltily, and not without a lot of heart-searching. Mrs Cranborne was a handsome widow of about thirty-six — although vilest torture would never have persuaded her to admit to more than twenty-seven — and she had at one time been a very close acquaintance of the earl's.

Truth to tell, Mrs Cranborne's interest in flowers was of the very slightest, limited to sniffing appreciatively at a bouquet — after checking, of course, to make sure that the sender was currently in favour. It is very doubtful that she would have been at Lyddington Court at all, had she not discovered by the luckiest chance that Lyddington was on his way home.

The earl, upon attending an embassy function in Italy — much against his will, it must be said — told the ambassador of his proposed return. The ambassador happened to be acquainted with Felicia's elderly aunt, Lady Broome, and the old lady, knowing of Felicia's interest in the earl, had passed on the vital piece of information.

When Lady Valeria had most fortuitously popped up to town, it had been quite easy for

Felicia to cultivate an interest in plants in order to gain an invitation to Lyddington Court, especially when she had hinted a little sadly about a youthful attachment between herself and the earl that had never really died.

That story was true in part at least. Eighteen years ago, she had known him rather better than her parents had ever suspected, and she would have been glad to marry him, if he had had more money. But neither of them had been sufficiently in love to throw caution to the winds, and when the wealthy Miss Comberley and the wealthy Mr Cranborne had appeared at about the same time, their ways had parted — apart from an occasional flirtation, and one encounter on the Continent three years ago.

Now, Felicia had decided that it was time she was settled in life. Dull Mr Cranborne had died six years ago, almost without his wife noticing the fact, and Felicia, a wealthy widow, was free to follow her fancy, rather than to look to the practicalities. Her fancy had lighted on Lyddington, and she saw no reason why he should not be brought to feel the same way. This visit would be the start of her campaign.

Two others guests were Marion Blakemuir and her daughter Alicia. Mrs Blakemuir was, at thirty-eight, still pretty and slender, with liquid brown eyes and a mass of brown curls to match. Her daughter was slightly shorter, with a more rounded figure. Her eyes were hazel and her hair a slightly lighter shade, and she was almost nauseatingly sentimental about anything to do with nature and flowers.

Mrs Blakemuir was unashamedly on the catch for a titled husband for her daughter, and had decided that Lyddington would do very well.

Miss Judith Hartington was a bit of a mystery. She had seemed very anxious to come and was clearly knowledgeable about flowers and gardens, but she also appeared to be rather nervous. She was a tall, thin girl with straight hair, deep-set eyes and a long thin nose; indeed, everything about her appeared to be thin. She was under the chaperonage of her friend Mrs Briar Storringe, whose husband was in the army and involved in some sort of manoeuvres at present.

As Lady Valeria took tea with her guests for the first time since their arrival, she could not suppress one tiny guilty pang. After all, there were only two ladies in her party of six whom she could be quite sure were not pursuing Lyddington either for themselves or for their relations — and even out of those two, Mrs Storringe might be out to promote Miss

Hartington's cause.

Her ladyship was not used to feeling guilty about anything, particularly with regard to her treatment of her brother, so she quickly comforted herself with the thought that if so many of them were after him, then they would probably all get in each other's way most of the time. In any case, Lyddington had been an eligible widower evading all manner of traps for the past fifteen years. No doubt he wouldn't be caught until he was good and ready. Lady Valeria allowed herself a small smile as she took in Mrs Cranborne's elaborate gown and rapacious look. Perhaps it was just as well that Lyddington was sleeping in the gatehouse!

* * *

Frances was working in the older part of the wilderness that afternoon. She and her father had decided not to make many changes there, but there was some undergrowth that needed to be trimmed away so she had set to with her pruning knife and was making good progress. Of course, it was not really the time of year for pruning, but there was a lot of dead wood preventing some new buds from looking their best, and Frances had decided to clear it away. That would give Peter Rance something else to put on his fire! The thought of him made her shiver slightly, and so, pulling herself together, she got on with her task with renewed vigour.

She was often alone in the garden, but she never minded. She enjoyed the opportunity for reflection. After a few minutes, she paused in her work, taking a little time to enjoy the peace of the garden only disturbed by natural sounds. No sooner had she stopped work, however, than she started to feel that she was being watched. Stepping out from where she was working, she looked around, but there did not appear to be anyone about. She admonished herself for being foolish, but continued to feel uneasy.

She had almost succeeded in convincing herself that her fears were entirely imaginary, when she heard the crackling of twigs, and a rustling that might indicate someone's approach.

'Who's there?' she called. 'Higgins, is that you?' There was no response; just a lingering, watchful atmosphere, with a hint of malice to it.

She was starting to think that it might be as well to leave this work and move to a more frequented area, when she heard footsteps and moments later the earl came into view, his firm manly features bearing what could only be described as a hunted expression.

'Hide me, for the Lord's sake!' he exclaimed, when he saw her. 'It's those confounded women! They're here!'

'My Lord . . . ' began Frances, about to remonstrate with him. Then hearing admiring female voices coming closer, she said, 'In here, My Lord,' and moved aside to let him through, and in amongst the bushes. There was barely time for him to thrust himself past her and for her to push back the undergrowth and take her place once more, before the ladies appeared.

Frances took off her hat and bowed slightly, but remained where she was, afraid to expose the earl.

'Ah, Master Sutcliffe,' said Lady Valeria. 'Hard at work I see.' She turned to her companions. 'The wilderness will be remaining, and will be incorporated into the new plans.'

Miss Renshaw looked carefully at the plants, then at Frances.

'Is this one of the new gardeners, Valeria?'

'Yes, Master Sutliffe and his uncle are transforming the gardens for us.'

'I trust they come adequately recommended,' said the beautiful Mrs Cranborne languidly, as she raised a large bud in one kid-gloved hand, then let it go as if it were unworthy of further notice.

'Most certainly,' said Lady Valeria with some hauteur, taking this comment as a slight upon her own excellent judgement. 'Master Sutcliffe is to go over the plans with us tomorrow evening after dinner.'

Frances bowed in acknowledgement and the guests moved on. As soon as the coast was clear, Frances stepped forward to allow the earl to come out of his hiding place. He was looking a little dishevelled, somewhat shaken and furiously angry. He opened his mouth, undoubtedly to give voice to a loud expletive, whereupon Frances hurriedly said, 'My Lord, pray recall! You may be overheard!'

The earl closed his lips tightly, then spoke, his voice furious, but in an undertone.

'That does it! By Heaven a man should be allowed to swear at the top of his voice in his own garden if he wishes to! My bloody sister! How dare she! How dare she? If I have told her once, I have told her a thousand times, I will not have her arrange a marriage for me!'

He drew closer to Frances, put his arm around her shoulders and spoke more pointedly in her ear.

'One of those cursed females in that group is the most virulent man-chaser that ever drew breath, and she's got my scent in her nostrils. And I shouldn't be surprised if the rest of them are after me too! Damn her!'

Frances was finding that his closeness and the intimacy of his warm breath on her face as he whispered in her ear was sending rather strange shivers down her spine. Anxious that she should not betray this heightened awareness of him, and moreover not being too sure whom the earl might be damning now, she merely whispered, 'My Lord, you may be doing them an injustice. Perhaps they are really here just to see the gardens.'

'And perhaps I am the queen of the fairies,' retorted the earl, with heavy sarcasm. 'No, they are hounds in hot pursuit, and I am their fox; but I'll prove too wily for them, mark my words! Thank Heaven I thought to stay in the gatehouse with you! Well, all my dependence is upon you, young Frank. There's nothing like another man to give a fellow courage!'

So saying, he turned, paused, then gripped Frances warmly by the hand and darted away in the opposite direction to the one which his guests had taken.

Frances remained looking in the direction in which he had gone for some minutes. As she stood there, she started to review the different guests in her mind. Which one, she wondered, was the virulent man-chaser? She thought she had a shrewd idea. It must of course be Mrs Cranborne, the very fashionable and worldly-looking woman in the vivid red gown, with her hair dressed high upon her head. There could certainly be no doubting her femininity! The earl might rail against her now, but how long would it be before he succumbed to her undoubted wiles? Frances glanced down briefly at her own working garb of waistcoat and breeches, then resumed her task with renewed savagery.

It was only some time later that she recalled the feeling of malice that she had experienced so vividly, before the earl's appearance. If his presence had not been responsible for that — and surely it could not have been — then who else had been frequenting the garden that day?

The earl was just congratulating himself on avoiding his visitors, when he came suddenly upon his estate manager, apparently hurrying towards where the ladies had gone. On seeing the earl, he lost a little colour, bowed, then straightened up and put up a hand to ease a neckcloth that seemed to be suddenly too tight.

Privately, Lyddington thought that he looked the picture of guilt, but out loud he simply said, 'Good day, Masters. This is unusual territory for you. Were you looking for me or my sister — or for Sutcliffe, perhaps?'

'Er . . . no . . . yes . . . that is, I was just . . . just taking a little air, you know, My Lord. I was feeling a trifle . . . ah . . . '

'Don't mention it,' replied Lyddington. He put an arm on Masters' shoulder in the companionable way that he was accustomed to do with 'young Frank,' but something about the way that the young man stiffened made him withdraw, and say quickly, to fill the embarrassing silence, 'Now that I've seen you, I have something to ask you. Would you be so good as to dine with us tonight?'

The young man whitened yet again, opened his mouth then closed it, saying nothing.

The earl went on, 'I seem to be the only man amongst a crowd of females, and it don't appeal to me. Say you'll bear me company. I'm thinking of asking Sutcliffe as well.'

Masters swallowed rather unhappily, then said, 'Forgive me, My Lord, but I beg you will hold me excused.'

'You have a prior engagement?'

'I . . . no, My Lord, I have not,' answered Masters, trembling at his own temerity. 'But I feel it would not be wise. I am an employee of yours — a servant in effect. I should feel I was stepping out of my proper station in life.'

He said all this without looking once at the earl.

'But damn it all, if I don't object . . . ' exclaimed Lyddington.

'My Lord, I beg you will excuse me,' said Masters desperately, bowing, then walking away.

'Extraordinary,' murmured the earl to himself, before walking back to the house.

* * *

That evening, Frances received a very nasty shock that was almost her undoing. She was in her room, having gone up to wash ready for dinner. Ruby was not with her, being about her housekeeper's duties.

Fortunately, she had been jotting down her account of the work done that day, a discipline from which she never allowed herself to lapse. She had therefore not begun to change, and was still wearing her wig, when, with very little warning, her door opened and she heard the earl's voice.

'Frank, my boy, forgive my sudden entrance, but I've had a splendid notion! You could come for dinner at the Court tonight! No need to sit on your own.'

'And protect you from all those women, My Lord?' asked Frances, thankful that she was sitting with her back to the door so that he could not see the shocked expression on her face. Laying down her pen, she stood up and turned to face him. He was still dressed in the breeches and shirt that he had been wearing that day, but he had cast aside his coat and as he was changing, his shirt was half-unbuttoned and pulled out of his breeches.

Cursing her inclination to blush at the sudden sight of his state of undress, she feigned a coughing fit. Unfortunately, however, this only exacerbated her problem, for the earl in response fetched a glass of water from her dresser and brought it to her after first patting her vigorously on the back. As a consequence, he was now much closer to her than before. She took a reviving drink, and felt a little better.

'Forgive me, My Lord,' she said at last, putting some distance between them by setting her glass back on the dresser. 'I do not really have any suitable evening clothes,' she went on. 'My uncle and I never bring such things when we are working.'

'Damnation!' said the earl frowning. 'What, nothing at all?'

'Not to appear before ladies, My Lord.'

'Confound it! And you're too slight to wear anything of mine. Well, as Masters don't appear to care for my company, and you have nothing to wear, I suppose I'll have to go alone, a solitary Daniel into the lion's den,' replied Lyddington regretfully. 'But I'll tell you what, Frank, we'll go to Bedford tomorrow afternoon, order you a set of evening clothes, and then spend a convivial evening at the Swan!'

Frances felt a sudden upsurge of panic.

'But My Lord . . . '

'Yes, yes I know, your work. You're a conscientious young devil, I'll say that for you. That's why I said we'd go in the afternoon. You can get plenty of work done in the morning.'

'My uncle is depending on me in his absence . . . ' said Frances rather feebly, feeling that she was rapidly running out of excuses.

'I'll set all right with your uncle, never fear.' He paused for a moment, then said in a slightly hurt tone, absently unbuttoning the rest of his shirt as he spoke, 'What's the matter, young Frank? You'd rather go roistering with a younger fellow, I suppose. I must be getting old, I think.'

Anxious not to hurt him, and yet even more concerned to avoid a convivial male evening at the Swan, Frances racked her brains, and came up with a brilliant and absolutely valid excuse.

'No indeed, My Lord,' she said earnestly, 'but tomorrow I am committed to seeing Lady Valeria and her guests after dinner, so that I can go through the plans with them.'

'Hm,' said the earl, thrusting his hands into his breeches pockets, thus pushing back the edges of his shirt and thereby exposing the full extent of his manly chest. Frances averted her gaze, and busied herself tidying her papers with fingers that suddenly seemed to have become all thumbs.

'Tell you what, Frank,' he said to her. 'We'll go into Bedford as I suggested, and get you measured up. It may be that the tailor might have something in your size — garments not collected, or something of the sort. Never mind your work for one day! We'll go in the morning, rather than in the afternoon, then we can have something to eat together. We'll return in the afternoon and if we're lucky, you might have something more formal to wear. Then you can dine with us, and save me from that devilish harpy. What say you?'

Frances took a deep breath.

'Very well, My Lord,' she said with a sigh, keeping her face averted.

Lyddington gazed at her searchingly, then crossed the room to put an arm around her shoulders, thus completing her confusion.

'I see what it is, young Frank,' he said kindly. 'I suspect you're afraid that one of these young females will take a fancy to you, and so it may be! But don't worry; there's safety in numbers! As there are two of us, we'll be able to keep to our port after the ladies have withdrawn, and with any luck, we'll get roaring drunk and not see them at all after dinner!'

'You are forgetting the plans, My Lord,' said Frances, laughing a little weakly. His proximity had never affected her so much before — but then she had never been close to him in this state of undress — and her heartbeats and temperature were doing rather strange things. She tried to tell herself how ridiculous this was — after all, she was used to working in the open, and this was certainly not the first time that she had seen a bare-chested man.

It was, however, the first time that one such had put his arm around her shoulders. To bring herself down to earth, she tried to tell herself that he smelled sweaty and unpleasant, but this was not true.

The earl, in common with many men of his time, had no high opinion of baths, and seldom indulged in them; but he frequently swam in clement weather, and it was a very common thing for a stable lad to be asked to work the pump over him in the yard. No, there was nothing repulsive about him, so for the sake of her peace of mind, Frances was very thankful when he released her and walked over to the door.

'But for now,' he sighed, 'I have tonight to get through. Well, thank God I'm returning here. Enjoy your solitary state. Do you have any wine, or shall I send a bottle over?'

'Thank you, My Lord, I am well provided for,' replied Frances. She would probably not drink any wine at all on her own, but she naturally did not say so.

'When does your uncle return, by the way?'

'Very soon, My Lord,' said Frances hopefully.

'Excellent. Then he can come and dine as well.'

He was about to go, when he turned back, and said, with unmistakable sincerity, 'You performed a friend's office for me today, young Frank. Had it not been for you, I'd have been confronted with those devilish women in the wilderness. I'm very grateful to you. Thank you.'

'Not at all, My Lord,' replied Frances, taking the hand that he held out to her.

'Oh, and by the way, Stop callimg me 'My Lord' all the time. It's unnecessary between friends.'

'Very well, my . . . sir. But what shall I call you?'

'Well, m'sister calls me Spencer; and you'll find that some of the females she's got staying will do the same, but all my male friends and acquaintances call me Sarrell.'

Frances waited until she had heard the sound of his door close before she sat down on the bed, feeling an unaccountable desire to weep.

'All his male friends call him Sarrell' she said, in the voice of one about to make a startling and not entirely welcome discovery. 'But I want to be a woman for him.'

6

The earl had determined not to look anything remarkable for his sister's dinner. If anything, he wanted to blend into the background. He liked women, and the company of women; but he enjoyed the company of his own sex too, and to be just one man in a room full of ladies would be rather too much of a good thing.

In order not to draw attention to himself, his lordship had gone for sombre colours. This was rather a mistake. He had looked magnificent, the night that Frances had seen him in full court rig-out. Tonight, quite unintentionally, he looked absolutely killing.

He had put on a black coat embroidered with jet and black beads, and black breeches to match. A snowy white waistcoat was found to have a small stain on it, so his lordship opted for a scarlet one, in the mistaken belief that it would look horrible with his unpowdered chestnut locks, whereas in fact, it simply drew attention to their vibrant glow. With his toilette completed by white stockings and black shoes, Lyddington decided that he looked absolutely dreadful.

Mrs Felicia Cranborne, seeing him for the first time in many months, decided that he was a man worth dying for; Alicia Blakemuir, who had previously thought him old and brash, revised her opinion; and Marion Blakemuir, who had wanted him for her daughter, now wondered whether such a man might not be wasted on a chit of eighteen.

The earl had taken great care not to arrive much before the hour of dinner, and indeed appeared only just in time to make his bow before the butler came in to announce that the meal was served. Somehow, by some means only known to herself, Felicia Cranborne managed to walk into dinner with the earl, leaving the rest of the ladies to be shepherded in by Lady Valeria.

At the dinner-table, Lyddington took the head, with the resourceful Mrs Cranborne on his right, and Mrs Storringe on his left. Lady Valeria took the foot with Miss Renshaw and Mrs Blakemuir either side of her. The two youngest members of the party, Miss Alicia and Miss Judith, sat in the middle opposite one another. Miss Stevenson had been invited, but had sent her apologies as she had a slight cold.

None could have doubted that Mrs Bartlett had put forth her best efforts for this particular meal. For some, however, the meal was of secondary importance to the conversations that were taking place during its course.

The earl looked up from his helping of fowl in plum sauce to see Mrs Cranborne regarding him as if he, too were something edible. As soon as her eyes met his, however, her smile became softer and warmer.

'How long it is since we were in Rome, my dear Spencer?' she said in her charming, low-pitched voice. 'And what a vast amount of time you managed to spend among those old ruins! You made me feel quite neglected.'

'Since I was there to see the ruins, to have departed without visiting them would have been rather perverse,' replied the earl, determined not to be diverted from his food.

'True,' replied Felicia, smiling. 'But then those of us who know you and . . . admire you, are charmed by your occasional — perversities.'

'You do me too much honour, ma'am,' replied Lyddington, determined not to call her by her given name. Then he turned with some relief to Mrs Briar Storringe on his left. That lady showed no wish to behave towards him with anything other than cool friendliness, and he enquired after her husband's military career with some interest.

Mrs Storringe was a slight woman with a rather boyish figure, a mass of rather mousy curls, and an open, confiding manner, but the manner could be deceptive. In fact, she was far more astute than most people gave her credit for.

She and Captain Storringe had been married for five years, but had not been blessed with children as yet. Mrs Storringe, being a sensible woman, tried not to repine, travelled with her husband whenever she could, and when that was not practicable, gained much pleasure from the cultivation of the garden of their comfortable town house, which was situated in Salisbury.

She did not know Lady Valeria well, but they had chanced to meet at a rout in London and had fallen into conversation. In the course of this, each had discovered the other's interest in horticulture. On the strength of this, Lady Valeria had issued an invitation, and Briar had managed to have this extended to include Judith Hartington, whose mother was rather anxious to take her mind off an unsuitable attachment.

'Your husband is on exercises at present, I believe?' asked the earl.

'Yes, in Buckinghamshire,' replied Mrs Storringe.

'Not far away, then.'

'No, but it might as well be the other end of the world when he has too much to do,' she replied ruefully. 'Were you ever a military man, My Lord?'

'No, ma'am. I was the only son to grow to manhood so any career other than estate management was out of the question.'

'And do you regret it?' she asked, tactfully refraining from pointing out that his estate had seen very little of him over the past few years. The earl was about to answer but Mrs Cranborne, who felt that his attention had been diverted from her for quite long enough, spoke first.

'Ah, what regrets some of us cherish,' she cooed, her eyes snapping a little angrily because her quarry had been conversing so easily with insignificant little Mrs Storringe. 'The things we might have done — the opportunities we might have missed.'

'I cannot imagine a woman of your resource ever missing an opportunity,' said Mrs Storringe in the mildest of tones, as she took a mouthful of syllabub. Mrs Cranborne looked suspiciously at her, but then decided that anything that that little mouse said could surely be taken at face value.

'You may be sure that I never make the same mistake twice,' she replied, with a predatory look at the earl. His lordship, seeing her expression, suddenly choked over his wine and had to call for a glass of water.

As he sipped it, he saw Felicia smile, and to him, in her feathered head-dress and with her rather prominent nose and sparkling eyes, she looked just like a bird of prey ready to pounce.

Quelling a most unmanly feeling of panic, he steered the conversation into the unromantic topic of land management until, to his great relief, Lady Valeria rose to signal the departure of the ladies.

'You will surely not wish to linger alone, Spencer,' murmured Felicia as she left. 'It has been so long since we last . . . talked together.'

Aye, and it'll be as long again, if I have any say in the matter, said the earl to himself as he sank his first glass of port. 'Damnation! Does the woman have no restraint at all? Thank God I'm staying at the gatehouse! Well, two things are certain at any rate: one is that I'm not sitting through another devilish meal like that without male support; and the other is that I'm not rejoining that gaggle of females!'

So, while the ladies entertained themselves, some of them well satisfied, others less so, the earl finished off his bottle of port, left by another door and went back to the gatehouse, whereupon finding that Frances had gone early to bed, he spent an hour or two with a book and then retired himself. The ladies waited in vain.

* * *

Later that night, Felicia sat examining her face in the mirror, looking for the slightest trace of a wrinkle. Eventually, well satisfied with her examination, she rose and walked towards the bed.

She was quite determined to have the earl. She had been determined before she had come to the Court, even though she had not seen him for some time. He had been a handsome young man, if a trifle rough and ready, when she had turned him down in favour of the wealthy Mr Cranborne. Even then, she would have been very willing to become his mistress, but he had seemed strangely reluctant to take that step.

After they had married and gone their separate ways, they had seen little of each other, but Felicia had not forgotten him, and she was convinced that he had not forgotten her. In her youth, Felicia had had a small but sturdy talent for self-conceit that had been diligently nourished by her doting parents, despite all attempts to the contrary by various governesses, who never stayed long. Finally, by the time she burst upon the ton, a beauty, it was true — if a little sharp-featured and hard of eye — it was well-nigh impossible for her to believe that any man could look at her and not instantly desire her.

Lyddington had looked at her and desired her, but his destiny had lain in a different direction, and his initial desire had not survived separation. Hers had, however, and she was now hot in pursuit. She had a fancy to marry again, and it might soon be too late. Her beauty was still undeniable, but now appeared at its best in candlelight. Her sharp features had begun to gain an angular quality in some lights which was decidedly unappealing, and her figure, although still good, had lost its supple quality. Decidedly, Lyddington must be caught, and caught soon.

* * *

Riding into Bedford the following morning, Frances was grateful that the earl had found her a comparatively docile horse. She had not ridden a great deal for some years, and hardly at all astride — for most of her riding was done when she was at home, in Plymouth. So when the earl had said to her, 'Well, young Frank, what kind of a beast appeals to you today? One that's a little mettlesome?'

She had replied. 'Oh no, My Lord, I beg

you! I am much more used to walking than riding, and must ask you to find me a very good-tempered mount.'

'Very well, but on one condition,' Lyddington had replied pointing his finger at her. 'I asked you to call me Sarrell, and I would like you to respect my wishes.'

'Very well — Sarrell,' she had replied, and, with a smile, he had given instructions for the groom to saddle Blackberry.

The horse proved to be as sweet-tempered as her name, and no trouble at all. As they set off, Frances glanced across at her employer's profile and reflected upon his consideration with gratitude. There were men — and she had met some of them — who, on hearing about her nervousness with horses, would have deliberately given her a mettlesome one for their own amusement. Lyddington, she knew instinctively, would never do such a thing. She had begun to understand why his people thought so much of him; why they were prepared to see behind the outbursts of temper and the Lyddington bellow, to the kind heart that he undoubtedly possessed.

'Well, Frank, and what do you think of our Bedfordshire scene? Dull, ain't it?'

'It's certainly not very exciting,' agreed Frances, looking about her at the almost uniformly flat countryside.

'Beats me why our ancestors ever settled here,' remarked the earl as he rode, sitting easily in the saddle, the reins in one gloved hand, the other on his hip. 'I suspect that whatever we did to please the king didn't really please him all that much. Still, it's my home, for all that, and a man has to belong somewhere. Tell me, Frank, where is your home when you are not gardening, and who tends it for you?'

'My uncle has a house near Plymouth,' she replied truthfully. 'That is where we live when we are not working.'

'And your parents?'

'They . . . they are dead, My Lord — Sarrell,' she corrected quickly, after a sharp glance from his lordship.

'Sad. And have you no female relatives to care for hearth and home, and patiently await your return?'

'I — have a cousin,' replied Frances, after a moment's hesitation. She and Thomas had always maintained the fiction that there were two people, his daughter and his nephew, in order that she should be able to assume a female role whenever she wished. At their own house, she never played the man, and was known in their small area as Miss Frances Sutcliffe. As they were often away, she was not acquainted with many people.

'Living with you?'

'Yes . . . yes, she looks after the house for us.'

'And is she of your age and temper, Frank?'

'Yes, My . . . Sarrell, we are much alike in . . . in every way,' said Frances, becoming a little flustered.

'Pretty?'

'Very pretty,' said Frances recklessly.

'Perhaps I should pay a visit to the Plymouth area,' mused the earl playfully. 'Methinks a pretty girl with your nature would suit me very well. Careful, young Frank,' he added quickly, catching hold of the rein, for Frances had jerked involuntarily, causing Blackberry to shy a little.

'Have you travelled much?' asked his lordship as they rode through the town of Houghton Conquest. It was quite a busy place, big enough to have a school of sorts, and there were plenty of people going about their business. Frances could not help but notice that their journey so far had resembled a royal progress. They had not yet ridden past anyone who walked by without a curtsy or a touch of the forelock — which courtesy the earl never ignored, sometimes speaking, sometimes merely nodding if he and Frances were conversing.

'A little within this country, in order to

execute my uncle's commissions, but abroad, not at all,' replied Frances. 'But I should very much like to do so. You have travelled extensively, have you not, sir?'

'I have. My father sent me on the Grand Tour, and it was the best thing he ever did for me. Well, you know how much I love it, for during the past twelve years, I have spent nearly as much time abroad as I have spent at home.'

'I suppose you speak French and Italian.'

'Yes I do. French very badly, although enough to make myself understood, and Italian rather better. Why did you never go on the Grand Tour yourself then?'

Unable to think of a convincing reason, Frances simply murmured, 'My father's death . . . '

'Oh yes, of course. I beg your pardon.'

Thankful to have escaped closer questioning on this topic, Frances merely inclined her head.

'Well, there's still time,' resumed the earl, 'and you ought to see Italy. From what I can gather from your garden designs, much is drawn from the Italian scene, or at any rate painters' ideas of the Italian scene. Next time I go to Italy, we'll see if your uncle can spare you. I've a fancy to take you under my wing.'

'Thank you, sir,' said Frances, a little taken

aback. 'You are very good.' For a brief, unguarded moment, the prospect of travelling around Europe with him seemed almost irresistibly attractive — until she remembered her disguise.

'Oh, and by the way,' said his lordship as Bedford came into view, 'I don't like 'sir' from you any more than I like 'My Lord'. It makes me feel like an elderly relative, and if you do it any more, I'll tan your breeches.'

'Very well,' murmured Frances, thankful that the press of persons on the road made it necessary for him to ride ahead, and thus not see her blushes.

They left their horses at the Swan and walked to a small tailor's shop in Silver Street, which the earl thought might just have something for them. Here luck favoured Frances. She had come fully provided with her own measurements taken by her faithful Ruby — whose outrage at the whole expedition had to be seen to be believed — for she was quite determined that no tailor was going to measure her. However, when they entered the shop, the earl going first naturally, and making his wishes known, it turned out that a local gentleman of just Master Sutcliffe's slight build had ordered some clothes and being in debt had found himself unable to pay for them, so the tailor had retained them.

There were two sets of evening attire, comprising coat, waistcoat and breeches, one set with the emphasis on blue, the other inclining towards brown, and also some shirts, not to mention coat and breeches for everyday wear.

'We'll take the lot,' said the earl largely, without any reference to Frances. 'Pack 'em up, will you?'

'But My . . . but Sarrell, I don't need all these,' protested Frances in hushed tones. She had come prepared to buy some new clothes, but not a whole wardrobe.

'Not immediately, perhaps, but you'll soon have occasion to wear them,' replied the earl cheerfully.

'I don't think so, My Lord,' replied Frances. 'The blue set will be quite sufficient.'

'Damned if it will,' retorted Lyddington, beginning to look less than pleased. 'If you're dining in my company, you'll need more than one suit of clothes.'

'But I cannot afford . . . ' began Frances in desperation, speaking in an undertone.

'Oh,' exclaimed Lyddington, his brow clearing. 'Don't worry about that, young Frank. I'm paying for these.'

Frances might have lived much of her adult

life as a man, but when it came to accepting presents of clothing, she found suddenly that her reaction was entirely female.

'No!' she cried, her hand going to her throat in a wholly feminine gesture that would have given her away to the earl had he not been too angry to notice. 'I cannot allow it.'

'Fiend seize it! I can do what I damn well please!' declared the earl, utterly losing his patience and turning to the tailor, who had been watching these proceedings with a good deal of interest. 'Have the blue set wrapped up and sent round to the Swan straight away. The rest can be sent to Lyddington Court with the bill.'

The earl took hold of Frances' arm and marched her out of the shop. Once outside, he rounded fiercely upon her, and bellowed, 'What the hell do you mean by arguing with me before a shopkeeper?'

Frances whitened a little. 'I . . . '

'Damnation, boy, have you no respect for me at all?' The voice was not as loud as the Lyddington bellow was wont to be, but the tone was as furiously angry as any she had heard from him, although she had never had that anger turned upon herself before.

'But, sir, I did not know . . . '

'You knew bloody well that you were to

have new clothes. Do you think me so penny-pinching as to buy only one coat? Or perhaps,' he went on with awful sarcasm, 'you expected us to hunt around the back streets to see if we could find something that had not been worn too many times?'

'No, by no means, My Lord, but . . . '

'Then why the devil did you dispute with me in such a way? 'Pon my honour, I don't know when I've ever been so humiliated. God knows why I bother with you.'

He strode aggressively up Silver Street, making no allowances for other road users, and rendering it very difficult for a rather distressed Frances to keep up with him. At length, as he reached the lock-up on the corner, he was forced to halt by dint of a heavy press of people following a cart, behind which a man was being beaten as far as Bedford bridge.

'My Lord,' she said diffidently, venturing to touch him on the arm.

'And another thing,' stormed his lordship. 'I've told you already, no 'My Lord', and no 'sir'. Or I swear I'll beat the servility out of you, devil take me if I don't.'

Frances drew herself up to her full height. She was beyond embarrassment now.

'All right, do it,' she said, looking him straight in the eye. 'Beat me if it will make you feel better. You say you don't like to be argued with in front of a shopkeeper. Well, I don't like it either, and I don't like to be made to feel like a pauper. Yes, I do have respect for you; more respect than I have for any man, save my uncle, but I am not servile and I will not allow you to dictate my actions.'

The earl looked at his young companion for a long moment, then slowly a grin spread across his features, and he clapped Frances across the shoulders in his own inimitable style.

'Damme if I don't like your pluck,' he said. 'Forgive me if I made you feel like my pensioner. Such was not mine intention, believe me. If it concerns you, take the clothes as thanks for allowing me to share your home at some inconvenience to yourself. Or, if that won't do, then let us share the cost. I value your friendship much too highly to remain at odds with you, young Frank.'

'Very well, Sarrell,' replied Frances, looking away and suppressing the oddest desire to weep at this reconciliation.

'Come, let's hurry,' said the earl. 'We want to get to the Swan before the crowd turns at the bridge.'

Frances did not dispute with him. She had no desire to see the man being whipped again, his back by now being no doubt very bloody.

They arrived at the Swan, where Lyddington was obviously well remembered, although he could not have been there for some time, and one of the serving wenches smiled at him very roguishly, which attention he received with a broad wink.

They were about to go and take some refreshment, when suddenly the earl blenched and pulled Frances with him into a doorway.

'What is it?' asked Frances.

'Would you believe it? It's the Cranborne woman!' muttered Lyddington. 'Damn that harpy! For pity's sake keep out of sight, Frank. I do believe she's coming in here! Can't a man have any peace?'

'I don't suppose she even knows you are here,' whispered Frances soothingly. Then the carrying tones of Mrs Cranborne were heard quite distinctly.

'I believe Lord Lyddington is intending to take refreshment here,' she was saying.

'That I can't say, ma'am,' replied the landlord. 'But his horses are still here.'

'Damn you, Hoskins,' muttered the earl under his breath. 'That's the last time I make use of your hospitality.'

'Then we will wait for him,' Mrs Cranborne was saying. 'Come, Judith. Be sure and tell us when he arrives, Landlord.'

The landlord bowed, showed the ladies to a room where they could be comfortable, and then withdrew. No sooner had he done so, than he found himself seized, and dragged into one of the smaller rooms.

'Devil take you,' said the earl accusingly. 'If you ever tell another female anything about my whereabouts, I won't be answerable for the consequences. Now, has a package arrived for me yet?'

'No, My Lord,' said the landlord warily.

'It will. Have it taken over the bridge to the King's Arms. Also my horses. Discreetly.' He dropped some gold into the landlord's hand. 'Don't let me down. And if that har — ' Frances gave him a nudge with her elbow. 'If that lady asks about me again, you can say that we left suddenly, but you don't know when — and don't volunteer any information.'

'Very good, My Lord. I'm sorry to have — '

'No matter, no matter,' said the earl with a dismissive gesture. 'You're a good fellow, Hoskins.'

Frances and Lyddington left the inn on foot and crossed the bridge, then walked the short distance to the King's Arms. As the earl was bending his head to enter the hostelry, Frances, who was behind him, chanced to look round, and saw the figure of Masters, the estate manager riding into town. As she looked, he half glanced over his shoulder, then rode on a little more quickly.

Once inside, they ordered a simple meal of an excellent meat pie with vegetables, washed down with ale, followed by bread and cheese. Lyddington was used to consuming ale in handsome quantities with most meals, and he expected his companion to do the same. After their argument, she did not want to anger him by showing further ingratitude, so she was very thankful when, after the second flagon — which she had forced down with some difficulty — the earl commanded that a jug be left on their table. She hoped that he would be so busy consuming it himself that he would not notice her lack of consumption.

'Now, Frank, you will dine with us tonight?'

'You are very good,' murmured Frances.

'Devil a bit,' retorted the earl. 'You know very well that you're coming to protect me from all those she-wolves — and one she-wolf in particular. Masters won't do it. You know I asked him to dine with me last night?' Frances nodded. 'Well, do you know what he told me? Said if it was all the same to me he'd rather not do so.'

Frances was beginning to think that she

knew the earl quite well, for beneath his careless tone, she was sure that he was hurt by Masters' attitude.

'I expect he was reluctant to overstep the bounds between master and servant,' she said soothingly.

'Yes, that's more or less what he said,' agreed the earl. 'Strange, though. It did not sound as though the decision gave him any pleasure. I may be wronging him, but he strikes me as being a man with something to hide.'

'It's odd you should say that,' commented Frances, 'But I saw him just now as we were going into the inn. I had the distinct impression that he had seen you, but did not want to be seen.'

The earl grunted non-commitally, then picked up the jug.

'Come, Frank. You are not bearing your part with this ale. Allow me to fill your tankard.'

Frances reluctantly drank a little more, and they talked further on indifferent topics. She was just marvelling to herself how at ease she felt with him, when he suddenly destroyed her composure by saying, 'Well, it's about time to set out. Are you coming to water the horses?'

'Not for me,' replied Frances, thankful that

she had heard this term used before, and so did not take it at its face value.

'I envy your capacity,' said the earl wryly, as he rose to leave the room. As soon as he had done, Frances got up hurriedly, desperate to find some place where she could make herself more comfortable, and knowing that she would never manage the eight-mile ride back to Lyddington Court unless she had done so.

'Can I help you, sir?' asked a waiter.

'Er . . . I . . . er, no thank you,' replied Frances, wondering how on earth she could contain herself until they reached home. Then, as she stood undecided in the hallway, she heard a door close upstairs, and saw two ladies move away from the door at the top of the stairs and descend. She stood politely to one side, then as they left the inn, she ran up the stairs, and knocked on the door of the room that the ladies had just left. If a maid was in there, or if the door was locked, then she was done for. Fortunately neither was the case. In an instant, she was inside and moments later, she had discovered a most necessary item, and comfort was restored.

As quickly as she could, she ran downstairs and made her way to the stables, where the earl was waiting.

'Where the devil were you?' asked Lyddington good-humouredly.

'I thought I saw someone I knew pass the inn, but I was mistaken,' she replied.

'That's a mercy,' replied the earl with some relief. 'We've had quite enough of seeing people we know today.'

They mounted their horses, but it was not until they were clear of Bedford that the earl said, 'Would you like to hear why I hold the fair but rapacious Mrs Cranborne in such dread?'

'I'm a trifle curious, I must admit,' replied Frances.

'Well, we were nearly affianced at one time — but it never happened, thank God, and we went our separate ways. But we continued to meet from time to time. Then a while ago, nearly three years, I think, I was in Rome and I chanced to meet her at a masquerade. And as you know, a man has needs, and she was willing, so — I had her.'

Frances made no reply, simply because she had no idea what a man might say in these circumstances. For herself, she felt a sudden, irrational surge of hatred for the absent Mrs Cranborne that made her feel quite hot.

'Your silence condemns me,' said the earl, misreading her reaction. 'Of course, I should have had the sense to go instead with a charming Italian lady who would have played the game by the proper rules. But at times, you know, a persistent woman can have a certain allure, and well . . . oh, never mind, I shan't try to excuse myself. I notice you don't ask me whether the experience was a pleasurable one. Well, it was pleasant enough, although I've had better. But ever since then she seems to feel that she has some kind of claim upon me.'

'Perhaps she is in love with you,' ventured Frances.

'In love? Not she,' said the earl with a scornful snort. 'Or if she is, it's with my title and my property. But she'll not have me. She may be wily, but I'm wilier. And of course, I have you to defend me, have I not?'

'To the death,' replied Frances dramatically, her hand upon an imaginary sword-hilt.

Lyddington threw back his head and laughed.

The remainder of the ride passed very companionably, Frances pressing the earl to describe some of the scenery through which he had passed on his travels, which he did with great patience.

As they left the stables, on their arrival, they were met by Lady Valeria in a state of high temper.

'Back at last, I see,' she said coldly, her eyes upon Frances. 'Well, I suppose I cannot expect you to take your responsibilties seriously while your uncle is away, but thanks to your scandalous neglect, some wicked person has succeeded in mutilating parts of the garden.'

7

'Mutilating?' repeated Frances, unable to take in the news.

'Yes, mutilating,' retorted Lady Valeria. 'I hold you entirely to blame for this, Sutcliffe.'

'Enough, Valeria,' said the earl impatiently. 'The lad came with me at my command, and not without protest. If there is any blame to be apportioned, then I'll take it. Now, show us what is amiss immediately.'

Lady Valeria led them round to where Frances had been laying out the water garden. It was not as if it had never been: it was worse than that. The area that had been dug out had been filled in carelessly, and stones that had been used to give a natural effect to the base of the garden had been strewn around, whilst plants that had been set to give the garden shelter had been broken down and trampled into the dirt.

Even Valeria was silent, looking again at the wreckage of something that had had the potential to become so beautiful. Frances crouched down to examine a plant gently with her hands, its stem crushed beyond salvaging, its leaves torn to shreds. Quickly she stood up, and taking a few steps away, rapidly brushed her sleeve across her eyes.

Lady Valeria, feeling a hint of regret for her hasty words, took a hesitant step forward. The earl, thinking that she meant to castigate his protégé even more for carelessness, halted her with a gesture.

'He's only a lad,' he said under his breath and, walking across, he put his arm around the shoulders of the disconsolate figure in a much more gentle manner than he was wont to do.

Frances blinked hard. If he said anything kind, that would be the end of her composure, and probably her disguise as well.

'Good thing we bought you some new shirts today, Frank, after the curst mess you've made of that one,' said the earl dispassionately, looking at her sleeve where dirt and tears had combined to make a muddy mark, much resembling the one on her face. 'Go and wash yourself,' he went on matter-of-factly, 'then we'll see what's best to be done.'

Frances nodded, not quite trusting herself to say anything. She almost ran to the gatehouse, amazed that what should be so absorbing her thoughts was not the damage done to her precious garden, but the fact that she had just fully realized that she was in love with the earl.

'You make too much of a pet of that lad,' remarked Lady Valeria after she had gone. 'He'll be following you around like a puppy.'

'Not he,' retorted the earl, looking at the scene of the vandalism. 'He's got too much independence of mind. When did you discover this, Valeria?'

'Only shortly before you arrived. In fact,' admitted her ladyship, 'I suspect I was so severe with Sutcliffe because I was still in my first anger.'

'Hm,' grunted his lordship. 'Had you visited the site earlier this morning?'

'No. One of the gardeners came to tell me what had happened. I asked him that same question myself. It seems that Sutcliffe was supervising that work very closely himself, and when he was not there, they were to work on something else. So that part of the garden was deserted.'

'Not completely deserted,' said Lyddington grimly, as he looked once more at the ruined garden. 'Someone was very busy. And what about your ladies? Where the devil were they?'

* * *

Shortly afterwards, the three of them were assembled in one of the small upstairs salons. On Frances' return, Lyddington had escorted her firmly inside, ordered wine, and insisted that she sit down and drink it.

'You've had a bad shock,' he said. 'It's not every day that you find your work wantonly destroyed. Tell me, when did you last see the garden as it should be?'

'This morning, shortly before we left for Bedford,' said Frances, in very subdued tones. 'I had had some new ideas about the siting of plants, and I wanted to make some sketches. Oh, if only I had not gone!'

'Balderdash,' said Lyddington forthrightly. 'If someone wants to make mischief then he'll find the opportunity. You could just as easily have got up and found that it had been done in the night.'

He paused for a moment.

'If you visited them this morning, then all must have been well until about eight, when we left. And Valeria, you say that the gardener had only just informed you of what had happened?' His sister nodded. 'At about one, then. So what are your ladies doing now? Mrs Cranborne and Miss Hartington are accounted for, as we saw them in the town.'

'They are taking a walk around the lake — indeed they should soon be returning in order to prepare for dinner. Mrs Storringe — such a sensible woman — is leading them.'

There was a sudden interruption as Frances dropped her wineglass — mercifully empty — onto the floor.

'Oh, good heavens!' exclaimed her ladyship. 'No, no, do not attempt to clear it up! I shall ring for someone.' Frances looked from where she was picking up the larger pieces to see the earl regarding her very keenly.

'This has been too much for you,' he said roughly. 'Come, you're all knocked to pieces. No more work for you today, and I'll walk with you to the gatehouse to make sure that you don't. But mind, I'm still expecting you for dinner.'

Lady Valeria was giving instructions to the maid who had just entered. The earl made as if to take Frances' arm, but she turned slightly as he did so and by chance he caught hold of her hand instead. Their eyes met, and to her, it seemed as if she had touched fire. Perhaps his lordship was similarly affected, for certainly he almost threw her hand from him and stepped back as though he had been burned. There was a long silence.

'Well, get you gone, boy,' he said at last, in tones much harsher than he was wont to use. 'Why the deuce do you linger here?'

After one startled and rather hurt glance,

Frances left the room hurriedly, even forgetting to bow to either the earl or his sister.

'Now who is being severe?' asked Lady Valeria, after the glass had been cleared up and the maid had left the room. 'That was rather uncalled for, Spencer.'

'Perhaps you are right,' replied Lyddington, filling his glass for the second time since Frances had left. The previous glassful he had tossed off in one gulp. 'However, you had the right of it before, too. The boy should not be encouraged to dangle after me. Such hero worship is . . . unhealthy.'

After a short silence, Lady Valeria said to him, 'I believe you were asking me about the whereabouts of the ladies? But I cannot believe that any one of them would be likely to do such a thing. What would be the motive?'

'Jealousy?' suggested his lordship, torn between guilt at his harsh treatment of Sutcliffe, and interest in the matter in hand. 'These plans are good, and the garden is undoubtedly going to be fine.'

'Yes, but all of them have lovely gardens of their own. And in any case, such a task would take a lot of strength, and would undoubtedly result in very dirty clothes.'

The earl's eyes gleamed.

'Exactly so. Send for your dresser, Valeria. I believe I have a little job for her.'

* * *

Frances did not go straight back to the gatehouse. She felt after that last encounter with the earl that she needed fresh air. When she had looked into his eyes, she could have sworn that he had been as moved at the encounter as was she. His harsh dismissal, so unlike his usual easy camaraderie, had come as a shock to her.

She also had to think about what to do about the fact that Briar Storringe was of the party. It was the shock of hearing this news that had caused her to drop the glass.

She and Briar had been very close friends at the seminary that they had attended several years ago, and they had maintained a rather irregular correspondence, although they had not seen each other for a long time. Briar would certainly be at dinner tonight, and would undoubtedly recognize her.

If only she could send a message to warn her! But she did not know the indoor staff at the Court well enough to have discovered who could be entrusted with such an errand. She sighed inwardly. Her mind was too full of other things to grapple with this particular problem. At least she was forewarned. She would just have to rely on Briar's acting skills.

Almost despite herself, Frances found herself walking in the direction of the ruined water garden. She found it just as shocking as before, but after closer examination, she felt rather optimistic than otherwise. True, the plants were mostly destroyed, but some could be salvaged, and the clay bed of the garden, although filled in, appeared to be intact, whilst the stones could always be regathered.

She stood upright from her crouching position, and flexed her back. Before she could leave the site, she became aware of the same unaccountable feeling of menace that she had felt before in the wilderness. It was nothing that she could put her finger on but just a sensation that something malignant was watching her, and this time rejoicing in the destruction of her work, and longing to do her further harm.

Quickly, and not without some anxiety, she looked around, and at first there was no one to be seen. Then, as she looked harder, a figure detached itself from the background. It was Miss Marigold Stevenson, as usual without a hair out of place. She was dressed in woodland colours, which explained why Frances had not spotted her immediately.

Without thinking, Frances ran across to her straight away.

'Have you seen the water garden?' she asked, uttering the first question that came into her mind. 'Did you know that it had been destroyed?' Later, it would occur to her that if Miss Stevenson was the vandal, this might not be the wisest course to pursue, but right now, she did not think of that.

Marigold Stevenson looked thoughtfully at her, her head on one side like a bird, her face rather expressionless than otherwise.

'Destroyed? Yes, I knew it. Part of my garden was destroyed. Did you know that, Mr Sutcliffe?' Frances nodded. 'The mess was terrible. I cannot bear mess. Neatness and order are what please me.'

'What are you doing here?' asked Frances curiously.

Marigold looked around.

'I came to see the garden, of course. But I do not like it. It is far too untidy. Good day, Mr Sutcliffe.'

Treading very carefully, she made her way around the side of the house and out of sight. Frances wondered what she could be doing there. It was rather too early to be arriving for dinner, and it would be rather strange to make a special visit to see either the earl or his sister, when dinner would ensure an opportunity of speech with both of them. Perhaps Miss Stevenson had been responsible for the destruction of the garden? She had certainly not appeared to like it, but surely the resulting mess would have been just as displeasing to her. Also, there was the fact that to have moved some of the stones would have required quite strenuous effort. Would someone so delicate in appearance as Miss Stevenson be capable of such an effort?

Frances decided that it was about time she obeyed the earl's order to go home and rest. To tell the truth, she was still feeling a little shaky. She looked around her and listened for a while, but the feeling of menace had now gone. Thoughtfully, she made her way back to the gatehouse.

* * *

After the conversation with his sister, the earl left the room and was crossing the hall, when he chanced to see one of the footmen just entering the kitchen.

'Jem!' he called. The footman turned back. 'M'Lord?'

Instead of giving any kind of order, or simply swearing, the earl stood and stared at him for a long time, a circumstance which the footman found singularly unnerving. Indeed, it was all he could do not to glance down to see if there was a smut on his breeches, or a dirty mark on his shoes. Then with a grunt and a shake of his head, his lordship made for the door.

'M'Lord, is there anything . . . ?'

'What? No, nothing. Get you gone.'

Well, that was a relief, thought the earl to himself. Jem was a tall, handsome fellow, and very popular with the local girls, by all accounts, but Lyddington had not felt anything when he had looked at him.

A well-travelled and experienced man, he was fully aware that there were men who found their own sex attractive. He had never been able to understand it himself, but was much inclined to let people get on with their own private business. However, when he and young Sutcliffe had touched and looked at one another, he had felt such a tug of attraction that he had begun to wonder, with some panic, about his own sexuality. Now he told himself that must surely have been fatherly feeling, coupled with sympathy for the stress that the young fellow had just undergone. He would meet young Frank again without the slightest problem. However, it might be as well to avoid undue familiarity at present — just in case.

With this in mind, the earl greeted Frances

with rather more formality than was his wont, when they met in the parlour before going over to the Court together. They both looked rather splendid, Frances in her new blue, and Lyddington again in black and red. He looked so magnificent that Frances, seeing him for the first time in this striking dress, wondered whether she might even die of love on the spot. She was glad of the joke they made of bowing very formally to one another, for it gave her an opportunity of hiding her feelings.

She had not forgotten that she had the forthcoming encounter with Briar Storringe to worry about. What would her old school friend say? Might she be fooled completely by the disguise? Frances did not dare to hope so. Briar would never give her away deliberately; her only hope was that she would not do so inadvertently, through surprise.

She need not have worried. The pact that they had made in girlhood had not been forgotten by Mrs Storringe. That lady, on hearing that the Sutcliffes were in charge of the project, had pricked up her ears. The news that Mr Thomas Sutcliffe was assisted by his nephew had interested her vastly, as she knew that Frances had no cousins still living. The fact that this nephew was called Francis had interested her even more, and she had resolved to be prepared for anything. So, when she was confronted by her school friend in blue satin breeches and coat, with a darker waistcoat, she did not turn a hair. Instead, she made her curtsy, murmuring at the introduction,

'I am pleased to meet you, Mr Sutcliffe. I have heard a great deal about you from your cousin, who was a school friend of mine.'

Not surprisingly, Frances was speechless at this remark; but she was not permitted to linger, for the earl, anxious about his safety, immediately introduced her to Mrs Felicia Cranborne, and then beat a hasty and, as Frances thought, a rather cowardly retreat.

The beauty had put forth her best endeavours tonight, and was looking superb in a very low-cut gown of shimmering green, with a white petticoat embroidered with silver flowers. She looked a little put out at the retreat of the earl, but, never one to repine, she turned to Frances and smiled at the young figure in front of her in a decidedly predatory way.

'Mr Sutcliffe,' she murmured. 'So yours is the skill that is bringing about the garden transformation. I am all admiration.' She widened her eyes a little at the end of the speech, hinting rather less than delicately that her admiration was not just for the garden.

Frances cleared her throat.

'You are too kind, ma'am,' she replied, repressing a sudden urge to run out of the room. 'But the skill is chiefly my uncle's.'

'Ah yes. I don't believe that we are to see your uncle here tonight?'

'No, ma'am. He is away on business with the nurseryman.'

'And so you are left in charge? You seem over young for such a responsibility.'

'I can assure you, Mrs Cranborne, that I am well able to cope.'

'Oh, I am sure that you are very . . . capable,' replied Mrs Cranborne, tapping Frances' sleeve in such a flirtatious manner that Frances was very glad when dinner was announced shortly afterwards.

At the table, Frances was placed to the right of Lady Valeria, and she suspected that this had been done in order to facilitate horticultural discussion. With Lady Valeria on her left and Miss Renshaw on her right, she was able to enjoy interesting and unalarming conversations about gardening, and was therefore able to relax.

Marigold Stevenson was also dining with them tonight, looking neat and trim, and conversing politely with no sign of awkwardness in her bearing. Frances found herself forced to conclude that she had merely been taking a constitutional in the grounds, when she had seen her earlier.

When at last the ladies left the table, Lady Valeria said to her brother, 'Now, do not keep Mr Sutcliffe at the brandy for too long, Spencer. You know that he is to go over the plans with us this evening.'

As soon as the ladies had left, the earl resumed his seat with a sigh.

'Well, thank the Lord for that. Come and sit down here, my boy. Port for you, Frank, or do you prefer brandy?'

'Port, if you please,' said Frances — judging it to be the lesser of two evils — as she changed her place at Lyddington's bidding. Fortunately, since she had sat at some distance away from the earl, she had not had to contend with his view of a man's drinking capacity, and consequently had drunk very little at dinner.

The earl passed her the decanter.

'I had an interesting meeting this afternoon, Sarrell,' she said, after they were both settled with their port.

'And what was that?' asked his lordship, cracking nuts between his long fingers.

'After I left the Court, I decided to take another look at the garden.' Seeing the earl's disapproving look, she went on hastily, 'Yes, I know that you said I should go straight back home, but I wanted to see it again to make sure that it was real and that I had not imagined it. While I was there, I saw Marigold Stevenson.'

'Thunder'n'turf!' exclaimed Lyddington. 'Did you speak to her?'

'Yes, I did. She betrayed no emotion, even when we spoke of the garden, but she did say that she could not abide mess of any kind.'

'I ruined part of her garden,' mused the earl. 'Might not she have destroyed part of mine — in revenge?'

'Perhaps,' agreed Frances. 'But would she wantonly create disorder? I wonder whether she would be capable of such a deed.'

'And furthermore,' added Lyddington, 'would she then be able to sit brass-faced at my table as if nothing had happened?'

They sat in silence for a while, then the earl said in frustrated tones, 'Well, who else is there? M'sister's abigail made a discreet search of the ladies' rooms while they were out today, and no muddy clothes or shoes were found.'

'Peter Rance?' said Frances at last.

'Mm,' murmured his lordship. 'It might be as well to keep our eye on him. But come, I think if I'm not to have my head bitten off by m'sister, we had best join the ladies.'

He made as if to rise, but Frances said in

thoughtful tones, 'There is just one more thing.'

Lyddington resumed his seat.

'Out with it, then,' he said.

'It is just that before I saw Miss Stevenson, I had a most unpleasant sensation of being watched.'

The earl shrugged. 'Miss Stevenson herself — before you saw her?' he suggested.

Frances shook her head. 'No — it wasn't her. I can't really explain it. I have felt it before — in the wilderness that time when I hid you. I felt it just before you appeared. It was a horrible feeling — malicious . . . '

The earl got up from his seat, walked round to her and put his hands on her shoulders. It was as much as she could do not to lean her cheek against one of them.

'Well, whatever it is, I can see it's disturbed you,' he said reassuringly. 'I'll tell my men to be alert. But I'm sure you are letting the events of today work upon your mind. Try not to think about it.'

Frances nodded, smiled, and rose to her feet, but she was only partially reassured.

When they got to the saloon, they found that the plans — another copy — had been spread out across a table, and the ladies were very willing to gather round and hear what Frances had to say.

Lyddington, having already seen them, would gladly have stood back, but when he realized that to do so would be to encourage Mrs Cranborne to start up an intimate conversation, he joined the others around the table.

He was amused to see that while Frances was totally absorbed in explaining the plans and answering questions about which plants were to be used in which setting, Alicia Blakemuir could not take her eyes off the young gardener. He wondered what her ambitious mother thought to that, but a glance at Marion Blakemuir revealed that she was eyeing him, Lyddington, with considerable interest. He edged a little closer to Miss Renshaw. At least her interest in plants and gardening was unassumed, he thought with relief. Miss Stevenson, who might have been expected to hold the plans in the greatest contempt, shyly drew near to look, almost despite herself. Lyddington could not help feeling that it would take someone far more brazen and self-assured than was she to be present that evening if she had only that day perpetrated a malicious act of vandalism.

Eventually, tea was brought in, and the party around the table broke up, some ladies remaining to look at the plans, Felicia Cranborne and Marion Blakemuir both attempting to monopolize the earl.

Briar Storringe drew Frances to one side with the words, 'Come, sir, I would like you to tell me all about what your cousin is doing now.'

As soon as they were out of earshot, Briar said *sotto voce*, 'Don't be alarmed, Fran; I shan't give you away! But what can have possessed you? Why this masquerade? And what a fine figure you make in that dress! Tell me all!'

'Very well,' said Frances hastily, looking round in a guarded way that escaped everyone's attention except for Lyddington's. 'But not here or now, Briar.'

'Then when? I am almost consumed by curiosity, I assure you,' said Mrs Storringe, her eyes sparkling.

'As always,' retorted Frances. 'All right, then, tomorrow morning at seven, by the sunken garden.'

'Seven!' squeaked Briar.

'Sh! Yes, seven, and don't be late.'

Not long after this, the party broke up, the ladies retiring to their beds, Mrs Cranborne with a very old-fashioned look at the earl, which made him very glad that he was sleeping at the gatehouse.

'You are already acquainted with Mrs Storringe, I gather,' said the earl casually as they strolled back together.

'Yes, a little,' agreed Frances.

'In fact,' he went on in even tones, 'I suspect that it was the mention of her name that caused you to drop your glass this afternoon. Am I right?'

'I . . . was surprised,' admitted Frances, inwardly cursing his perspicacity.

'It might be wise to be a little cautious there,' Lyddington advised. 'From what I have heard of Captain Storringe, I do not believe he would be a complaisant husband.'

'Nor does he need to be on my account,' said Frances earnestly. 'I am not romantically attached to Mrs Storringe.'

They had by now reached the gatehouse.

'Nor to anyone, I suppose you will tell me,' replied the earl.

Frances stopped in her tracks, and the earl did likewise. 'You are mistaken, My . . . Sarrell. There is someone, but . . . '

'Your affections are not returned?' questioned Sarrell.

'Something like that,' replied Frances sadly.

'Try not to be too down-hearted,' said the earl kindly, gripping her by the shoulder, as they walked into the house. 'It will pass — believe me.'

'Will it?' she replied forlornly, before following his tall figure up the stairs.

8

The following morning Frances, a customarily early riser, smiled as she dressed in her gardening clothes, thinking about Briar having to struggle out of her bed at such an unaccustomed hour.

She made her way to the rendezvous in good time, but it was not until nearly twenty past seven that Briar appeared.

'I did say seven,' said Frances reproachfully. 'Do you want me to be completely discovered?'

'I did my best,' replied Briar defensively, shaking out her brown day dress which was, in truth, looking a little rumpled. 'Not all of us are used to such early hours. And now, tell me everything, you wicked creature.'

'It's quite simple,' replied Frances, as they sat down on an old stone bench. 'After my cousin Edmund died, Papa desperately needed a helper in his business, and I had to have something to do. I could not bear to be idle at home, and governessing or being someone's companion was not for me. It took a bit of doing, but I managed to persuade him to allow me to pose as Francis

Sutcliffe, his other nephew, and Edmund's younger brother.'

As Frances was speaking, Briar's look of wry amusement turned swiftly to one of concerned disapproval. Frances was not really surprised. As she had been speaking, her whole masquerade had suddenly started to sound shocking rather than practical, as she had always thought it to be.

'Your father needed your help . . . Frances, for how long has this masquerade been going on?'

'Ever since Edmund died,' said Frances evasively.

'Frances, give me a straight answer, if you please,' said Briar sternly.

'You sound just like Miss Harvey,' exclaimed Frances, hoping to divert her friend's mind. However, seeing from the stern look that still adorned her normally sunny features that this was a hopeless idea, she added in a subdued tone, 'For six years.'

'Six years!' exclaimed her friend, aghast. 'But surely you have not maintained a male role for all that time?'

'No, of course not,' said Frances defensively. 'When we are at home at Plymouth, I become Frances Sutcliffe, young lady of the house.'

'That is no answer,' said Briar, sounding to Frances' ears even more than a little like Miss

Harvey, who had been one of their strictest teachers so many years before. 'Tell me everything.'

'Well, when I am at work, I am always as you see me now,' replied Frances. 'For the most part, employers deal with my father, and not with me. I am as well acquainted with gardening techniques as any man, I can assure you. No one ever expects to see a woman working as a gardener. People usually see what they want to see.'

'And you have managed to fool everyone? I don't believe it!'

'Well it's true,' said Frances, a little nettled at this refusal to believe in her acting ability. 'I have succeded in fooling everyone — except for you, my dear friend, and you don't count, because you knew me already.'

'Even the perspicacious Lord Lyddington?' murmured Briar, determined to shake her composure.

'Even Lyddington,' agreed Frances, turning her head to hide a blush. But Briar, knowing her friend rather well, spotted this tell-tale sign.

'Ah! I think I detect a chink in the male armour! Can it be that you nourish a tenderness for him?'

'Cetainly not,' said Frances, quickly and unconvincingly.

'You do!' crowed Briar. Then, seeing her friend's face, she changed tone immediately. 'Oh, my dear, what will you do?'

'I don't know,' said Frances hopelessly. 'He treats me as a man — his friend! He has taken me shopping to buy the things I was wearing last night . . . '

'You have allowed him to buy you clothes!' exclaimed Briar, more shocked than ever. 'Fran, how could you?'

'Please try to understand,' begged Frances. 'He doesn't think of me as a woman. He likes me to drink with him, and . . . and he calls me Frank, Briar.'

Here, her friend smothered a giggle.

'Yes, I can see it must be vastly amusing to you,' she went on, 'but all I can see is that I am caught in a trap; forced to play the thing that I am not, and afraid to reveal the truth about myself for fear of earning his scorn.'

'But if he really has a regard for you, he might understand,' murmured Briar.

'He has a regard for a man called Francis Sutcliffe,' said Frances leaping to her feet. 'Can't you see that I stand to lose everything here? My work; everything that most interests and absorbs me; my opportunity to go about the world freely; my . . . his friendship. If I told him . . . ' She stopped, then went on slowly and painfully, 'If I told him and he

. . . he returned my . . . my affections, then all might be well, but . . .'

'Might?' queried Briar.

'Yes, might. Do you think he would be likely to marry his gardener's daughter — especially one who has, as you have pointed out, spent most of her adult life dressed as a man?' Briar looked away abruptly. 'But if he rejected me, could I be sure that he would keep my identity secret; would he feel honour bound to tell my next employer of my deception? Or perhaps he would think it a good joke to regale his friends with in the London clubs.' Her voice nearly choked on a sob. 'No, Briar, it's too risky. I must leave things as they are,' she added with a sigh.

After a brief silence, disturbed only by the early morning bird song, Briar began gently, 'But be frank!' Before she could finish her train of thought, they both exploded into helpless giggles, which did much to release the feeling of strain in the atmosphere. 'Be honest,' Briar managed at last, 'has there ever been a man before who has made you want to tell him?'

Frances smiled ruefully and shook her head. A hasty step was heard, and a look of panic crossed her face.

'Lyddington!' she breathed. 'He mustn't

find us together.' She darted away along one of the paths and only just in time, for moments later, the earl did emerge into the clearing where they had been talking, closely followed by his dogs.

Frances was just near enough to hear him say, in surprised tones, 'Good morning, Mrs Storringe. You are up and about early.'

Briar was a little flustered at Frances' sudden departure, but she concealed this by bending to make a fuss of the dogs. In the back of her mind was the need to prevent them from sniffing out Frances' trail until she was far enough away for it not to matter.

'Yes indeed, My Lord,' she replied. 'It is a beautiful morning, is it not?'

'It certainly is. I had not suspected any of m'sisters guests to be early risers, though. A relic of campaign days, perhaps?'

'Well, not really,' said Briar, adding inventively, 'I rather like rising early when my husband and I are away from one another. I know that often he has to rise early to be about his duties, and this way I do not feel that we are so very far apart.'

'What a romantic notion,' remarked the earl, slashing at a nettle with his cane. 'Shall we walk?'

Briar agreed, thinking rather uncomfortably of the reluctance with which she had risen from her bed. In some absurd way, this now seemed somewhat disloyal to her dear captain.

'I trust you are enjoying your stay at the Court,' said the earl after they had walked a short way.

'Indeed yes, thank you, My Lord. My mother is very knowledgeable about plants, and I have learned a great deal from her. Unfortunately however, we are not in a position to cultivate a garden at present, so I am enjoying the chance to look at yours.'

'There's very little to see yet, I fear. The garden's still in the making as you know.'

'I think that makes it even more interesting,' responded Briar spiritedly. 'Especially if I am granted the opportunity to return in later years, and see how the scheme has progressed.'

The earl inclined his head slightly to signify polite agreement to this scheme.

'I hope it will live up to your expectations,' he replied.

'It don't matter, for I shall gain something from my visit either way,' she said roguishly. 'If the results are satisfactory, I shall copy your design shamelessly; if I don't like what is achieved, I shall observe all the mistakes you have made, and take care not to make the same ones myself.'

Lyddington laughed. It was good to be able to enjoy the company of a woman who did not regard him in the light of a quarry to be pursued at all costs.

'Whatever the mistakes may be, they most assuredly won't be mine,' he replied. 'The Sutcliffes are doing the job — and I can't even be blamed for hiring them, for m'sister did it. But going by the plans, and what has been done so far, they seem to be making a satisfactory job of things.'

'Yes, I have heard good reports of them,' said Briar carefully. 'But then my informant, being a relation, is likely to be biased.'

'Quite possibly,' agreed the earl. 'Is Miss — Sutcliffe, is it? — like her cousin?'

'Very like him,' said Briar, with perfect truthfulness. 'They are much of an age, and very close — like brother and sister, in fact.'

'Such cousinly closeness sometimes ends in marriage,' murmured his lordship in a colourless tone.

'Not in this case, I am sure,' said Briar firmly. 'They are far too alike.'

'But then likeness — like beauty — is very much in the eye of the beholder, is it not?' returned her companion. 'My opinion may not be the same. I wonder whether I will ever have the pleasure of meeting Miss

Sutcliffe in order to assess this likeness for myself?'

'I should not be at all surprised,' returned Briar gaily. 'And now, if you will excuse me, I must return to the house. My maid will have apoplexy if I am not in my bed.' Almost at once, she realized her mistake, and blushed guiltily.

'Surely not, knowing your romantic habits as she must do,' replied Lyddington acutely. 'Or perhaps you had another reason for being in the garden so early?'

'Your Lordship can hardly expect me to divulge it,' parried Briar, trying to recover herself.

'Your business is your own, naturally,' said the earl politely. 'But if romantic rendezvous are to your taste, may I ask that you refrain from making them with the young and inexperienced?'

'For example?' prompted Briar.

'Let us say, for example, with Frank Sutcliffe. He is very young, and I would not have him hurt.'

Briar tried not to laugh, but in the end found it quite impossible. The earl smiled quizzically, but said nothing. As she looked at him, the most outrageous idea came into her mind, and she simply could not resist saying, 'My lord, you are too modest. Did it not occur to you that I might be in pursuit of you?'

He looked so horrified that she laughed again, and ran back to the house before any more could be said.

Lyddington shook his head in bewilderment. Surely he was not going to have to avoid yet another member of the party! He had been so convinced that she only had eyes for Captain Storringe. The more he thought about it, the more he was sure that she had just made that last remark in order to throw him off the scent. But what scent? A real romance with Sutcliffe? Except that Sutcliffe had assured him that there was nothing between them — and young Frank was his friend. Anyway, it was too much to think about before breakfast.

The dogs ran on ahead to the kitchens, and Lyddington was about to follow them, when a figure caught his eye. He stepped back instinctively, seeing the furtive manner in which it was moving. It was undoubtedly a woman, but only being slightly acquainted with some of his guests, he did not realize until she was passing quite close to him that it was Judith Hartington.

His first impression had been a correct one. She was looking anxiously from one side to the other, her eyes full of concern, her hands clutching at the edges of her shawl.

He waited until she was as close as she could be before stepping out in front of her with a cheery greeting.

'Good morning, ma'am!'

The effect was catastrophic. Miss Hartington lost even the little colour that she possessed, her hands flew to her face, she uttered a piercing scream, took a few steps back, then picked up her skirts and fled back towards the house.

The earl started after her, but before he could reach the door into the drawing-room, his sister emerged, full of righteous anger.

'Spencer!' she exclaimed, her bosom swelling with indignation. 'What were you doing to distress Miss Hartington so? Upon my honour . . . '

'No, upon my damned honour!' retorted her brother forthrightly. 'If I can't say good morning to someone I meet while strolling in my own garden, I should bloody well like to know what I can do!'

'Spencer . . . ' began her ladyship, a trifle more uncertainly.

'All I did,' repeated the earl firmly, 'was to step out in front of her and say 'good morning'. Why is that so disturbing to her? Has she got a guilty conscience?'

With a snort, her ladyship turned away back into the house, and Lyddington also turned on his heel and made his way to the kitchens where an adoring Mrs Bartlett presently served him with an excellent breakfast.

9

Frances was becoming increasingly anxious for her father's return. With him away, the whole burden of decision-making fell upon her shoulders. This was not something that normally worried her; it had happened before on odd occasions; and if she were honest with herself, she enjoyed having the responsibility. Such responsibility meant, however, that she needed to give all her mind to her work, and anxiety about her relationship with Lyddington was inevitably sapping much of her nervous energy.

She had managed to avoid going into Bedford with him in order to sample the night life, but it had not been easy. Moreover, she had not been able to avoid further social interaction.

He had invited her to go to the Lyddington Arms with him on two occasions, and judging this to be a lesser evil than a further visit to Bedford, she had agreed to go.

She had not really been surprised at how welcome he was there; after all, he spent his money freely, and all present benefited from his largesse.

Nevertheless, it was a constant source of wonder to her, the way that he seemed to invite deference coupled with a relaxed easiness in his company. Every man rose at the earl's entrance, and every man doffed his cap, but during the course of the evening, the earl would take part in all manner of conversations, some initiated by him, some by others. No matter was too small for his interest; nobody's difficulty too trivial for him to be concerned about. As with his servants, he might not always remember all the names, but he knew all the family connections and circumstances.

An outing to the Lyddington Arms with him became a fascinating social occasion, on which she discovered a great deal about local customs and personalities, and even more about the personality of the earl himself.

Her enjoyment of his company was, however, tainted by the dread of discovery. She was not at all sure whether it was more nerve-racking to dine with the company and be forced to converse in manly fashion with the ladies of the party, or to dine with Lyddington tête-à-tête, and suffer his closer scrutiny and intimate conversation.

On the whole, she thought that possibly the latter was preferable. When the whole company was present, there were other problems. Alicia Blakemuir had started to look at her rather soulfully, for one. Fortunately Mrs Blakemuir clearly did not relish the thought of an alliance with a tradesman, so Alicia would not be allowed to go too far, nevertheless, it was a worry.

In addition, Mrs Cranborne, with a view to making the earl jealous, had started to address her in decidedly caressing terms. Lyddington seeing which way the wind was blowing, was eyeing the proceedings with gleeful relish, so she could hope for no help whatsoever from that quarter.

No, on the whole, dinner alone with Lyddington was preferable. She put down her pen, and got up to look out of the window, her eyes not seeing the scenery in front of her, but dwelling instead on the previous evening, the two of them sitting at the table, legs stretched out before them, glasses in hand.

Lyddington had now seemed to accept the fact that his young friend had a capacity for wine that was far inferior to his own, and had ceased to plague her with constantly filling her glass, or teasing her about her small consumption. So while he drank several glasses to her one, they would sit relaxed, still in day clothes — for they did not bother to change for one another — and talk about anything that came into their heads.

For the most part, Frances preferred it when the earl talked about his travels abroad, for he had travelled extensively, and being a naturally curious person, he had taken in a good deal.

Sometimes his amatory adventures came into the discussion, and then she was glad that the glow of the candlelight hid her blushes, but although he did speak of conquests that he had made, it was never with any boastful intent, but simply because they happened to be an integral element of a situation that he was describing.

The more time they spent together, the more she enjoyed his companionship and the more she worried about what his reaction might be if he were to discover that she was a woman, and about how all this would be lost to her.

She was thinking about this, and not for the first time, when there was a commotion outside, voices, and the stamping of horses and the jingling of harness, then the famous Lyddington roar, this time with a sense of urgency.

'Frank! Ho there! Hurry!'

With a sense of foreboding, she rushed downstairs, quite forgetting in her haste that she was not wearing her wig. On reaching the front door, she found it already open, with Lyddington and another man carrying Thomas Sutcliffe across the threshold.

'Frank, you must prepare yourself for a shock,' said the earl. 'I'm afraid he's been attacked.'

'P . . . Papa?' stammered Frances, her hands going to her cheeks, her face whitening. At first glance, her father appeared to be covered in blood.

Lyddington gave her one, acute glance before taking a deep breath and saying firmly, 'His bedchamber, young Frank. Make sure his bedchamber's ready. Get someone to help you.'

Frances glanced once more at her father before hurrying upstairs, glad of something to do. She was on the point of calling out for Edward, when he appeared from her father's room.

'Edward, is the master's room ready?' she asked urgently. 'There's been some kind of accident.'

'An accident?' Edward blenched. He had been with Thomas Sutcliffe for over twenty years. 'Oh, Miss Frances . . . '

'Ssh, now. There isn't time. Is the bed made up?'

'Oh yes indeed. I'll just go and get a warming pan ready.' As soon as he had gone,

Frances hunted for a clean night-shirt. She had only just got everything ready, when Lyddington and his groom brought in their precious burden, and set him down on the bed. Now that Frances had time to look at him more closely, the blood was not so alarmingly widespread as she had thought at first. He was obviously badly wounded, however, and the bloodstains contrasted shockingly with his pale face. Frances saw his chest rise and fall, and permitted herself a small sigh of relief.

Following the groom was a short, stout man carrying with him a leather bag.

'Thank God, the doctor chanced to be passing this way,' said the earl. Frances made as if to go towards the bed, but Lyddington took hold of her arm with something less than his usual vigour.

'No,' said his lordship. 'No, my . . . my friend. You wait downstairs, you are in no frame to help. I'll be down to tell you the news.'

With one, brief scared look at Lyddington's face, she left the room, and hurried downstairs to the study where she had been working. Such was her agitation that she could only sit and sob, and she was still brushing away her tears when the earl opened the door softly.

'How is he?' she asked urgently, rushing over to him.

'The doctor will not commit himself,' replied Lyddington, putting an arm around her shoulders with unusual gentleness, and then almost immediately withdrawing it, leaving her with an acute sensation of loss. 'It appears that someone went for him with a knife. No vital organ has been damaged, but the attack was a violent one, and he has lost a lot of blood. The next twenty-four hours will be crucial.'

'How did it happen? What do you think can have occurred?'

'Of that we cannot be sure until your . . . your father can tell us himself,' replied the earl. 'It seems certain that he was on his way home; had nearly arrived, in fact. I had rid over to Woburn, and was on my own way back when I saw a riderless horse, and then found him lying on the ground. By great good fortune, the doctor also came by, returning from a visit to a patient. Although I made a swift search while Ruddles and the doctor got him into the gig, there was no sign of the assailant.'

'But why would anyone want to attack him? He's a good, kind man; he would never hurt anyone himself so . . . ' She brushed away her tears impatiently with her sleeve.

'Who can say at this stage? We must explore every avenue,' said the earl after a slight pause. 'In the meantime, try not to worry about him. Dr James knows his business.'

He walked to the door.

'You are leaving?' said Frances in tones of anxious disbelief.

'I must, for the present,' replied Lyddington. 'I want to take a thorough look at the spot where it happened. At the time, all my efforts were concentrated on getting Thomas back here. Now, I want to go and see if there is anything to be discovered.'

'Be careful,' said Frances urgently. 'If you were in the vicinity when the attack took place, then my father might not have been the real target.'

'That had occurred to me,' admitted the earl. 'I shall take Ruddles with me, but I don't expect a second attack. Even if you are right, whoever is responsible will have got away from the scene as quickly as possible. I shall be back as soon as may be to take my turn in Thomas's room. Edward is staying there for now, and I have sent for my own valet, who has some experience of sick nursing.'

'You are very good,' murmured Frances. Then she added with a gallant attempt at humour, 'I'm surprised you have not pressed

Mrs Cranborne into service.'

'Believe me, things would have to be a good deal more serious than they are for me to ask for help from that devil's daughter,' said Lyddington forthrightly before leaving the room.

Although he had spoken in jest, Frances felt a little reassured. If Lyddington thought that matters could be much worse, then perhaps there were more grounds for hope than she had supposed.

Immediately upon leaving the house, Lyddington and Ruddles, who had been awaiting his master's convenience, set out towards the Millbrook road. There was much that the earl wanted to discuss with 'Master' Sutcliffe, he told himself savagely, but now was not the time, not when the doctor had only just left, and Thomas's life hung in the balance. Perhaps it was as well that there was this other matter to occupy his mind.

It was, as the earl had said, only a short distance to where the incident had taken place.

'Any poachers around in the area at the moment, Ruddles?' asked his lordship as they rode.

'Poachers wouldn't normally attack a man the way Mr Sutcliffe's been attacked, M'Lord.'

'Possibly not. But if he were afraid of discovery, and seeking to get away?'

'Not on your land, M'Lord. If it were Sir Alfred Froome, now . . . '

The earl grunted. Sir Alfred was a local landowner who was well-known for his harsh and unbending attitude towards poachers.

'In any case, it's a funny time of day for poachers,' went on the groom.

'I know that,' said his lordship scornfully. 'But I have to consider every possibility. Come to think of it, I would probably have heard at the Lyddington Arms if there had been any.'

'You'd be the last person anyone'd tell,' retorted the groom, with the freedom only accorded to very old and trusted servants.

'Oh, you'd be surprised what I find out,' replied the earl.

'Well, I don't know of any,' said his groom after a moment's thought. 'Not that are regular, so to speak. And Your Lordship hasn't been around here long enough to make any enemies.'

The earl turned in the saddle to look at Ruddles.

'You're the second person who's suggested that I might be the target. Why me and not Sutcliffe?'

'Well, why go for a gardener, My Lord?

You're the one with the power. He's only obeying your orders after all.'

The earl gave a crack of laughter.

'I? Give orders? I thought it was m'sister did that.'

The groom laughed too.

'Every man on this estate knows that it's you as is the master here,' he replied.

'Perhaps so,' retorted the earl. 'The question is, who's going to break the news to Valeria?'

By now, they had reached the spot where the attack had taken place. They dismounted, and tied up their horses a short distance away, so that they would not disturb the ground further.

'I'll just keep looking round, M'Lord,' said the groom, taking a serviceable looking gun from the saddle.

'Well, I'll be damned!' exclaimed Lyddington staring at the firearm. 'You really do think I might have been the target.'

The earl spent some time examining the grass carefully. It had been much disturbed, because of all the activity that had taken place that day. After a short time spent in thought, Lyddington called out, 'Ruddles, come over here.'

'What is it, My Lord?' asked the groom, leaving his post some short distance away.

'There's a devil of a lot of blood on this grass,' said the earl.

'Well, he was badly wounded.'

'Yes, but he was on horseback. If you wanted to attack a man who was on horseback, what would you choose?'

The groom said nothing, but patted his gun significantly.

'Exactly so,' replied the earl. 'So who would attack with a knife?'

'Someone who wasn't prepared?' suggested the groom. 'He didn't expect to see Sutcliffe, but when he did, he suddenly decided to attack him.'

'On impulse, you mean?' Lyddington rubbed his chin thoughtfully. 'It could be so — in fact it probably is so, because no one knew of the exact time of his return — even young Frank didn't know that he was coming back today. But tell me, Joe, if we two were on horseback, and I started to attack you with a knife, what would you do — assuming that you weren't armed?'

'Gallop away hell for leather, My Lord.'

'Exactly so,' said the earl again. 'Which leads me to think that by some means the attacker induced Sutcliffe to dismount before he attacked him.'

'A highwayman would do that,' remarked the groom.

'And how would he manage it?' asked the earl wryly, touching Ruddles's gun with a stick that he had picked up. 'No, Joe, everything points to the attacker knowing Sutcliffe, and being known by him. He would therefore be able to induce him to dismount without suspicion.'

'If it were done like that,' said the groom, 'then it need not even be a man that was the attacker.'

The earl grunted. 'Well, hopefully, Thomas will soon be in good enough frame to tell us something of what occurred.'

They were about to go back to their horses, when Ruddles suddenly said, 'A moment, My Lord.' A few steps away from where they had been standing, he put his hand into a longer clump of grass, and produced a knife with ominous-looking stains upon it. The earl looked down at the slightly curved blade.

'No doubt young Frank will correct me if I'm wrong, but I think that's a gardener's knife,' he said.

* * *

'Of course you must dine with our guests tonight,' said Lady Valeria, after her brother had declared his intention to absent himself from the table on the evening of the attack.

'To refuse to do so simply because the gardener is ill in bed would be to carry eccentricity to its very extremes.'

The earl coloured a little, but replied mildy enough, 'The man's life is in danger. You are speaking as if he simply had a cold in the head; and he's rather more than just a gardener, my dear.'

'Perhaps so,' admitted her ladyship grudgingly. 'But I cannot remember your showing half this concern when I fell through the ice on the pond, and caught an inflammation of the lungs.'

'Valeria, that was thirty years ago! Allow me to have gained a little human compassion in that time.'

Lady Valeria snorted in a most unladylike manner.

'Human compassion my eye,' she retorted. 'Just because you've conceived some sort of attachment for that lad . . . '

The earl turned away so that his sister would not see his expression. At present his feelings for 'that lad' were so confused that he did not understand them himself. He certainly did not wish to discuss them with his sister.

'Thomas Sutcliffe is dangerously ill, perhaps dying,' he said, walking over to the window and looking out of it, his back to the room. 'The attack occurred on my land and I feel a degree of responsibility; and yes, I am concerned about young Sutcliffe. Thomas is practically his only relative, and he is very young.'

'No younger than you were when you took on the earldom.'

'I was — shall we say — made of very different stuff?' retorted the earl, smiling inwardly at his private joke. 'But enough, Valeria. I will dine with you and your guests, and Soames can attend to Sutcliffe, but if he sends word that Sutcliffe is worse, I shall go over straight away.'

With this, her ladyship was forced to be content.

That evening the talk was all of the attack upon Thomas Sutcliffe, to which the ladies reacted as might have been predicted.

'How terrifying to think that the perpetrator might still be in the vicinity,' murmured Mrs Cranborne, shuddering artistically, and swaying towards Lyddington so as to give him an even better view of her over-exposed bosom, were such a thing possible.

'Oh, do you think so indeed?' exclaimed Alicia Blakemuir, her hand at her throat. 'Mama, do you think that we should perhaps return to town?'

Her mother, however, was of sterner stuff

and, moreover, was still weighing up the chances of snaring Lyddington, either for herself or for her daughter.

'Nonsense, my dear,' she said firmly. 'I am convinced that His Lordship can be relied upon to catch the perpetrators.'

Lyddington acknowledged this compliment with a slight inclination of his head, but said nothing.

'We must make sure that we have the protection of some reliable man at all times,' purred Mrs Cranborne as she smiled at the earl, her eyes full of meaning.

'I will make certain that one of the grooms or footmen is always at your service,' he replied impishly.

Mrs Cranborne's own smile grew a little thinner, but she said sweetly, 'What a comfort that you have our interests at heart.'

'As long as you don't expect me to call in the militia,' put in Mrs Storringe in matter-of-fact tones. Then she coloured a little as she recalled the nature of her last exchange with the earl.

Lyddington, who had now drawn his own conclusions about Mrs Storringe's presence in the gardens, laughed easily.

'Only if you would like an excuse to see your gallant captain,' he remarked. 'When do you expect his current duties to be complete?'

With that, the conversation turned to other matters, but in her place at the top of the table Lady Valeria, conversing politely with Gertrude Renshaw on her right and Judith Hartington on her left, was secretly very worried.

Marigold Stevenson had been invited to partake of dinner that evening. The arrangement had been that she should give a talk afterwards on 'the qualities of the Bedfordshire soil, and whether these same affect garden flowers favourably or adversely'. All the ladies had agreed to take turns to give the company the benefit of their specialist experience. So far, Gertrude Renshaw's had been the most erudite, and Felicia Cranborne's had been the most trivial. Miss Renshaw had spoken about tree-moving: how it could be achieved, and whether it was a wise procedure. Mrs Cranborne had spoken about bouquets. But as her talk chiefly revolved around the men who had presented them to her, most of whom appeared to be of doubtful character, its horticultural nature was really open to question.

Lady Valeria had not particularly been looking forward to Miss Stevenson's talk. On a previous occasion, Marigold had spoken about 'weeds and their remedies'. Her way of speaking had been so dull, that Lady Valeria had nodded off partway through, and had only just woken up in time to give a vote of thanks. Nevertheless, it was a surprise to her, and a matter of concern, when Miss Stevenson failed to appear without a word of explanation. Eccentric she might be, but she was punctilious in all matters pertaining to etiquette.

Lady Valeria could not help feeling rather worried. She had not said anything in front of the other ladies, for after the dreadful attack upon Thomas Sutcliffe, she was afraid of causing anxiety. She resolved to have a quiet word with Lyddington when he rejoined the ladies after his brandy. No doubt he would be delighted to miss hearing about the Bedfordshire soil. As for the ladies, they would just have to make their own music, or play cards.

As luck would have it, however, she was not to get her chance to approach him. As soon as the ladies left, the earl sent a message over to the gatehouse to discover how Thomas was faring.

He poured himself a glass of brandy, but after only one mouthful, he put it down and rose decisively to his feet. On his way out of the dining-room, he called another footman to him.

'When Jem comes back, send him up to my room. I'm going to change.'

The earl had to change without the help of his valet, as Soames was doing duty at the gatehouse, but this was no problem to him. He had indeed needed assistance in order to don his silver grey coat and breeches and salmon pink embroidered waistcoat earlier that evening, but to put on his customary riding dress required no help, and very little time at all. He was just sanding a note he had written to his sister when there was a knock at the door.

'Come in,' he called, picking up his coat.

'Beg pardon, M'Lord,' said Jem from the doorway, 'but Mr Soames says that Mr Sutcliffe is holding his own, but might get a touch restless later.'

The earl grunted, shrugging himself into his coat, and picking up his hat.

'Have my horse saddled and brought round. I want to go down to the village. Oh, and give this to my sister — but not till after I've gone.'

'Very good, M'Lord,' replied Jem, taking the proffered note. Only his rigorous training at the hands of the butler enabled him to keep a straight face.

The Lyddington Arms was not unduly busy that night. Sam Pewsey was there serving his customers, and showed his usual delight in being able to welcome one who was not only his landlord, but also his most generous customer.

The earl greeted all present with great geniality, called for drinks all round, and once he had his tankard in his hand, looked round with apparent carelessness, but nevertheless made his way unhesitatingly to a table in the corner.

Sitting at this table was Jed Hawkins and he was gratified, but not alarmed, at the earl's approach. Lyddington was known to enjoy a very relaxed relationship with his fellow men, and it was not the first time that they had sat together enjoying Sam's hospitality.

'How's business?' asked the earl amiably. Jed grunted, then rather belatedly added 'M'Lord' on the end. His business was one subject into which he did not wish anyone to enquire.

To say that he was a thief would have been unjust; he was more in the nature of Shakespeare's Autolycus — 'a snapper-up of unconsidered trifles'. Publicly, he was a kind of carter, travelling about between Dunstable and Bedford, visiting various of the villages in between. He was very ready to deliver anything that needed taking, and ran a very useful line in pedlar's goods. There were though a good many items on his cart whose origins were shrouded in mystery and about which their purchasers were careful not to enquire.

Valuable as was the service that he provided however, Jed's greatest asset was his ability to recall and relay news and gossip. Nothing of importance could happen to the good folk of Toddington without the good folk of Ampthill discovering it, if Jed was in the vicinity. Very little escaped his eye.

Seeing that Jed's tankard was empty, Lyddington called for more ale and after it had arrived, he said, 'And what about news? What's the latest story?'

Jed looked a little uncomfortable, and buried his nose in his tankard.

'Nothing that'd interest you, M'Lord,' he muttered.

'About me, is it?' speculated the earl interestedly. 'Out with it then, man. I'd like to know what I've been credited with.'

'Well, M'Lord, I . . . ' began Jed, then he finished, 'You wouldn't like it, M'Lord. Let me tell you instead about the cattle running wild in Dunstable.'

'Devil take the cattle,' said his lordship mildly. 'I want to know what's being said about me.'

'Well, seems you've been seen riding about with that young gardener fellow,' began Jed cautiously. The earl shrugged his shoulders, but said nothing. Jed took up the tale again reluctantly. 'Some people have noticed that you seem to favour him, and that he's a good bit younger than you.'

'Yes? Well?' There was nothing in Lyddington's expression to give him away, but his manner of speaking had become a little abrupt.

'Seems some people have seen a likeness between the young fellow and Your Lordship's brother that died — in childhood.'

'A likeness — between young Sutcliffe and Hugh?' began the earl rather puzzled. 'But Hugh was only twelve years old when he died, so . . . ' Realization began to dawn on his face until, much to Jed's relief, he slapped his knee, threw back his head, and roared with laughter.

'By God, that's rich,' he exclaimed as soon as he was able. 'So local opinion has decided that young Sutcliffe is my bastard! I'm not sure whether I want information from you if you've become a purveyor of such nonsensical stuff!'

Jed assumed a look of righteous indignation, but before he could find words adequate enough with which to defend himself from such slander, the earl went on, 'Never mind that. It'll die down soon enough; or mayhap I'll do something outrageous to take people's minds off it. I've something else I want to ask you about, and that's the attack on Thomas Sutcliffe. Is it the only such that there's been, or have there been more?'

'Done with a knife, wasn't it, and very savage?' asked Jed. 'No, no more like that; leastways, not that I've heard about. Those that I've talked to — and there aren't that many so far — are saying . . . ' He looked a little uneasy. Lyddington wondered fleetingly whether it was because Jed Hawkins was so obviously genuinely concerned about what was happening that he found out so much.

'Yes?' prompted the earl.

'People are saying that a madman must be responsible. All that blood . . . '

'Mm,' agreed his lordship, musing that gossip did indeed spread like wildfire if the earlier events of the day were already being noised abroad. 'Any ideas?'

'Somebody with a grudge against you and Mr Sutcliffe?' hazarded Hawkins.

'Both of us? Why so?' asked the earl, furrowing his brow.

'Stands to reason, M'Lord. If it weren't for you, Mr Sutcliffe wouldn't be here, would he?'

'Well, let me know if you hear anything to the point,' said Lyddington, dropping some coin into his hand. He moved on to talk to some others, and soon the conversation was all of weather, crops, and livestock.

Lyddington did not stay at the inn very late, and he did not drink deeply either. Somehow, with Hawkins' words still clear in his mind, he wanted to be alert during his ride. He was very confident of his ability to look after himself if threatened; and resented having to consider the possibility in his own back yard. He rode home at his usual pace, outwardly relaxed, but inwardly alert and, as he arrived back at the stables, was conscious of a mild feeling of elation.

Quietly, he let himself into the gatehouse, and went upstairs to take his turn at Thomas Sutcliffe's bedside.

10

Lady Valeria's feelings towards her brother the following morning were not of the most amiable. She had had a nagging concern about Miss Stevenson, that not even Mrs Storringe's spirited piano playing or Miss Blakemuir's indifferent watercolours — displayed at her mother's insistence — could shake off.

Truth to tell, her ladyship was beginning to tire of this party. The atmosphere in the drawing-room whilst they were waiting for the earl's return had been full of expectation. Miss Blakemuir had kept looking towards the door, Mrs Cranborne, whilst too experienced to do anything so gauche, had had a decidedly predatory look in her eye, and she had wandered round the room examining all kinds of things just as if she were pricing them, thought Lady Valeria to herself.

She had begun to wonder wearily how many of her guests, apart from Gertrude, were really interested in flowers and gardens at all, and how many were simply on the catch for her brother. At least she could acquit Miss Stevenson of that — which brought her back to the anxiety which had nagged at her ever since the previous evening, and had even cost her an hour or two's sleep.

She had really wanted to share this concern with her brother, but his note, brought by Jem after the writer had left the premises — as she had ascertained — did little to endear the earl to her.

Dear sister (it had read)

Pray excuse me for the rest of the evening, but I am gone down to the Lyddington Arms on an important errand. I hope that this will not inconvenience you.

Spencer.

Important errand, my eye! Lady Valeria had thought to herself as she read it, but she had long ago accepted that try as she might, if her brother was set upon a certain course, there was no changing his mind. She did reflect, looking at the note again in the light of day, that he might have made his apology sound a little more regretful, but that was Lyddington all over.

When her ladyship entered the breakfast parlour, she discovered that the earl had broken from his customary early habits that day and had decided to breakfast with his sister and her guests, then take his walk a little later. He was looking a little pale, his sister decided, and she commented upon it.

'Must have been bad brandy,' said the earl more cheerfully than one would have expected from one who had cravenly disappeared in order to drink himself silly at the Lyddington Arms.

There was good reason for his cheerfulness. Although the table was laid for eight, Lyddington and his sister were the only partakers at present. The ladies were so used to their host's early morning walks and absence at the breakfast-table, that none of them had troubled to come downstairs in pursuit of him. Truth to tell, Mrs Cranborne preferred to let her skin settle down a little first thing in the morning before exposing it to the public gaze.

'I wonder you are not ashamed to look me in the eye,' remarked Lady Valeria, helping herself to coffee.

'Ashamed?' he replied, sitting down again and getting on with his breakfast. 'I thought you would be pleased to see me at table this morning.'

'Don't be obtuse, Spencer,' snapped his sister. 'I am referring to your shameful disappearance last night — and when I most particularly wanted to have speech with you.'

'Oh that,' replied the earl calmly. 'I had

very good reasons — not that it did me very much good, mind you.'

'I am not surprised,' said Lady Valeria with some satisfaction. 'Perhaps you are too old to stomach the brew that is served at the Lyddington Arms. You had much better keep to what is in your own cellar.'

'I'm not talking abut Sam Pewsey's ale, dammit,' exclaimed Lyddington. 'Stap me, but sometimes I think it's the best thing about coming home! If you must know, I went to see what I could find out about the attack on Thomas Sutcliffe — but learned nothing that I hadn't already surmised.'

'Well, I suppose that does excuse you in part,' conceded her ladyship grudgingly. 'Although I think you might have guessed that no useful information could be had from the drunken sots who emerge from the Lyddington Arms. But it does not alter the fact that I have had a matter troubling me since last night, and have been waiting to share it with you.'

The earl, his mouth full of cold beef, signalled to his sister to proceed.

'Spencer, I am worried about Miss Stevenson,' said Lady Valeria. 'She was invited here last night, but she failed to appear.'

'Well, she wasn't in the Lyddington Arms,

if that's what you want to know,' said the earl casually, when his mouth was empty.

'Don't be flippant, Spencer,' said his sister severely. 'This is most unlike her, and I am very concerned. Can you remember whether her house was in darkness?'

The earl laid down his knife, and rubbed his chin. At length, he said, 'When I set off, I really couldn't say. But as I was coming home, I thought about my last encounter with her fence, and looked towards her house. It was definitely in darkness, and I wasn't very late either.'

'Perhaps she mistook the day, and has gone visiting,' murmured Lady Valeria, looking very unconvinced.

'I've not had my walk yet,' said her brother. 'I'll go down to the village and see if I can find anything out.'

* * *

The earl's enquiries in Lyddington Over yielded no fruit. He was greeted with courtesy by the villagers, but no one could throw any light on Miss Stevenson's whereabouts, not even her neighbours. Her house was completely shut up, with no sign of life whatsoever.

A stroke of inspiration caused him to make

enquiries for the maid, but this too was fruitless. The girl, a local tradesman's daughter, had gone down with a putrid sore throat, and Miss Stevenson had been managing without her for the past few days.

Finally, Lyddington decided to call upon the vicar. The vicarage still stood where it always had, nestling against the wall of the churchyard, for the church and the vicarage both stood on church land, and therefore could not be moved, unlike the rest of the village.

The Reverend Richard Crawley welcomed the earl courteously, and invited him into his study for some wine.

'Yes, my wife and daughter are both well,' he replied in answer to his lordship's enquiry. 'They have gone to stay with my wife's sister in Yarmouth for a few weeks. And what about yourself, My Lord? Do you plan a long stay this time?'

'I'm not at all sure,' replied Lyddington, taking the wine he was offered with thanks. 'My plans are uncertain. I may stay.'

'Your tenants will be glad if you do,' said the vicar. 'Many of them fear what may happen if your sister is given free rein again!'

The earl gave a short laugh.

'I think she must have gone her length this time. I would move the village back, but I fear that the disturbance would be just as great as before, and most people appear to have settled very well. You're the only one I feel sorry for, Crawley. Do you feel very isolated here?'

The vicar smiled ruefully. He was a tall, thin man, very much the same age as the earl.

'Well, a little, perhaps; although I must say that at times I enjoy the peace and quiet! There are times when I feel that I should be nearer to my flock, and the church will be harder for people to get to in bad weather.'

There was a short silence, then the earl said, 'Would you like me to build you another church in the village?'

The vicar looked quite overwhelmed.

'My Lord, I . . . '

The earl raised his hand.

'You don't need to answer me now. Think about it, and let me know. I do mean it, you know.'

'I know that,' answered the vicar. 'You are well known to be a man of your word.'

'Amongst other things,' murmured Lyddington. 'Now, Crawley, a small matter you might be able to help me with.'

'Name it, My Lord.'

'The whereabouts of Marigold Stevenson.'

'I take it you have tried her house.'

'Her house, her neighbours, everywhere I

can think of, but with no success. You are my last port of call.'

'If she is not to be found in the village, then I cannot imagine where she might be — unless she has gone to visit her old governess who lives in Toddington. But why this sudden concern, My Lord?'

'M'sister expected her for dinner last night, and she didn't appear. Apparently, that's most unlike her.'

'It is indeed,' agreed the vicar concernedly. 'I can write down the name of her governess in Toddington, if you like.'

The earl thanked him, and left shortly afterwards.

'I am sorry that I have been of so little help,' said the vicar as they parted at the door. 'Please let me know if you discover anything.'

Lyddington nodded and left, whistling to his dogs, who had been nosing about in the vicarage garden.

The obvious way back home from the vicarage was to walk straight up the drive, which lay almost immediately before him, but the earl was unattracted by such a formal route, so as soon as he had entered the park gates, he turned to his right, and headed out towards the lake, intending to walk part way round it. The dogs darted away from him, frisking about, one of them going to drink, the other showing a suspicious tendency to dig for rabbits.

For a short time, he stood at the edge of the lake, looking roughly in the direction of Bedford. His estate was situated to the western side of Ampthill Hill, his house nestling in its shelter, and thus receiving all the afternoon sun, but less benefit until the morning was quite well advanced.

The morning was pleasantly warm, unlike some of the June days that he had spent in Italy, when the temperature could at times be greater than was tolerable. Watching the geese and the ducks on the water, and listening to the wind rustling in the trees, he was suddenly conscious of being glad to be home.

He had never been in love with Alfreda, his wife, but the suddenness of her death, and the shocking manner of it, had shaken him thoroughly; his one desire had been to escape England and all that it held. He knew that he was very fortunate in having Lady Valeria as a sister, for he had always known that he could leave the estate in her capable and willing hands.

After a while, being abroad had become a habit with him — a way of avoiding the London season, with all the matchmaking mamas, he had to admit ruefully to himself.

So he returned home from time to time. But never until now had he felt this affection for the place — this feeling that here was where he belonged. Of course, the welcome that he had received from all his people had only confirmed that. His people; of course they were!

Suddenly, he was conscious of a feeling of guilt that he had not been here when the village was moved, when Bobkiss retired, when the Sutcliffes were hired. He should have had a hand in all those matters. It was time that he settled down to being a squire. For once, the idea gave him, not a feeling of restlessness, but one of quiet satisfaction — as if that was how things were meant to be.

Then, of course, he could marry again — he was only forty, after all.

Suddenly, he shook off his mood of reverie, and began to walk towards the house, whistling to his dogs as he went. He would be glad of a little something in the kitchen after his walk.

Huddled amongst the trees, and shrubs was the ice house, the scene of many happy games of childhood, when Lyddington, then young Lord Meadhurst, because his father was still alive, had played hide and seek, usually with Tom Bobkiss, the agent's son. They had lit fires, climbed the trees, and dared each other to go inside, for it was strictly forbidden. Even after all these years, Lyddington rubbed the seat of his breeches ruefully as he remembered the sound hiding that he had received from his father after the discovery of his trespass.

As he stood looking and remembering, the dogs caught up with him and began sniffing round, investigating the surroundings.

'I fear there are no rabbits around here,' said the earl. 'Come Toby, come Gaby.' He was turning away towards the house, when one of the dogs started to bark excitedly. Turning back, he walked to the entrance of the ice house. Toby was snuffling at something on the ground.

'What have you there, boy?' asked the earl as he bent down to look. It was a woman's reticule. Allowing both the dogs to sniff it, he said, 'Go seek!' and the two dogs immediately explored the area, but soon returned, their search fruitless.

He tried the door of the ice house, but it was tightly shut, and all his efforts would not release it. He could not tell whether it was locked, or simply jammed.

'Hallo! Is anyone in there?' he called out urgently, as he banged on the door, but there was no answer. Briefly regretting the fact that he was on foot, he hurried in the direction of the house, and hailed the first outdoor servant that he met.

'Hey, you there! Fetch the key to the ice house and something to prise open the door; and bring help. I fear someone may be trapped inside.'

Hoping that the gardener would have the wit to obey his instructions, he hurried back to the ice house. There had been too many mishaps recently for him to risk the possibility of leaving anyone in there unattended for a moment longer than was necessary.

It was not long before two stalwart fellows arrived with the key, and a fearsome-looking instrument called a ring dog. They were accompanied by Frances, carrying blankets.

'That was a good thought,' said the earl.

'If anyone has been trapped in there then they will need all the warmth they can get,' replied Frances.

The earl tried the key first but without success, so the two outdoor men applied themselves to the door with the ring dog. In the end, it took their combined efforts, and those of his lordship as well, before the door gave way with a tremendous crack, throwing them all off balance.

Lyddington entered, both of the servants holding back for fear of what might be found.

Inside the ice house, there was a space between the outer and the inner door leading to the chamber which housed the ice. The door to the inner chamber was closed, and the outer area was filled with straw to provide insulation for the ice. It was not a large area, and it did not take Lyddington long to spot the pale-blue cotton of Marigold Stevenson's gown. Quickly, he knelt next to the crumpled figure. She was lying quite still, curled up as if to protect herself. Her gown was muddied and a little torn, and there was an ominous stain near the hem. Bending close down to her, Lyddington made an important discovery.

'I'm bringing her out!' he called. 'She's alive!'

As he carried the limp figure through the doorway, it was hard for the onlookers to imagine that there could be the slightest vestige of life in her. She had always been slim and delicate-looking; now she seemed to be positively ethereal.

Quickly, Frances stepped forward with the blankets, which she and Lyddington wrapped around the unconscious figure of Marigold Stevenson.

The earl turned to the two men, saying to one, 'You, run ahead of us to the house. Warn them to have a warm bed prepared, and to call the doctor.' And to the other, 'You, secure that door. I don't want anyone else straying in there and getting themselves trapped.' Then, finally, he spoke to Frances. 'Come, young Frank, let's get her to the house as quickly as possible.'

* * *

'How do you think she got herself trapped in there?' asked Frances as they hurried along. Miss Stevenson was a mere featherweight for the earl to carry. 'Was it an accident, do you think, or . . . '

'Or another attack,' finished the earl for her. 'Impossible to say at this stage, as the door wasn't locked. We'll have to wait until she regains consciousness and strength.' Neither of them voiced the thought that was in both their minds: if she regains it.

Both were too preoccupied with the task in hand to remember what lay beween them — the discovery of Frances' sex — and by the time they had recalled it, they were at the house, and here Lady Valeria took over, instructing her brother to carry Miss Stevenson upstairs to the yellow bedroom, which had been swiftly prepared.

Judging herself to be superfluous now, Frances wandered back to the gatehouse to find that Lyddington's valet and Edward had matters very well under control. Thomas Sutcliffe was still too ill to speak, but the wounds were beginning to heal well. He was a little feverish, but not excessively, and she began to allow herself to hope that he would soon be well.

Meanwhile, Lyddington was starting to feel superfluous too. Having handed Miss Stevenson over, he found himself banished — quite properly — from the bedchamber, with nothing to do. Before he went downstairs, he insisted on having a few words with his sister.

'What is it, Spencer?' asked her ladyship very much in the tones of one having to deal with the unreasonable demands of a small child. 'Can you not see we are busy?'

'Certainly I can, but this is important, Valeria.' His quiet tones and the lack of profanity in his speech caught her attention far more than the Lyddington roar would have done, and she came out of the room, pulling the door to behind her.

'Quickly then, Spencer.'

'Preserve the gown as it is, if you please — and her shoes,' he said in an undertone. 'And would you check for any cuts and bruises — particularly about her head and hands?'

'You think this was another attack?' asked his sister anxiously, thinking of the slight figure on the bed. Next to the rosy-cheeked maid who had been preparing her nightgown, she had looked paler than ever.

'Perhaps. But will you do as I ask?'

His sister nodded, after which he wandered thoughtfully downstairs.

* * *

Although Thomas made good progress initially, the fever that had passed him by earlier on, attacked him with a vengeance when all danger was thought to have passed. For two days, his life hung in the balance. Frances, Lyddington, and Edward, together with the earl's valet, all took their turn at his bedside, whilst Ruby ran the household, making sure that food was always ready when needed. Out of respect for the earl, the doctor came every day, and Frances was very glad to see him, for Thomas's fever mounted alarmingly. Her thankfulness abated somewhat when the doctor insisted on bleeding him.

Frances could not believe that that could do him any good after all the blood he had lost already, but reflected that some of the things that she did as a gardener would probably seem absurd to an outsider, and so kept her peace.

Marigold Stevenson also needed careful nursing, and naturally this task was organized by Lady Valeria. Mrs Storringe proved to be practical and helpful, as did Miss Renshaw, but the other ladies seemed to be either unable or unwilling to help, and were usually to be found drifting about the house like spectres, hoping for a sight of Lyddington, who seldom appeared, occupied as he was with his own nursing duties at the gatehouse. Indeed, Mrs Cranborne had come in search of him once, but when she discovered that the earl was asleep after his period of duty in the sick-room, she did not remain.

Frances was very grateful for his willingness to help, for her father needed round-the-clock attendance. Nevertheless, when she had an opportunity for reflection, she often wondered how she would explain her conduct to him; there was much that needed to be resolved between them. Although they were co-attenders at Thomas Sutcliffe's bedside, they seldom met, for they tended to take different turns.

Cravenly, Frances was glad of it. She found herself dreading what he might say. She did not know how she could bear it if his anger was so great that it drove them completely apart.

As for Lyddington, now that he had discovered Frances was a woman, he wondered how he could ever have been so stupid as to think that she was a man. Even in boys' clothes, there was a grace about her that was undoubtedly female. Everything about her now seemed to betray her femininity. There was, moreover, something about her tender gentleness in dealing with her father of which he caught a glimpse, that almost made him envious of the sick man.

But as time went by, and Thomas's health improved, his sympathy gradually changed to anger, as he realized how fully he had been duped. As he sat at Sutcliffe's bedside with nothing to do but think, his mind went back to the time when he had called for her help that first time they had met. How she must have laughed at him then! He then recalled their trip to Bedford, when they had seemed to be so companionable, and he had bought her those new clothes. How foolish she must have thought him!

When finally Thomas's fever abated, the earl had worked himself up into a fury, which was all the worse for having been contained for so long. On the day that he asked her to meet him in the drawing-room, his anger was such that he could barely ask civilly for an interview, let alone wait patiently to be alone with her before confronting her.

'Now, Miss Sutcliffe,' he said savagely, as she closed the door. 'You can tell me what the devil you mean by this charade! And take off that bloody awful wig!'

His verbal attack came quite without warning, and Frances almost jumped with surprise and shock. She reached up hesitantly then took off the wig, allowing her blonde hair to fall about her shoulders, giving her an air of vulnerability. The sight should have softened Lyddington, but it didn't. She opened her mouth to speak, but before she could do anything, the earl spoke again.

'And don't dare to tell me to mind my language in your presence either. I've spoken my mind to you for too long to worry now. Or rather, I thought I knew who I was speaking to; now I'm not so sure.' He ran his hands through his hair, then burst out, 'God in Heaven, Frank, I thought you were my friend!'

'But I am, I . . . '

'How the deuce can you be? You're a woman! I thought you were a friend, and you turn out to be a woman!' He spat out the last word as if it were a term of abuse.

'But I can still be your friend . . . '

'Dammit, I don't even know what to call you!'

'My Lord, please . . . '

'Oh, splendid! You want to tell me all about it now, I expect! Well, let me tell you — '

'Damn you, Sarrell, you won't even listen!' The volume of her voice and the violence of her language surprised her almost as much as it surprised him, and at least it stopped him in his tracks. She took a deep breath before going on.

'The pretence — if pretence it was — was not to deceive you — not to deceive you personally, I mean. And it is not all pretence. My name is Frances Sutcliffe — but Frances with an *e* and not an *i*. I am not playing at what I do. I am a gardener. I know almost as much as my father does about this work — more about some aspects of it. Be in no doubt, Sarrell, I pull my weight.'

'But why then this masquerade? Gardening is an acceptable interest for a woman. My sister — '

'Oh yes, your sister, My Lord,' interrupted Frances scornfully. 'Gardening is a hobby to her, and I expect that she would say it should be the same to me.

'When my father's own father died, he was discovered to be much poorer than had been thought. There were large debts to be paid, some of them left by my uncle, father's older brother. My father knew he must either live upon his relations or turn to a trade and, as he had always been skilful at gardening, he decided to adopt that as his profession.

'My cousin Edward came to live with us after his father died. He was more like my father than his own, and he wanted to help Papa in his venture. They set up a gardening business together and were much in demand. Then, six years ago, Edmund died of a fever.

'There was a great deal of work coming in, and Papa desperately needed my help. We had no family fortune to fall back upon and besides, I needed an occupation. By playing the part of Francis Sutcliffe, I enable my father to take on more work than would otherwise be possible, and so the business can support us both.'

'Support you both!' retorted the earl. 'Don't give me that! I know what your father is paid to the last penny. He can well afford to support you!'

'Yes, he can now,' replied Frances defensively. 'But it is only in the past few years that his business had really begun to flourish, thanks to people like you who want to turn their gardens upside down and don't know how to set about it. My father could not possibly fulfil all his commissions without me.

'And in any case, what makes you think that I would be happy to sit idly at home whilst my father always works away? Perhaps I should sit primly over my stitchery, or paint watercolours of flowers, or pick them and arrange them in vases? I cannot be idle, My Lord. I have to have an occupation.'

'Well, and so there are occupations,' stormed the earl, driven against the ropes.

'Oh really,' replied Frances, her arms folded, her feet astride. 'And what do you suggest?'

'Well . . . well . . . ' began the earl hesitatingly, then gathering inspiration and continuing with much more confidence, 'Something that would not necessitate the wearing of that devilish indelicate attire!'

'Well, you bought it,' said Frances, goaded.

'Yes I did, but that was when I thought you were a man, and my friend, damn your eyes,' roared the earl. 'Stap me, but you've been playing me for a fool all this time! And laughing at me behind my back, I've no doubt. Who else has been laughing at my expense, I wonder? Mrs Storringe, of course.'

'I did tell Briar, yes,' began Frances defensively.

'Of course you did! She's fortunate to have been honoured with your confidence! How many other gentlemen have been the butt of your secret jokes, I wonder? And then there's your father. I did think him a man of honour, but maybe I was mistaken. I suppose the only one I can really acquit with confidence is your servant, who naturally has to do what you tell him.'

'Sarrell, you are not being fair!' exclaimed Frances, now so distressed by this scene that she could feel that tears were not far away.

'I do beg your pardon,' he replied, with a parody of a courtly bow. 'I had no idea that fairness was involved in any of this. Tell me, before I go, was I ever to be told about all this, or was I to remain simply an amusing topic of conversation to while away a winter evening for you and your father when there was no gardening to be done?'

Frances looked at him in horrified silence.

'I believe I have my answer,' he said coldly, distressing her far more by his rigid self-possession than he had ever done by his ranting and raving. She took a step or two towards him, then halted, appalled by the bitterness in his eyes.

'Sarrell,' she whispered. 'I would have told you . . . was going to do so — I don't know when, I . . . '

'Then forgive me if I keep to my own opinion on this matter,' he replied, his hand on the door handle. Then for a moment the old blustering Lyddington returned as he burst out, 'Dammit, I don't know whether to bow or kiss your hand! I don't know what the devil you are any more!'

* * *

After the earl had left, Frances stood in appalled silence. That he might be angry that she had not confided in him she had accepted as inevitable, but it had never occurred to her that he might think that she was laughing at his expense. Looking back at what had happened, she wondered how she could have been so stupid as to fail to grasp this possibility. Even Ruby had tried to warn her, she remembered now, but she had not listened — more fool her!

The earl never appeared to be a proud man as such; indeed, Lady Valeria was often heard to bemoan the fact that he was quite tiresomely plebeian in his tastes. But he was very confident in his own masculinity, and in his ability to relate to both men and women in an easy manner. Frances now perceived that she had struck at the root of this confidence and, after all, no man likes to think that he has been made a fool of.

She was going to have to make the earl listen to her again, and accept that she had never intended to strike at him personally. She could only hope that having vented the famous Lyddington temper upon her, he might soon be more ready to listen to her.

Her father's condition was still such that she was able to excuse herself from dining at the Court that night. Lyddington had had his belongings removed there as soon as Thomas was out of danger, and was now braving the onslaughts of Mrs Cranborne and others back in his own house.

That night, as soon as she was satisfied that her father was settled, Frances wandered along to the room that had until lately been occupied by the earl. She looked around, but the servants had been very thorough. No trace of him was left. It was as if he had never been there.

She walked over to the window to draw the curtains, even though there would be no one sleeping there and, as she turned back to pick up her candle, her eye was caught by something white, partially concealed by the bed hangings. She went to investigate, and found that it was one of the earl's handkerchiefs, crumpled but quite clean. For a moment, she nursed it to her cheek until she heard the door click, and turning, she saw that Ruby had walked in. The little dark woman only had to hold out her hand for

Frances to rush over, rest her head on her shoulder, and burst into tears.

★ ★ ★

The following day, a note was brought to the gatehouse addressed 'F. Sutcliffe' and written in Lyddington's sloping hand. It said simply: 'I won't betray you' and was signed 'Lyddington'. This provided Frances with some measure of relief up to a point. At least it meant that after they had finished here, she could continue with her work.

On the other hand, it was distressingly brief and formal, and carried no overtones of forgiveness. The fact that he had signed himself 'Lyddington' when he had so often commanded her to call him Sarrell was in itself depressing. If she could have had her way, she would leave the Court tomorrow, but there was the commission to be finished, and she could not desert her father when he was still not in full health.

The previous evening, she had admitted to Ruby that she was in love with the earl. Now, she acknowledged to herself that to go away and never see him again was a thought almost too dreadful to contemplate. Perhaps though it was preferable to seeing him, and knowing that he loathed and despised her as a liar and a cheat.

Reluctantly, she got ready to go out. The garden could not be avoided. It was the very reason she was there after all. Her work with the garden would surely come to occupy the whole of her mind as it had always done and perhaps provide her with much needed solace in the long, lonely years that were to come.

11

'What do you mean?' asked the earl exasperatedly of his sister. They were in the library where Lyddington had been writing a letter, and whence his sister had come directly from Miss Stevenson's sick-room.

'Oh Spencer, don't be so obtuse,' said his sister impatiently, seating herself next to the desk so that she could face him. 'I meant exactly what I said. She does not remember anything.'

'Damn!' exclaimed his lordship, striking the table with his fist and rising hastily. 'She must remember something!'

'Spencer, she is not doing this just to annoy you,' declared her ladyship. 'I have questioned her gently but quite firmly. She recalls going out for a walk in the hopes of seeing some flower in bloom — although she cannot remember which one. She recalls leaving the house and closing the door behind her, but she remembers nothing else until waking up in the room upstairs.'

'And what does the doctor say? Does he think that she will soon recall everything?'

'He cannot tell. In such cases as this, the

shock of the attack — if she was involved in some way, which is by no means certain — and then the incarceration in the ice house, might be so great that it might be some time before she regains her memory.'

'Very inconvenient,' said the earl with a sneer. 'Or perhaps convenient for her?'

'Why so?'

'Oh come now, Valeria, now who's being obtuse? Upstairs, we have either an innocent witness or a violent attacker. If the former, well, loss of memory is surely a merciful gift of nature. If the latter — it could be a very convenient ploy.'

Lady Valeria thought for a moment, then shook her head.

'Oh no, Spencer, I cannot believe it of her. The whole affair was far too messy for someone so fastidious. And surely, she was taking a great risk, shutting herself in the ice house like that. Besides' — she studied her fingernails — 'she has been told how you rescued her, and is disposed to become a little sentimental about you.'

'Oh my God, not another!' exclaimed the earl, covering his eyes. 'What is it about me, Valeria? Why do they pursue me? I'm not even good-looking!'

'Well it can't possibly be your charm and pretty speeches,' said his unsympathetic sister. 'How fares Thomas Sutcliffe?'

'Better, I believe,' responded the earl, flushing a little. 'But still not well enough to be questioned about the attack upon him. Which puts me in mind of something: I still need to establish what sort of knife was used.'

He collected the knife from where he had locked it up in the book-room, and made his way round to the side door, where he stood hesitating in a way that was quite unlike his normally decisive manner. A few days ago, he would have gone quite happily to seek Frances out. Now because of what lay between them, he felt unable to do so. He had been quite in the right, he told himself defensively. She had deceived him, and made a mockery of him. Why the devil then was he feeling guilty?

He set off walking aimlessly, and found himself quite by chance in the kitchen gardens. At once, his thoughts went to how he had found Frances there at the mercy of Peter Rance. He recalled how anxious she had looked, and then how her anxiety had turned to relief when she saw him, and he felt a fierce surge of protectiveness towards her.

Suddenly, he had a sensation of being watched. He turned around looking about him. There was no sign of anyone, and at once he called out, 'Hallo there!'

He heard rapid footsteps, and almost immediately Fred Thompson, the head of the kitchen gardens came into view. Lyddington walked over at once to speak to him, but he was still left with the certainty that it had not been Thompson's presence that he had sensed.

Fred was surprised and gratified to have his master in his domain, and would cheerfully have shown him every plant, flower and fruit to be seen, with detailed histories of each. The earl managed to avoid this by asking bluntly, after the pleasantries were over, 'What of Peter Rance?'

'That I couldn't say, M'Lord. He's not been seen at work for several days now, although one of the under-gardeners thought he saw him yesterday.'

'Where was this?'

'Over by the lake, M'Lord.'

'What is he like to work with?'

The gardener scratched his head.

'The men don't like him. They'd just as soon have nothing to do with him.'

'I know he's always been strange,' agreed the earl, 'but never as bad as this, surely?'

'Not until the parterre went. You see, M'Lord, that was his task — trimming the parterre — and I'll say this, he did know what to do, and he could do it. Now he's well, lost, if you take my meaning.'

'Then I suppose I must take my share of the blame,' said Lyddington ruefully. 'Do you think he would be violent?'

Thompson thought for a moment, his brow furrowed.

'I couldn't say, M'Lord. But I will say this: Your Lordship's got no cause to go blaming yourself. He was one that was likely to go strange, whatever.'

Suddenly recalling the purpose of his errand, Lyddington drew the knife from his pocket and unwrapped it.

'Yes, that's a gardener's knife, no doubt about it,' said Thompson, as soon as the reason for its presence had been disclosed to him.

'Could you tell me what type of task it might be used for — or in what part of the garden?'

The gardener shook his head.

'Any gardener would have a use for a knife like this,' he said.

'So you can't tell me if it belonged to anyone in particular,' said Lyddington resignedly.

'No. Might I take it for a moment, M'Lord?' The earl willingly handed it over, and Thompson examined the handle. Then he added, 'It's one of ours, not one of Mr

Sutcliffe's.' He pointed to a small 'L' carved on the handle.

'Well, I'm blest!' exclaimed the earl. 'Even the garden tools are marked with my initial! Thank you, Thompson. Will you take care of this now? Let me know if any man seems to be missing his knife. I'll want to talk to him.'

'Very good, M'Lord.'

The earl turned away, walked a few steps and then turned back.

'You haven't got an 'L' carved on you anywhere, by any chance?' he asked quizzically.

'Not on the outside,' replied the gardener seriously as he touched his hat.

Feeling a little humbled by the man's obvious loyalty, Lyddington made his way out of the kitchen gardens and into the wilderness where, strolling deep in thought, he rounded a clump of trees and was confronted all at once with Frances.

Both changed colour, Frances turning a little white, and Lyddington flushing somewhat. In their embarrassment, they both began to speak at the same time. Then, having stopped abruptly, they looked at each other, neither being sure how to proceed.

Had things been as they were one week previously, there would have been no problem. Lyddington, as master of all he surveyed, would naturally take precedence over a male employee. As a gentleman, however, he would just as naturally allow a lady to speak first. Having discovered Frances' sex, he was totally at a loss as to where he stood, and his lifelong training as to male behaviour in any situation could not help him.

Frances, for her part, was ready to defer to him as before, but was anxious not to do anything that might rekindle his anger that had raged about her head at their previous meeting.

At length, the earl gestured to Frances to walk beside him and they set off through the wilderness. Automatically, Lyddington went to put his arm around Frances' shoulders, then withdrew, digging his hands into his pockets.

Frances was left with an acute feeling of loss, which she tried to cover up by saying, 'How is Miss Stevenson?'

'Recovering well, according to m'sister — but apparently she remembers nothing of how she came to be in the ice house — or how she came to have blood on her dress. She sustained no cuts at all, so the blood cannot be hers.'

'Do you think that she is telling the truth — about not remembering?' asked Frances.

The earl shrugged.

'M'sister thinks so; and there was a big bump on her head. Valeria also maintains — and I'm inclined to agree — that she would never have got herself into such a state voluntarily. So we are no wiser, as yet. I don't suppose your father . . . ?'

Frances shook her head, saying worriedly, 'The fever has gone, but he still shows no sign of regaining consciousness. However the doctor seems hopeful of a complete recovery, so I will not allow myself to become too downcast. I think that we can manage without Soames now, if you would like him back.'

'Let him return in time to dress me for dinner,' replied Lyddington after a moment's thought. 'Then he can sleep in his own bed, poor fellow. He can return to you to relieve your Edward in the morning.'

Frances smiled her thanks and they walked on a little way in silence. Lyddington was about to tell her about the knife, when she spoke, and with her words destroyed the better atmosphere that was beginning to be built between them.

'My Lord, I would like to thank you for your note . . . '

'For my promise not to give you away, you mean,' he interposed, his face set. 'You need have no worries on that score. I have no wish to broadcast my foolishness to the world.'

'Please,' she begged him, her frustration at not being able to convey her meaning clearly showing in her stance and her expression. 'Please understand that I have never sought to ridicule you or . . . or deceive you . . . ' Her voice faded away.

'Forgive me if I find that difficult to swallow,' said the earl politely, but still without a hint of humour or understanding in his voice. 'From the very beginning, you have done nothing but deceive me and make a mockery of my overtures of friendship to you. God in Heaven, and to think I preferred your attitude to that of Masters! I would rather you had coldly and disdainfully refused my company as did he, than accepted it and served me such a trick!'

'But I have not deceived you out of malicious trickery, any more than I deceived any of the other people we worked for!' she protested, tears not far away.

'Oh, I beg pardon!' exclaimed the earl with awful sarcasm. 'So the deceit becomes less culpable if it's perpetrated upon a greater number. I suppose if you had succeeded in fooling the whole world, then your action would become an honourable one?'

'Well no, but . . . '

Until now, the earl had conducted himself

with dignified restraint. But Frances' deceit had hurt his pride and his feelings. Moreover, his discovery that she was a woman had awakened emotions towards her that he was not yet ready to confront. As a consequence, he completely lost control of his temper.

'Hell and devil confound it!' he roared. 'You're half man, half woman, with the worst half of both! You've neither a man's sense of honour nor a woman's femininity! Why can't you bloody well be one or the other? And I still don't know what to call you!'

Having thus given vent to his feelings, he strode off in the direction of the house, whereas Frances, heedless for once of who might see her, ran to the orangery and hurling herself down upon one of the benches in there, cried as if her heart would break.

After leaving the scene of this their latest quarrel, Lyddington returned to the house and proceeded to give voice to his rage by ripping up at Masters for some small omission, pulling a bell rope so viciously that he broke it, and by bellowing at a footman for getting in his way.

Eventually, he decided that fresh air would be helpful, so he took the dogs out for a run. Once in the grounds, he managed to incur his sister's fiercest wrath by striding past her and her guests with his dogs, and allowing the animals to gallop through a muddy puddle, thus bespattering several ladies, all without one word of acknowledgement or apology.

This latter achievement so pleased him that he returned to the house in a much better humour, and after he had looked in on Masters with a blunt apology, and tossed the offending footman a guinea, (causing him to say to his colleagues 'I'd get in his way again for that!') he went upstairs to change out of his muddy clothes. He was glad to be without Soames, so that he could be alone with his thoughts.

Standing on a small table in the window was a miniature of his father, and he picked it up and looked at it for a moment — the man who had so wasted his substance that his son had had to recoup his fortunes through an advantageous but loveless marriage. Thomas Sutcliffe faced with a similar problem had used his own skills to build a new life for himself — and with great success and, of course, Frances had played her own part in achieving that success. Lyddington put the picture down, thinking to himself that he had to admire both the Sutcliffes for their hard work and ingenuity.

Dammit all, he thought to himself as he took off his coat. I think I could forgive her if she had not played the boy so completely. But she took everything that I said and did without a blush; accepted all my confidences so readily. I can't forget that.

As he stood lost in thought, he caught sight of himself in the mirror, his shirt unbuttoned, his hands thrust into the pockets of his breeches, so that the ends of the shirt were thrust back and virtually the whole of his chest exposed.

Suddenly, his mind went back to the time when he had entered Frances' room unexpectedly, and had at one stage stood talking to her, in virtually the same pose that he was in now. He thought of her coughing fit when he had entered, her endless fiddling with her papers, her reluctance to meet his eyes, and the air of tension about her.

Then he recalled how they had sat together one evening, and he had recounted to her one of his more racy adventures. She had leaned forward to move one of the candles, her face coloured, as he had thought, by its glow.

As he looked at his reflection, the puzzled expression disappeared, to be replaced by a smile. Moments later, he started to chuckle. Almost immediately afterwards, those of his household nearby were relieved to be able to report that his lordship was laughing 'fit to burst'.

12

That night at dinner, the earl was very poor company. From elation at discovering that there were very definite signs of feminine modesty in Frances, he had swung to despondency, as he recalled the way in which he had sworn at her, and he wondered whether she would ever forgive him.

If she were the man that he had thought she was only a short time ago, he could slap her on the back, call himself every kind of fool, and they could get drunk together. Now, however, his approach had to be altogether different, and he felt very unsure of himself.

His sister, watching him from the other end of the table, wondered whether he was quite well. He had only toyed with the braised fowls in oyster sauce — one of his favourite dishes — and was even now pushing a fragment of pigeon pie around his plate in a manner that was quite unlike him.

Mrs Cranborne watched him with predatory eyes. His valet, no doubt in deference to the preponderance of sick people in the vicinity, had arrayed his master in unrelieved black, embroidered with jet. Mrs Cranborne found him quite devastating in his abstraction, and decided that tonight must be the night.

'You seem thoughtful, My Lord,' she purred. 'I hope your thoughts are pleasant ones.'

His lordship, only hearing the half of this, smiled absently, and murmured in agreement. Taking this as encouragement, her heart gave a little leap.

'I have to say that my own thoughts are very agreeable,' she went on, looking at him through her lashes. It was a coquettish, girl's trick that she could still just about get away with in candlelight.

'Then I trust that they may continue,' replied the earl, still with only half his mind on what he was saying.

'Or perhaps be brought to fruition?' murmured Mrs Cranborne, unable to believe how well this conversation was going. 'Do you remember Rome, My Lord?'

At this moment, Lady Valeria gave the signal to rise, and Mrs Cranborne was forced to go with the rest. But the bow that the earl gave her, with his hand on his heart, as she was leaving, convinced her that he was now ready to take up their relationship from where they had left off in Rome.

It was some time before the earl felt ready

to rejoin the ladies. He had resolved to seek out Frances the next day, and put things right with her, even if he was still not sure what he was going to say. After all, they had been friends, even if on a mistaken basis, and he now felt the loss of that friendship quite keenly. Dammit all, he was missing her this evening, for example!

They had talked about so many things together, in a frank and open way — not like the conversation that he had just had with Mrs Cranborne, to which he had only given half his attention, and which could have meant anything or nothing.

He liked women; liked talking with them, flirting with them, dancing with them, making love to them; but with Frances, he had thought that he had had something different. Could that kind of easy friendship be possible between a man and a woman? Could one even have it all — friendship and love, both within one relationship? It was a novel idea to him and suddenly rather an appealing one.

He thought about Frances sustaining her disguise for six years. That must have taken courage and self-sacrifice. All in all, she was a remarkable woman. Surely she must have longed at times for feminine attire, and all the knick-knacks that went with it.

What would she look like dressed as she should be, he wondered? Perhaps in blue — a similar shade to the outfit that he had bought her in Bedford, but without that ugly wig, and with that blonde hair — that he had seen now on several occasions — dressed becomingly. Would a low-cut gown suit her, and how low cut would it be?

Here, he sternly called his musings to a deliberate halt, before they became too engrossing. He still had the rest of the evening to get through, after all.

With a sigh, he rose from the table and went to rejoin the ladies. The first person that he met as he entered the room was Briar Storringe.

'My Lord, I have an apology to make,' she murmured, after he had greeted her politely.

'I am very sure you have not, Mrs Storringe,' he replied, smiling.

'Oh but I have,' she answered, not meeting his eyes in a way that was not really in accord with her normally open disposition. 'I gave you a foolish, wrong impression in the garden the other day, and I wanted to say that . . . that . . . '

'You were merely jesting,' concluded the earl. 'I felt sure at the time that you must be. Your loyalty to Captain Storringe is well known.'

There was a short silence, then Briar said, slowly and carefully, 'You should know, My Lord, that I had no assignation that morning.'

'Certainly not with any man,' agreed the earl, before wandering away, leaving Briar completely dumbfounded.

He felt in such a good humour now, that he even indulged Mrs Cranborne with — as he thought — a light flirtation, totally unaware of the encouragement that he was giving to her hopes.

The party being in rather a sombre mood, no one was very late to bed. Mrs Cranborne was one of the first to retire, giving the earl a very meaningful glance as she went. Lyddington remained till last, blowing out the candles as he went. He disliked being waited on all the time, and encouraged his servants to retire early, if he felt he could manage for himself. His valet would have been in his bed long since.

He entered his dressing-room and saw that the door that led to his bedroom was almost closed. This was unusual, but not unprecedented. He walked over to the door, and was about to push it open, when he realized that light from within the room was coming from candles set on one of the tables. This was unheard of. All of Lyddington's servants knew never to leave a lighted candle in an untended room. His lordship's personal tragedy had made him most strict on this particular point. It was inconceivable that Soames, who had been with him for the whole of his adult life, could have forgotten such a thing.

Pausing for a moment longer at the doorway, he caught just a tiny whiff of an exotic perfume. Lingering only to pick up his own candle, he was out of the room in a flash, and back down the passage. He had known that Felicia was determined to have him, but never had he supposed that she would go to such lengths.

'The cunning bitch!' he breathed to himself. 'Now where the devil do I go?'

Presumably the plan was that in a short while, Mrs Cranborne's maid would go in search of her mistress and, finding her in his lordship's bed, would start up some kind of a commotion to make sure that the disgraceful events were properly witnessed. A marriage would then be necessary to save the lady's reputation.

Clearly, it was essential for the earl to be elsewhere — preferably out of the house — at the crucial moment. With this in mind, he headed for the front door, then after a moment's pause, went instead to the steward's room, in order to collect the key to the gatehouse. He would surely be safe there. However Frances may have deceived him, her deceit had never had the manipulative quality that seemed to characterize this trick of Felicia Cranborne's.

His dogs had been curled up in the morning-room, but on hearing his familiar step, they both emerged into the hall, to follow at his heels. He was to be very glad that they did.

With no thought of concealing his presence, he walked towards the gatehouse with his usual brisk step. The dogs, distracted by the sound of some small animal, dashed round the side of the darkened building, and Lyddington reached in his pocket for his key.

Thinking he heard footsteps, he turned, and it was as well that he did so, for otherwise the blow which struck him would have done so full square and could easily have killed him. As it was, having received a glancing blow, he fell to his knees, and instinctively gave a whistle. The dogs bounded back round the corner, and the unknown assailant made good his escape.

By now unable to think clearly, Lyddington somehow managed to insert the key in the keyhole, unlock the door, stagger inside, and collapse on a small sofa which was set against the wall at the back of the hall. One dog flopped down beside his master in order to guard him. The other stationed himself across the still open front door.

* * *

Frances was usually the first down in the morning. Even when her father was well, he often took a little longer to appear at the breakfast-table. This was because he always wrote up his journal for the previous day first thing in the morning when he was fresh.

After getting dressed, she had looked in on him to discover from Edward that although his colour was much healthier, there was still no sign of a return to consciousness. She tried to recall the doctor's optimism, but she could not help feeling rather depressed, and her usual appetite for breakfast seemed non-existent.

Who will benefit if you fall ill as well? she said to herself, as she left her father's room.

On reaching the top of the stairs, she felt a draught of fresh air and, as she came down, she realized that the front door was open. Gaby got up from his station, and sniffed at her ankles, then on receiving a pat, flopped down again.

'Sarrell?' she called out, frowning. 'Sarrell, are you here?' A sound that was very like a groan came from behind the stairs. Frances spun round to be met with the sight of his lordship struggling to sit up. Still in his black evening clothes, with his face as white as chalk, the only colour about him was the smear of dried blood to the side of his face, and a rapidly growing bruise.

Frances fell to her knees beside him.

'My Lord, what has occurred? Oh, please, don't try to sit up,' she went on. 'Let me send for some help, and get something to bathe this wound. Promise me you won't move.'

The earl tried to nod his head, but finding that this was too painful, waved his hand in agreement. Frances ran out of the front door and round to the kitchen to get some water, and finding the kitchen maid there already, sent her across to the Court immediately to get help.

She hurried back to the hall, and found that Lyddington was now sitting up with his eyes closed, and that Edward, having heard something going on, had come downstairs to investigate and was even now about to administer some brandy.

Frances squeezed out the clean cloth that she had found in the kitchen, and began to bathe the earl's cut. The sudden touch of the cold water made him wince at first, but he allowed Frances to minister to him without argument.

'How did this occur, My Lord?' asked Frances, after the earl had taken a sip of brandy.

'I was on my way here,' replied his lordship, not able to remember for the moment why. 'I had the key in my hand — someone struck me down. If it hadn't been for the dogs . . . '

Seeing that he was tiring, Frances said, 'Don't try to talk any more. You need to rest. I will have your old room prepared upstairs, and you will be able to go up immediately.'

She was just turning away in order to do this, when the earl grasped hold of her wrist. 'Thank you . . . young Frank,' he said.

In a very short time, servants arrived from the Court, and, at Frances' instructions, carried the earl upstairs to his room, which had been prepared by Ruby. It spoke volumes for Lyddington's weakened condition that he uttered not a word of protest at this. At the same time, Ruddles was despatched to fetch the doctor.

By the time the doctor arrived, Lady Valeria had been alerted as to her brother's condition. She had judged it best to have nothing said about it at the Court, so as not to alarm the ladies, most of whom were still very unsettled after the attack on Thomas Sutcliffe, and Miss Stevenson's 'accident'.

'Well, at least his head is not broke,' was the doctor's verdict. Lady Valeria had been waiting for news downstairs in the gatehouse with Edward and Frances.

'I should have been very surprised if anything could break it,' replied her ladyship dispassionately, her tone deliberately vigorous in order to hide her feelings. She was very fond of her brother, and after the various mishaps that had occurred, was much concerned.

'You are a tough breed, if you'll allow me to say so, My Lady,' said the doctor with all the licence of one who had treated members of the family for the past thirty years. 'However, he has quite severe concussion, and must keep to his bed for a while.'

'For how long, Doctor?' asked Frances anxiously.

'He won't want to go anywhere for the rest of the day,' he replied. 'Try to keep him in bed for as long as you can, is my answer.' He smiled wryly. 'Knowing His Lordship, that won't be for long. But keep him from strenuous exercise — no riding for now, and make him rest as much as possible.'

After the doctor had gone, Lady Valeria turned to Frances.

'Well, it appears that you are to have the inconvenience of my brother staying with you again, at least for a time,' she said in dignified tones, 'although why he chose to come back here in the middle of the night is quite beyond me. I will despatch his valet over here at once, and please be so good as to let me know if there is anything more that you need.' She paused for a moment, then went on, 'This will be your second invalid to care for. It seems to me Master Sutcliffe, that you had better set up as a physician rather than a gardener. Will you be able to manage two of them?'

'There will be no difficulty,' Frances assured her. 'My uncle no longer needs constant nursing, and His Lordship, I think, needs only rest.'

'Well, Spencer will be wanting Soames, so I will send him anyway. But now, I must go and attend to my guests.' She turned to leave, but then paused and turned back, on her face an expression of anxiety that she could not conceal. 'You will let me know if there is any change?'

Frances hurried to her side, and laid a hand on her arm.

'Of course, My Lady. He will receive the best possible care, I assure you.'

Lady Valeria looked at Frances searchingly,

as if she was trying to find the answer to some kind of puzzle.

'You are . . . very fond of my brother, are you not?'

Unable to trust her voice, Frances merely nodded, Lady Valeria, after a moment's silence, nodded too, then turned and left.

* * *

There was no difficulty in keeping his lordship in bed for the rest of that first day. He was in considerable discomfort, and also felt some dizziness from time to time, although he refused to admit it. The problems began on the following day when, feeling very much better apart from a headache, he insisted on being allowed to get up.

'Devil take you, man,' said the earl to his valet. 'I don't mean to be molly-coddled like some ailing female. It's time I was up.'

'But My Lord . . . ' began Soames. Then seeing evidence that the Lyddington roar might come into play, he left the room in haste, saying something about getting his lordship's things together.

On his way out of the room, he met Frances, who was on her way to see how the earl was doing, and the valet begged for her support.

'Indeed, Master Sutcliffe, the doctor did say he was to remain in bed for as long as possible, and it's only been a day! And it was a very nasty blow. But he won't listen to me. Perhaps you . . . '

Frances sighed, and entered the bedchamber, where Sarrell was sitting up in bed. Thankfully, he had a good deal more colour than when she had first seen him the previous day, but he was sporting a rather jaunty looking bandage around his head, and his expression was a very determined one.

'Reinforcements?' he remarked to his valet, causing that faithful gentleman to colour up a trifle.

'I understand, My Lord, that you mean to get up today,' said Frances calmly. 'No doubt you have been told what the doctor said, but naturally you know better than the doctor.'

The earl opened his mouth to speak, but before he could say anything, Frances went on, 'Very well, then you had better do as you please, but with one or two conditions: that you do nothing more strenuous than walk round the grounds — and that not by yourself; and that you have a rest on your bed this afternoon.' So saying, she whisked herself out of the room before the earl could make any reply.

'Are you sure this is wise?' asked Edward,

when he heard the news that Lyddington was getting up. 'After what the doctor said?'

Frances shrugged.

'Perhaps not,' she replied. 'But I judged that if he were not allowed to do so, he might put himself into a passion, and surely that would be far worse for his condition.'

Edward nodded.

Lady Valeria had been alerted to the fact that her brother was getting up against all medical advice and consequently, when he descended the stairs looking remarkably well save for the bandage, she was waiting for him.

'Spencer, are you sure this is wise?' she asked mildly. Like Frances, she was all too aware of the possible danger to his health in rousing his temper.

'I'm damnably sure it's the only thing what will keep me sane,' he returned. 'You know I could never endure to be abed for long, Valeria. Some fresh air is exactly what I need.'

'Some fresh air!' she exclaimed. 'You are actually going out?'

'Certainly. A walk around the gardens will do me good.'

'But Spencer, what of your assailant? What if he should be concealing himself somewhere?'

'Fudge!' he exclaimed good-humouredly.

'The fellow was obviously a housebreaker. He'll be far too fearful at what he's done to return. And if he does, well, I'll have Sutcliffe to defend me.'

Frances tried to look manly and dangerous, but was not sure with how much success.

'Well, if you are sure,' murmured Lady Valeria doubtfully.

'There is just one thing you can do for me if you love me, Sister,' went on the earl, taking his hat from his valet and putting it on gingerly over his bandage 'and that is to keep that devil's daughter away from me.'

'If you mean Mrs Cranborne, then she is gone,' replied Lady Valeria.

'Gone!' exclaimed the earl, hardly able to believe his good fortune. 'When?'

'Yesterday morning. She came downstairs in the foulest of tempers, and ordered her carriage immediately. Since there was not the slightest reason to implicate her in the attack on Thomas Sutcliffe, and since she did not appear to have any relevant evidence either, there seemed to be no point in insisting that she stay. Oh Spencer, do take care!'

She spoke thus, for the earl's amused expression had broadened gradually during her speech, until at the end he was laughing so heartily, that she was afraid that he might do himself some damage.

'Valeria, that's the best news I've had since I came home,' he declared, as soon as he was able. 'Come, young Frank, let's be off. I'll enjoy my walk all the more, now!'

13

They made their way around the side of the house and into the gardens, walking slowly, the earl with his arm around Frances' shoulders. Perhaps it was because the earl felt that he needed a little extra support, or perhaps he had forgotten for a time what lay between them. Whatever the reason might have been, Frances kept quiet about it. The sensation of having him so close to her was far too sweet for her to risk curtailing it by a thoughtless comment.

For once, they were without Toby and Gaby. After the earl had been put to bed in the gatehouse, Ruddles had collected them, and he had taken them out that morning for a run whilst he exercised his lordship's hunter.

By mutual consent, they walked in the direction of the wilderness, crossing a small bridge over a brook that fed into the lake further down.

'Well, thank the Lord that hell-cat's gone,' exclaimed Lyddington, as they leaned for a moment on the balustrade, watching the lazy water trickling beneath them. 'Would you like to know what she did, and why I was in your house the other night, hm?'

'If you wish to tell me,' she answered.

'She only lay in wait for me — in my bed!' he explained. Frances gasped. 'I realized she was there when I saw a light burning in my room. Marriage was the bitch's object. Had I been there one minute longer, I reckon she'd have snared me!'

'So you came to us?'

'So I came to you,' he agreed. Their eyes met briefly, then Frances blushed and looked away. 'And got a blow to my head for my pains,' concluded the earl.

Again by unspoken mutual consent, they ended their contemplation of the little stream and walked on again.

'My Lord, do you really think it was a housebreaker?'

There was a long silence.

'If it was, it'll be the first we've had — and a very ignorant one, too. Anyone living around here — or anyone wishful to find out — would know that we have a houseful of guests and servants at present. And why go for me, when I had a pair of dogs at my heels? No, if he was a housebreaker, he was either vastly over-confident, or very stupid.'

There was another silence, then the earl spoke again, changing the subject.

'By the way, did I tell you that the knife

that was used by your father's attacker was a gardener's knife?'

'No indeed, My Lord. Is it known whose knife it was?'

'One of the estate's apparently, which I suppose would make it mine. And by the way,' he went on casually, 'I seem to recall telling you on many occasions not to address me in that way.'

'Yes, I . . . I remember,' said Frances, colouring fierily, as she remembered in what way he had promised to punish her if she erred in such a way again.

Perhaps a similar thought passed through the earl's mind, for he flushed a little himself, cleared his throat, then said aggressively, 'Devil take me, I still don't know what to call you!'

'Well . . . Briar calls me Fran, but my cousin Edmund used to call me Frankie,' she replied a little shyly.

'Fran,' said the earl thoughtfully, trying how the name felt on his lips. 'No, not Fran; it's too severe.' He looked wryly at her. 'Too . . . masculine, almost.' Frances chuckled, raised her eyes to his, then looked away. 'But Frankie,' murmured the earl. 'Frankie. Yes, that'll do.'

Thinking that the earl might perhaps be tiring, Frances steered them towards a small temple in which they might sit for a time. It was not one of the ornaments which had been erected on Lady Valeria's orders, it was considerably older, and parts of it had become very overgrown with ivy. There was a roof over the seating area, but the back of it was only joined at the sides and not at the roof. There was a broad step at the back on which a statue stood, with a false pillar on each side of it, closer to the sides of the structure than to the statue itself. Only the most determined viewer could see them, however, for the ivy had long since grown down to conceal the statue and the step completely.

Lyddington was happier to sit down than he would have admitted, and both sat in silence for a time, looking around them.

'What about this place — shall I tear it down, do you think?' asked the earl idly.

'Oh no,' replied Frances. 'Look, the marble behind the ivy is undamaged and of a beautiful colour,' she went on, getting up from her place and lifting it to show him. 'And the statue could be cleaned.'

'You have to admit, though, that it is rather preposterous,' answered Lyddington, rising to take a closer look.

'Oh yes, but something can be preposterous and beautiful at the same time,' protested

Frances, colouring a little in her enthusiasm. Then she realized that the earl was no longer looking at the statue, but at her.

'That is something I am just beginning to realize,' he answered slowly, and for a few long minutes they stood in silence, looking at each other. Then suddenly, the spell was broken as they heard the sound of approaching footsteps.

'In there!' said a furtive voice. 'We shall be able to talk undisturbed.'

Swiftly, the earl glanced round, then pulled back the ivy, mounted the step and held out a hand to Frances to pull her up next to him. Then he allowed the ivy to drop, and they were completely concealed.

It had only taken them a moment to conceal themselves; it now seemed to take an age for anyone to enter the temple. While they were waiting, a number of things became very noticeable to Frances: one was that the step on which they were standing, although it had appeared to be very broad, was in fact quite difficult to balance upon. The earl was standing with his back to the statue, and was able to hold on to it to keep his balance, but Frances, having got up nearer to one of the false pillars found herself thrust up against the earl, and had to rely upon him to keep her in place with his other arm across her body.

Frances looked up at him, but his expression was quite unfathomable in the gloom. At very much the same time, she became conscious of his breathing, and of the feel of his body against hers; a sensation she could hardly avoid, trapped as they were against each other within that small space, and quite unable to move without giving themselves away.

Once having looked at him, she found it quite impossible to look away; and equally impossible to turn her face aside when she realized that he was going to kiss her.

They did not embrace; movements of arms within that restricted space would have been unthinkable. Frances felt the earl tighten his grip on her waist whilst he brushed first her brow, then her cheek, then her lips with gentle kisses, before covering her willing mouth with his own firm one and kissing her deeply.

The existence that had been hers until now had allowed no opportunity for romantic dalliance, and this was the first time that she had ever been kissed, apart from the occasional fatherly embraces from Thomas Sutcliffe, and because of her masquerade, there had been precious few of those, even in private. But it seemed to her that here, in this tiny world, somehow removed from reality, kissing the earl, and being kissed by him came to her almost as easily and as naturally as breathing itself.

Eventually, Lyddington lifted his head and almost appeared to be about to speak, when they both became aware that the temple was now occupied, and that a conversation was in progress.

'I can't bear to think of you taking such risks,' said a male voice. The words were clear, but the tone was muffled, so it was impossible to identify the speaker.

'But you are taking risks as well,' was the reply from his female companion.

'No one will say anything,' he answered. 'I am my own master here. But you! If it should be discovered that you had come here . . . '

There was a short silence. Then the man spoke again.

'Surely, your mother must relent soon!'

'You do not know her!' was the answer. 'She will always be against us.'

'I can't listen any more, this is too damn' personal,' growled Lyddington, and he leaped down from his hiding place. Frances, immediately robbed of her means of balance, half jumped, half fell after him, and at once they were confronted with the sight of Judith Hartingon clasped firmly in Laurence Masters' manly arms.

'Well, I'm damned!' declared Lyddington.

If Frances and the earl were shocked, it was nothing to the feelings of the two lovers, suddenly confronted by two rather dishevelled individuals who seemed to have appeared from out of the wall by magic. Masters turned white and loosed his hold on Miss Hartington, who swayed so alarmingly that Frances got hold of her, and led her firmly to the tiny stone seat set inside the grotto.

'So you're your own master, are you?' the earl went on forthrightly. 'Well, in that case, I should like to know who the devil I am!'

'My Lord,' began Masters with great dignity, drawing himself up to his full height. 'I may have done wrong, but I venture to suggest that what you were listening to was a private conversation.'

'Accusing me of poking my nose in, eh?' queried the earl belligerently. 'That's exactly why we showed ourselves, because we could tell it was personal.' He turned to Frances, who was bending solicitously over the distraught Miss Hartington. 'Frankie, take the lady back to the house. I would have a few words with Masters alone.'

At these words, Judith Hartington rose to her feet, flinging herself dramatically in front of Masters, her bosom heaving.

'No, no! You shall not! I forbid it! You shall not harm him!'

Lyddington eyed her with an expression of total perplexity.

'Harm him? And why the devil should I do that, pray?'

Miss Hartington cringed a little, but stood her ground. For Lyddington, this was a very mild reproof, and Frances was left to wonder what she would do if ever she were treated to the Lyddington roar at close quarters. However, she felt that she ought to intervene, so she ventured to say, 'Sarrell, you do look a little wild. I think you are alarming Miss Hartington. And you have lost your bandage.'

'B-b-bandage?' quavered Miss Hartington, swaying once more and turning whiter than ever, were that possible. 'But I . . . '

'Hush, dearest!' said Masters urgently. 'Not at this stage.'

This exchange went unnoticed by Lyddington, who was exclaiming, 'Devil take the blasted thing!' and by Frances who was urging him to sit down whilst she retied it.

Once the earl's chestnut locks were restored to their confining ribbon, and his bandage was in place, he said, 'Now let's go where we can all sit down, and preferably where we can have a drink.'

They adjourned to the orangery, where

unfortunately the second of the earl's requirements could not be met, but at least they were fairly sure of not being interrupted.

'Now,' said the earl, when they were all seated, Judith and Masters very close together on one seat, and Lyddington and Frances a little further apart on another. 'I want the truth from you, Masters.'

'Very well, My Lord,' said Masters taking a deep breath. 'My father is agent to Mr Cuthbert Ferrier, whose estate is in Lincolnshire. Mr Ferrier is married to Judith's mother, so Mr Ferrier is Judith's stepfather. We . . . ' He tugged at his neck-cloth. 'Judith and I, well . . . '

'We became attached,' interrupted Miss Hartington, clasping hold of Masters' arm. 'But Mama would not hear of an engagement between us.'

'Mrs Ferrier's attitude is quite understandable,' said Masters, patting his beloved's hand. 'I do not have a noble name or connections, and my profession is my only asset. I tried very hard not to become attached to Judith, but . . . '

He smiled lovingly at her. His smile was returned with one of such sweetness, that he quite forgot what he was saying, and he had to be brought back to earth by a rather fidgety earl saying testily, 'Yes, yes, true love and all that. Go on, man, do.'

'Our attachment developed, and by the time Mrs Ferrier realized what was happening, we were in love.'

'It was not Laurence's fault,' declared Judith, looking anxiously at the earl's raised eyebrow, then looking away again. She seemed to find it impossible to look directly at him, but appeared fascinated with his bandage. 'I pursued him!'

'As indeed you appear to have done all the way down here,' murmured the earl.

'My Lord, you will unsay those words!' declared Masters, leaping to his feet, and squaring up to his employer.

'Why? Aren't they true?' replied the earl blandly, remaining where he was, and not even uncrossing his legs.

'Yes, they are true,' exclaimed Judith, pulling at Masters' hand, so that he sat down again next to her. 'Mama wanted to part us, but knew that if Laurence left in disgrace, his father might well leave too and deprive the estate of an excellent manager. So she looked around for employment for Laurence, and then heard from Lady Valeria that a new agent was needed on this estate, and so recommended him.'

'So how did it come about that your mother allowed you to come here, knowing that Mr Masters would be here?' asked Frances, speaking for the first time.

'I lied to her,' confessed Judith, blushing and hanging her head. 'I told her that I had received an invitation to travel with Briar Storringe — which I had, so that was quite true. And I told her that I might not be able to write as I did not know where I would be. Mama is very busy, as she is due to be confined quite soon, so . . . '

'And is Mrs Storringe aware of this deceit?' asked the earl.

'Oh no, no one,' said Judith earnestly.

'And when have you managed to meet? During my time, I suppose,' surmised the earl.

'No, My Lord!' exclaimed Masters indignantly. 'This was one of the few times when we have met during my working hours. Otherwise we have managed to meet at night, or sometimes when I should have been having my lunch . . . '

'So when you arranged an assignation with Miss Hartington in Bedford, you were not trespassing on my time or neglecting your duties to the estate?' remarked the earl conversationally.

Masters turned red, and Judith gasped.

'But how . . . ?' she began.

'How do I know? I suppose it was just

unlucky for you that Frankie and I were in Bedford on the same day. Well? Was there an assignation?'

'We did meet, I confess it,' admitted Masters. 'But I had business of yours to execute in the town.'

'And I had shopping to do,' put in Miss Hartington, as if her use of her time was in question as well.

'So we met and walked by the river for a short time — but only when your business was concluded.'

'Very well, Masters,' acknowledged the earl. 'I accept that you're too scrupulous to steal my time. The only other thing I'd like to know is how did Miss Hartington succeed in shaking off that bi — the redoubtable Mrs Cranborne?'

'She wanted to stay at the Swan,' said Miss Hartington. 'She hoped . . . that is . . . '

The earl grinned impishly.

'Enough. I know about her hopes. So, apart from your meeting in Bedford, were most of your trysts held in the garden?'

'Yes, My Lord, nearly always,' assured Masters.

'Then it would appear that we have discovered our prowler,' remarked Lyddington to Frances. Frances made no reply. It would have been comforting to think that all the unseen watchers had been Masters or his lady-love, but she could not believe it. The malice that she had felt on some occasions would certainly rule them both out.

'Would your scruples also account for the fact that you have been so reluctant to take up any of my invitations?' went on the earl.

Masters flushed slightly.

'I could not take the risk of meeting Judith at a social occasion,' he confessed. 'One of us would have been sure to give the game away. In any case, Mrs Storringe has seen me on Mr Ferrier's estate. If she saw me here in company with Judith, she would very likely feel it to be her duty to pass the news on to Judith's mother.'

'And then we should be parted for ever!' cried Judith, and she began to weep daintily into her handkerchief.

'Briar would never be so disloyal,' said Frances positively.

'Well, you should know,' said the earl softly. Frances coloured slightly.

Masters looking up from attending to Judith, was struck by a sudden thought. 'My Lord . . . ' he began.

His Lordship held up his hand. 'Whatever you're thinking, abandon it, and don't give voice to it if you value your skin,' he said tersely. 'As your employer, I'm entitled to enquire into how you conduct yourself, but my conduct is none of your affair, and don't forget it.'

14

That night, the earl insisted that Frances join the company for dinner. She had tried to decline, but he would brook no refusal.

'M'sister harbours suspicions about you, I think,' he said smoothly. 'It would be as well not to nourish them.'

'How would my absenting myself from your table do that?' asked Frances.

'You and I are supposed to be friends. We had one falling out — well, friends do that. But another — and so soon after we have sauntered amicably together in the grounds? It would start to look like a lovers' tiff.'

Frances coloured. 'My father . . . ' she began.

'Your uncle,' corrected the earl firmly. 'How will you maintain your deception if you keep making these kinds of slips? Your uncle is now well enough to be attended by your manservant. Soames can come over here as well while you are there, if that will ease your mind.'

Frances was forced to agree, but with many misgivings. She wore the brown suit this time and the earl made his appearance in dark green coat and breeches, with a lighter green waistcoat, embroidered with gold. He had wandered over to the gatehouse to meet her — having now moved back to his own room in the Court — and was waiting when she came downstairs.

'I like the blue better,' remarked the earl, looking her up and down as they stepped outside.

'Well thank you, My Lord,' replied Frances, shying away from his speculative gaze. 'For my part, I think you look very fetching in black and red.'

'Do you indeed,' murmured his lordship, as they made their way to the front door which was being held open for them by Jem. 'Well, if ever I want to . . . ah . . . fetch you for any reason, I shall know what to wear!'

No one regretted the loss of Mrs Cranborne. She was one of those women who never troubled to recommend herself to members of her own sex. As her knowledge of gardening was minimal, she had never contributed much to the discussions. Her sole aim had been to snare the earl; once she had been thwarted in that, she had beaten an angry retreat back to London and easier game.

They were sufficiently early for Frances to

be able to make enquiries about Miss Stevenson.

'She seems much better,' said Lady Valeria, 'but she still recalls nothing after leaving her home. At times, she wrinkles up her brow as if trying to remember, but when memories fail to come, she becomes so distressed that I cannot find it in my heart to press her.'

Frances nodded understandingly.

'There is no one more anxious than myself to see the attacker brought to justice,' she said. 'But my uncle would never want this to be done at the expense of Miss Stevenson's health'

'Thank you,' replied Lady Valeria. 'I felt sure that that would be your view, and you have put my mind at rest. Tell me, how is your uncle?'

'The fever is now gone, and we have hopes that he will soon be able to talk,' said Frances.

The earl had wandered over during this interchange and now spoke.

'I, too, have no wish to distress a sick person,' he said, 'but the sooner one of our two invalids speaks, the better it will be. I do not want to have the kind of person who committed that crime wandering freely about the neighbourhood.'

Both his listeners were in agreement with

this. The room was now filling up with Lady Valeria's guests, so further conversation on this topic became impossible, and soon afterwards, dinner was announced.

Truth to tell, Frances found herself hoping that the meal would last for ever, because then, she would not have to be alone with Lyddington. She tried to tell herself that she had been alone with him before; that it was absurd of her to dread something that had become so . . . commonplace? No, not that; to be with him could never be termed commonplace. But surely after sitting with him so many times over a glass of port, she was being very foolish to dread this occasion?

The truth was that now that the earl knew her to be a woman, the whole business had taken on a different complexion. What was once seen as a relaxed, companionable time, was now taking on some of the attributes of a clandestine meeting.

Moreover, if she was really honest she would have to confess that she had never felt entirely relaxed with him in such a setting, for at the back of her mind there had always been the fear of discovery. Now that fear had gone, but only to be replaced by the age-old wariness between man and woman.

As the meal proceeded, the forthcoming intimacy with the earl began to look like a huge black cloud on the horizon. She longed for dinner to take for ever, but to her shattered nerves, it positively seemed to fly past. Even Miss Blakemuir, always a slow eater, appeared to Frances to be shovelling down her floating island at unprecedented speed.

Shortly before the ladies were due to leave the table, a servant entered with a message for Lady Valeria. After a moment or two, her ladyship leaned towards Frances and said, 'Miss Stevenson has expressed a desire to have speech with you. Will you be so good as to go up to her room after we withdraw? One of the servants will direct you.'

'Of course,' answered Frances. Cravenly, her first thought was one of relief, that she would not have to remain at the table with the earl after the ladies had gone. Only then did she wonder whether it could be that Miss Stevenson had at last recovered her memory.

Very shortly after this, Lady Valeria stood up to go, and Frances, rising for the ladies, made as if to walk out after them.

'Where are you going . . . boy?' uttered the earl with relish.

'Miss Stevenson has asked to see me, so I promised Lady Valeria . . . ' Her voice trailed away.

'You can drink a glass with me first,' said

Lyddington firmly. He had resumed his seat, and looked every inch a nobleman, lounging at his ease at the head of the table. 'Come and sit here, my dear Frankie.' He gestured towards the chair next to him. She remained standing in her place, not moving and looking more than a little anxious.

'Don't be nervous,' he continued, smiling. 'What are you so afraid of, I wonder? Are you thinking that some of my stories might become too ribald? Or are you perhaps anxious that I might seek out a chamber-pot and make use of it in your full view, hmm?' She said nothing. 'You could always avert your gaze,' he added softly.

In her agitation, Frances did not detect the note of gentle teasing in his voice. Thinking only that he was still intent upon punishing her for her impudence, she pushed back her chair sending it crashing to the ground, and made for the door. Lyddington's languid pose was deceptive. Quickly he rose, his own chair tumbling over, and before she could reach the door, he was there before her, taking hold of her wrists with a firm but not ungentle grip.

'Please . . . let me go,' she said piteously.

'Or are you afraid,' went on the earl, as if there had been no gap in the previous conversation, 'that we might continue from where we left off earlier today?' And so saying he let go her wrists, pulled her into his arms and kissed her.

It was indeed as if the kisses that they had shared behind the ivy had been designed as a prelude to this embrace; he indulged in no preliminary caresses, but held her close and sought out her lips with his own, coaxing them to part and then plunging his tongue into her mouth.

She struggled a little, shocked by this sudden intimacy, and Lyddington, instantly responsive to her fears, slackened his grip and drew back, to whisper against her mouth, 'Don't be afraid, sweetheart. I'm sorry if I frightened you, but I just wanted to kiss you properly, that's all. I won't hurt you; I'd never hurt you; but kiss me back, won't you?'

This time, when his lips found hers again, her fears were forgotten in the joy of being so close to him and she slid her arms around his neck and returned his embrace with fervour. Pressed tightly against him, she could feel the beating of his heart, and the hardness of his male body, so different to hers despite the similarity of their clothing.

At last their lips parted and Frances realized that whilst her arms had been around his neck, she had all unconsciously managed to unfasten the ribbon confining his hair. She also discovered, with some consternation, that whilst the earl's left arm was about her waist, his right hand was resting lightly on her bottom.

'I've never embraced a woman in man's clothing before,' he remarked, noting her confusion and instantly removing his hand from its embarrassing position, 'and I have to say that it carries unforeseen advantages. But,' he went on, tugging the top of her waistcoat gently, 'I look forward to seeing the *décolletage*.' He leaned forward and kissed her again, this time briefly.

Suddenly shy, Frances stepped back, releasing herself from his now slackened embrace.

'I . . . I must go to Miss Stevenson,' she said hesitantly.

'Very well,' replied Lyddington, setting her chair to rights, and then going to the head of the table in order to pick up his own. 'I must remain here to recover my . . . ah . . . composure; but don't forget, young Frankie, we still have a good deal to discuss.'

'We . . . we do?' asked Frances, her hand on the door handle.

'Why certainly,' answered the earl, resuming his seat and pouring himself a glass of brandy. 'We need to talk about your future.'

As Frances left the room, Scrivens crossed the hall, and she was able to obtain from him directions to Miss Stevenson's room. As she mounted the stairs, she saw the butler pause and enter the dining-room. Sighing with relief that he had not done so a few minutes earlier, she climbed the staircase and made her way along the passage.

Downstairs, Scrivens entered the dining-room and bowed.

'I beg your pardon, My Lord, but there is a message for you from Mr Soames.'

'Indeed,' said his lordship. 'Out with it then, man.'

'It appears that Mr Sutcliffe is awake, and has remembered something.'

'Excellent,' said the earl with satisfaction. He drained his glass and put it down on the table. 'I'll go and — no, dammit, I'd best wait until young Frankie comes down.'

'Just so, My Lord,' replied Scrivens. Then he added diffidently, 'I should perhaps say that I came in a little earlier to inform you of this, but you were . . . engaged.'

'Ah.' Lyddington nodded, flushing a little. 'Was I so? I might perhaps remind you that everything is not always what it seems.'

'No, My Lord,' replied the butler impassively. 'But might I suggest a little caution? Had it been Jem who had come in, he might have taken the situation at its face value.'

'Damnation! You're right! Perhaps I should

take steps to regularize matters. I shall be rejoining the ladies shortly. Make sure that . . . ah . . . *Master* Sutcliffe does so as well after visiting Miss Stevenson.'

Scrivens bowed and left the room. Lyddington poured himself more brandy, and for a short time afterwards, he sat in a brown study. Then, draining his glass once more, he went to rejoin the ladies.

* * *

Upstairs, Frances, following the butler's directions, made her way to the room where Marigold Stevenson was lodged. The room was dimly lit with just one branch of candles on a cupboard near the window, and another single candle close to the bed, but well out of the way of the bed hangings, another sign of the earl's strong views about possible sources of fire. The only servant who had been dismissed from Lyddington's employ in recent years had been careless with candles.

A housemaid sat nodding near the empty fireplace, for it was a warm evening, and the fire had not been lit.

There was a slight movement from the bed. As Frances drew nearer she perceived the form and face of Marigold Stevenson, her brown hair tucked into a night-cap, but most uncharacteristically coming down from it in wisps.

'Master Sutcliffe?' she said faintly, struggling to sit up.

'Yes, I am here,' replied Frances, moving towards the bed. 'Let me help you.'

Miss Stevenson pulled herself up in the bed and Frances, leaning behind, found the pillows and made a resting place for her. Before she had even thought about it, she had tucked some of the stray wisps of hair under the edge of Miss Stevenson's night-cap.

'Thank you,' said the lady in a voice that was a little stronger. 'How kind — not like a man at all.'

Frances did not want to let this comment pass, but she was very anxious to hear what Miss Stevenson might have remembered, so, putting on one side any remarks that she might have made about the kindness of men, she said simply, 'I understand that you wished to see me.'

'Yes, that is so. Is your uncle recovering now? Such terrible blows that were rained down upon him — so much blood . . . '

Seeing that Miss Stevenson was becoming agitated, Frances interrupted hastily, 'He is getting better. He was very ill, it is true, but he is now improving daily. Miss Stevenson, do I understand you to mean that you saw the man who attacked my uncle?'

Marigold sat very still, staring straight ahead as if in some way the events of the attack were passing before her eyes once again.

'I was walking towards Marston in order to look at some wild flowers that are quite rare. I saw Mr Sutcliffe on his horse — although I did not realize at first that it was he. Then a man stepped out from the spinney and Mr Sutcliffe got down. Neither of them saw me at first. It looked like a meeting between friends. The man seemed to be taller and younger than Mr Sutcliffe.

'Then the man raised his hand and I saw that he held a knife. He brought it down with the full force of his arm, and Mr Sutcliffe fell to his knees, his hands raised to protect himself.'

Frances, her face absorbed, nodded as she recalled the wounds to her father's hands and arms.

'I cannot recall screaming, but I think I must have done so, because the man turned his head away from his horrible work and looked at me.' For a moment, Miss Stevenson paused, then looked at Frances, her distress clear to see.

'Never have I seen such a face, Master Sutcliffe. The look of it is burned into my memory, I think. His chin was unshaven and his dirty face was surrounded by his black hair. I could not tell what length it might be, because it was so tangled and matted. But it was his eyes that caught my attention: they were red-rimmed and they burned with a fierce, malevolent light.'

Frances caught her breath. All at once she was reminded of the time when Peter Rance had taken her arm and had so nearly forced her into the flames of the bonfire.

'He threw down the knife and began to run in the opposite direction. I knelt for a moment beside Mr Sutcliffe. He was still alive and I knew that he needed to have help very quickly. I ran towards the house with that only on my mind, but as I paused for breath by the lake, I thought I heard footsteps. I cannot tell now whether that was what I really heard or whether in truth it was the sound of the beating of my own heart.

'Whatever it was, I began to panic. I forgot about the need to get help, and thought only about my own urgent need to preserve my life. All I could see in my mind's eye was that dreadful livid face with the staring eyes.

'I saw the ice house and at once resolved to hide there. I ran inside and pulled the door shut with all my strength. I remember nothing more.'

She sank back exhausted. Frances leaned forward and said, 'Miss Stevenson, since you have been so frank may I ask you one question? I know you said that you found the appearance of the man distressing. Can you tell me if, to your knowledge, you have ever seen the man before?'

Miss Stevenson shook her head.

'Do you think I would ever forget it? I will dream about that face for a long time, I think.'

Seeing that she looked very tired, Frances decided to take her leave.

'One . . . one more thing,' said Miss Stevenson, as Frances made as if to rise. Frances waited patiently. 'I . . . I took the map; the garden plan. I found it in the steward's room when I brought the wine for His Lordship. I took it away and hid it behind the garden shed.'

'But . . . but why?' asked Frances.

'I didn't want it to change,' she said fretfully, plucking at the covers. 'I like patterns, straight lines and even numbers. These new ways have no order to them.'

'But they do,' said Frances softly. 'Otherwise there would not be plans.'

She got up softly, and this time Miss Stevenson made no protest. At the door, she paused, looked back and said, 'I want you to know that there are kind men in the world. Lord Lyddington carried you to this very room, and my fa — my uncle would never hurt a fly.'

Miss Stevenson's hands plucked a little at the bedcovers.

'My father treated my mother with systematic cruelty until the day she died,' she said painfully, 'and my uncle stood by and allowed it to happen. I have never seen sufficient kindness to equal the value of that.'

Frances went out, softly closing the door behind her.

* * *

In the saloon, Lyddington was eagerly awaiting news, but it was not possible to speak frankly with all the others present. The ladies crowded round Frances to discover how Miss Stevenson was, whilst the earl withdrew to the window, preferring to hear the complete version of events that would no doubt come his way.

He stood looking at the colourful group: Judith Hartington in yellow with a cream underdress; Briar Storringe in green; Miss Renshaw discreet but very well dressed in violet; Mrs Blakemuir in puce and her daughter in pink; and Lady Valeria very much the *grande dame* in dull gold and white.

Had Mrs Cranborne been present, she would no doubt have worn some loud, flamboyant colour to draw attention to herself, and the picture would have been spoiled. As it was, they made a charming representation of a gathering of the flowers that they all admired so much.

In the midst of the group, Frances, in sombre brown, made as much of a contrast as a sturdy wooden stake might provide at the centre of a bed of bright, ephemeral blooms. Lyddington smiled and, as if his mood had been transmitted across the room to her, Francis looked up and smiled back at him.

The ladies' curiosity satisfied, the little group dispersed like petals before the wind. Before Briar left Frances' side, she found a chance to say, 'I think that Lyddington suspects.'

'He more than suspects; he knows,' retorted Frances.

Briar, astonished, would have said more, but Miss Renshaw approached to ask Master Sutcliffe for some advice concerning her hot house, and so the moment was lost.

Soon afterwards, the ladies started to go up for bed, and Lyddington announced his intention of accompanying Master Sutcliffe to the gatehouse.

'Do you intend to stay the night there?' asked Lady Valeria in an undertone.

'No, I think not,' replied the earl without looking at Frances. 'But apparently, Thomas has started to regain his memory of what happened and I would like to hear what he has to say.'

'You did not tell me this,' said Frances accusingly.

'I have not really had the opportunity, since the news was brought to me whilst you were with Miss Stevenson,' said the earl mildly. 'But I can see that you are now longing to be gone, so let us be off immediately.'

'Well, come and see me before you retire,' said Lady Valeria to her brother. 'I would like to hear the latest tidings.'

Lyddington nodded his assent, and left with Frances at his side. It was a clear night, warm and still.

'Now, tell me the full story of what Marigold Stevenson said,' he urged.

Frances did as she was bid, finally concluding by saying, 'At first I thought that it must be Peter Rance; but when she said that she did not recognize him, I realized that it could not have been he, for surely she must have seen him before.'

'Did you ask her whether she destroyed the

water garden as well as taking the plans?' asked the earl.

'I could not find it in my heart to do so, for she was becoming so tired,' replied Frances, 'but I do not think that she did. This evening, she wanted to unburden herself, and if that had been a burden to her — which it must have been, had she done it — she would surely have mentioned it.'

The earl grunted. They entered the house, to be met by Edward at the door. Not trained or even encouraged to be impassive as was expected of servants in great houses, his relief was plain to see on his face.

'Mr Sutcliffe has regained consciousness,' he said happily, 'and he has been talking sensibly!'

Frances was so relieved that she had to raise a hand to dash away a tear. She had not realized how acute her fears had been until this moment, when many of them were removed.

The earl put his hand on her shoulder and gave it a comforting squeeze.

'That is indeed excellent news,' he said. 'We will go and speak with him immediately.'

'I'm afraid that will not be possible, My Lord,' said Edward apologetically. 'The doctor called in just a few minutes ago, and gave him a sleeping draught.'

'Damn and blast it,' said the earl forcefully. 'Now we'll have to wait until morning. I don't suppose he said anything about who his attacker was?'

Edward shook his head regretfully.

'All his concern was for . . . for Master Francis,' he said a little hesitantly.

'I won't come up now, then,' answered the earl. 'Has Soames returned to the Court, Edward?'

'Yes, My Lord, just after Mr Sutcliffe went to sleep.'

'Very well, then.' He turned to Frances. 'This is very good news — I really am delighted for you, although for my own part, I'm damned annoyed that I can't speak to him tonight. Oh well, I suppose it will keep until tomorrow. I'll see you first thing in the morning,' he promised, then with a nod, he walked away.

Frances stood looking after him until his figure faded into the gloom. After the passionate kiss they had shared, it was hard to watch him walk away after a perfunctory farewell, even though she knew that he could scarcely do more in Edward's presence. She had a moment's panic and a sudden impulse to run after him, but she suppressed it. If she did so, what would she say? Beg him to come back and stay? Blushing at her thought, she stepped inside and closed the door.

She went upstairs to look at her father. He was lying very still in bed but to her, his features appeared to have more colour and more promise of animation. They had been so important to each other for so long that she had not dared to imagine what she might do without him, even when the possibility of his not surviving had existed, for the thought would have been too dreadful to contemplate. Now at last, she could retire to her bed without having to worry about him. Instead, she had the question of what, if any, future there might be for her relationship with Lyddington to occupy her thoughts.

I won't think about that now, she resolved as she brushed her hair in front of the mirror. I can't make any decisions that will affect the business without consulting my father, and that cannot be until he is fully recovered.

She got into bed and pulled up the covers, convinced that she would not be able to settle, but the strain of the past days must have been greater than she knew, for within a very short time, she was fast asleep.

15

Frances was never sure what it was that awakened her that night. Once she was awake, she was simply conscious of a feeling of unease — a sensation that something was terribly wrong.

Quietly getting out of bed, she put on her dressing-gown and pulled open her bedroom door, to be engulfed immediately by smoke. Unexpected as it was, it took her completely by surprise and at once she began to choke. Darting back into the clean air of her bedroom, she pulled open the communicating door and shook Ruby awake.

'There's a fire!' she cried urgently. 'Hurry over to the Court and raise the alarm. I'll go and help Edward with father.'

Having seen that Ruby was properly awake, she went back to her bedroom, pulled a handkerchief from her drawer, damped it in the water jug, and used it to cover her mouth and nose.

Prepared now, she crouched down where the smoke was the thinnest. The fire seemed to originate from the same floor and as she moved out into the passage, she realized to her horror that it was coming from her father's room. Forgetting to be cautious, she hurried towards the blaze, wondering as she did so why Edward had not given the alarm. The next moment, the reason for his silence became all too plain, as she nearly fell over the body of the servant, huddled up on the floor almost in the doorway to her father's room.

Thinking him to be overcome by smoke, she attempted to rouse him.

'Edward, Edward, can you hear me?' she said urgently, her voice punctuated by coughs. 'Get up! We must get out and get help for my father!'

As she took him by the shoulders to shake him, she became aware of an ominous stain on the front of his clothing, and touching it with her hand, she felt that it was sticky. It became horribly clear to her that she would never be able to rouse Edward. At once, some sixth sense prompted her to look up, and through the smoke she saw the figure of Peter Rance towering over her, his eyes blazing, looking, as he stood with his back to the flames, like a figure from Hell. In his hand was a wicked-looking knife, already stained with blood.

Rance raised the knife high above his head and Frances lifted her arms automatically to shield herself. This was how her father's arms and hands were injured, she thought helplessly, and longed for Lyddington to come and rescue her. As if in response to her unspoken cry, a shout rang out along the corridor.

'That will do now, Rance,' called the earl, deliberately making his voice sound firm and reassuring, although the sight that met his eyes filled him with fear and dread. 'Get back to your duties.'

Something about the earl's authoritative tones penetrated the blackness of Rance's mind, and for a brief instant, years of habit prevailed. Rance straightened, turning towards the earl.

'M'Lord,' he muttered and went to raise his hand to his fore-lock. As he did so, he realized that he still held the knife. At that moment Lyddington knew that he had lost any control over him — but that brief interlude had been enough for Frances to escape Rance's notice and slip into her father's bedroom.

With a cry that was more animal than human, Rance launched himself at the earl and for a short time, the two were locked in combat at the top of the stairs, the knife glinting balefully as they struggled for possession of it. The earl was a tall, powerful man, but Rance's madness lent him such strength that at times it seemed as if he must surely prevail.

Suddenly there was an exclamation from downstairs, as the earl's figure was spotted by one of the servants who had come from the Court to help. It was hastily suppressed, but it was enough to take Lyddington's attention momentarily from what was happening. At once, Rance pressed home his attack, but with too much ferocity, for the earl, driven back against the newel post, only just managed to save himself from falling, whereas Rance tumbled headlong to the foot of the stairs and lay still. Ruddles crouched over him whilst the two menservants looked on. Moments later, and with a vigour that astonished them, he sprang to his feet with a shout and made for the door, taking them all so much by surprise that no one was able to seize hold of him.

'Don't let him escape!' called the earl. 'I'm going for the Sutcliffes!'

Once in her father's room, Frances took hold of the ewer and threw the water in it over the flames which were by now consuming the curtains at the window and the bed-hangings, but there was simply not enough there to have any effect. Hurrying to her father's bedside, she found him sleeping just as peacefully as if nothing had occurred. With a shudder, she realized that without someone to aid him, he would certainly have perished, all unconscious in the blaze, which by now had really got a hold on the room. It was by no means easy to rouse him because of the sleeping draught, and when Lyddington arrived, she was only just managing to pull him from his bed.

The earl hurried to her side and between them, they managed to support him to the door. There was a sound of heavy footsteps on the wooden stairs and some men appeared with buckets of water.

'About bloody time too,' growled the earl, as the men went past them.

Suddenly as they reached the head of the stairs, Sutcliffe straightened.

'Now I recall!' he said in a voice much like his old tones. 'The man who attacked me was Peter Rance.'

* * *

In the darkness, Ruddles and the two footmen hurried after Peter Rance. It was hard to believe that someone who had just fallen down a flight of stairs could spring up so nimbly and evade them, but so it was. They were not far behind him, but it was difficult to keep up, for he ran with a reckless disregard for his safety or for the well-being of anything in his path. There was no moon; and had it not been for the fact that he was running without any attempt at concealment, they would have found it difficult to pursue him.

It went through Ruddles' mind that even when they did catch him, he might prove to be impossible to restrain in his madness. They had had to come in such haste that they had no rope or cord with them.

So intent were they upon keeping their eyes on him that they did not realize where he was leading them until they were almost at the lakeside. Rance turned and looked round and Ruddles could almost feel his panic, although he could not see his face. Then with a cry, Rance turned and plunged into the lake, running whilst he could, then wading forward with all his strength until at last the water closed over his head.

Others had now reached the lakeside and two of them ran to get a boat, but in his heart Ruddles knew that it was too late: Peter Rance must already be dead.

* * *

Early the following morning, Frances sat in the room that had been allocated to her in Lyddington Court. After bringing them both out of the fire, the earl had insisted that they spend the remainder of the night in his house. Indeed, there really was no alternative. Thomas's room was unusable and most of the rest of the house was tainted by smoke. Morning would bring the opportunity to discover whether there was any structural damage.

Aside from any practical consideration, there was also the fact that Frances now felt that she would always see the body of Edward, lying symbolically next to the doorway of her father's room. The old servant, whose loyalty had never been in doubt, had proved that loyalty by guarding his master with his life, and Frances could not help shedding tears for the man who had also guarded her own secret so faithfully.

There was also a further reason for her to wonder about her own future. When she and Lyddington had helped her father out of the burning house, she had had no thoughts other than for his safety. Now in her mind's eye she could see herself clearly as she had appeared last night, in her dressing-gown with her blonde hair about her shoulders. No one who had seen her — and plenty had done so — could have doubted her sex.

Lady Valeria herself had appeared in her night attire to investigate, for it had been from her room that Lyddington had seen a flicker of light in the gatehouse that had seemed to him to be more than a candle's glow. She had been very kind, ensuring that rooms were prepared for both the Sutcliffes and for Ruby, and at the time, Frances had been far too concerned about her father to think about her ladyship's manner. Now, she recalled the constraint with which her ladyship had spoken to her, and she knew beyond any doubt that her masquerade was at an end.

Ruby had insisted on putting her to bed for the second time that night. They had cried together about Edward, and Ruby had offered to sleep in a chair in Frances' bedroom, but Frances had insisted that she would be perfectly all right, and had sent her off to sleep in a proper bed in the room that had been prepared for her.

She had been sure that she would not be able to sleep, and so it had proved. All the events of the night had gone round and round in her head making anything other than fitful sleep quite impossible. She had tried to read in order to make herself drowsy, but she found herself reading the same words over and over again, and the wise advice concerning the treatment of gardenias, comparatively new arrivals to English climes, made no impression upon her at all. Then, when it had almost seemed that she might drop off, there had been the visit from Lyddington.

In the early hours of the morning, there had been a tap on the door and Lyddington had entered, now fully dressed in his daytime wear. Frances pulled on a dressing-gown over the night-gown she was wearing — both kindly lent by Briar Storringe, who had also been woken by the night's events — and got out of bed.

'I have been down to the lake,' he said as he closed the door. 'It appears that Rance waded in and, whether intentionally or not, drowned himself. The men tried to rescue him, but it was too late. Had it been daylight, perhaps they might have succeeded, although whether that would ultimately have been for the best I very much doubt. The man would certainly never have been allowed his freedom again.'

'He killed Edward,' said Frances and immediately felt her eyes filling once more.

'I know,' replied Lyddington, closing the distance between them and pulling her into his arms. 'He was a brave man and I am sure that he saved your father's life by his actions. I suspect that Rance came to attack your father and that Edward, about his normal duties, barred his way, and because of that Rance struck him down.' He paused for a moment, then added, 'I have had his body removed, to be laid out in a more seemly manner.'

'Thank you,' murmured Frances. 'Poor Edward.' It was so comforting to be held close against Lyddington like this, leaning against his chest, that she felt that she could stay here for ever. It was the earl who stepped back, kissing her gently on the brow and then holding her by her shoulders at arm's length.

'It's time you settled,' he said. 'You're obviously worn out.'

'Do I look very bad?' she asked anxiously.

'Devilish,' he said frankly. 'Now, to bed with you. I know you don't think you'll sleep but you must try.'

'I have tried,' she answered plaintively.

'Well try again,' he said firmly. 'Come on, young Frankie. Obey orders for once. After all, I am the master here, you know.'

He spoke with such confidence as he guided her towards the bed. 'I am the master,' he said, and he knew it. But as for her, she felt as if her identity had vanished away, and she no longer had a role to play

— certainly not in this place. Feeling a sudden sensation of panic, she clutched hold of his sleeve, and said, 'Yes, I do know you are the master here. But tell me please, what am I? What is to become of me?'

Gently he removed her hand from his sleeve and walked to the door, then stood with his hand on the handle. There was a wry smile on his face.

'Well — you'll be the mistress, I hope,' he answered, then quickly went out before she could say anything.

Once it was light, she got dressed in her usual boy's attire. Her customary day clothes had been brought over from the gatehouse. As she always put her things away at night, they had escaped the taint of smoke. Her wig had failed to appear, so she tied her own blonde hair back in a simple queue.

As she studied her own reflection, she thought about how her days as a gardener working for her father were almost certainly over. She was surprised at how little she regretted it. Perhaps the burden of disguise had been greater than she had realized. Certainly, she had begun to feel a longing in herself for feminine things that she had not experienced before. No, the abandonment of the disguise in itself would not cause her any heartaches.

What of the future, though? It was not something to which she had given much thought before. Had anyone asked her about her future only a few weeks ago, she would probably have replied that she intended to go on working for her 'uncle'. Now, however . . .

Last night — or was it this morning — Lyddington had made matters quite clear: he intended to make her his mistress. She was in no doubt about her feelings for him. She was in love with him as she had never expected to be in love with any man. That was why she had never been able to see any future other than her work, of course. Now Lyddington had offered her a future — but it was not enough.

Their conversation had effectively ruined her chances of getting any sleep, so in what had remained of the night, she had turned the matter over and over in her mind. Nothing less than knowing that they would be together for always would be enough for her. Perhaps it was something to do with the gardener in her — the kind of mind that did not look for instant gratification, but for the long-term growth, each year building on what had gone before. Lyddington might be satisfied with a temporary liaison; for her, only marriage would do, and that plainly was not on offer.

She could not blame him. After all she had

spent six years dressed as a man, working with her hands, unchaperoned, unprotected. The wonder of it was that he was prepared to accept her at all. The fault, if there was one, lay in the fact that her desires refused to be limited by the constraints of logic.

She was just trying to decide how best to break the news to her father that she must end her employment with him and leave — she had not yet allowed herself to think about how she might part with Lyddington — when there was a soft tap on the door.

Glancing quickly at the mirror, Frances realized that her cheeks were wet with tears, without her even knowing that she had been crying. Wiping them away hastily, she called out, 'Come in.'

It was Lady Valeria, dressed immaculately in a blue morning gown. Frances looked at the small clock on the mantelpiece and was amazed to see that it was nine o'clock. She had not realized that she had spent so long in thought. Automatically, she stood as her ladyship entered and made a small bow.

'Excellent,' said the lady in icy tones, as she looked her up and down. 'And how long did it take you to perfect that little manoeuvre, miss?' Frances whitened. 'Do you mind if I sit down?' went on her ladyship, suiting her actions to her words. 'Though why I should even ask is beyond me really. I have always been brought up to observe all the courtesies, but when someone behaves towards me with such a lack of consideration, I find myself at something of a loss.'

'My Lady,' began Frances earnestly, 'if there has ever been aught in my manner towards you that has not been courteous, then I ask your pardon.'

Lady Valeria, having taken her seat, now rose again majestically.

'Not courteous?' she exclaimed in tones of outrage. 'When your whole person is an affront to decency? It is utterly beyond me how any young woman of decent family could stoop so low — or it would be beyond me, if I was not well aware that women of a certain stamp will go to any lengths to snare the man that they want.'

'My lady, that is not true! I — '

'Do you deny it, then? Can you deny that you want my brother?'

Frances could not find the words to reply, but she could feel her face flushing.

'Your face tells its own story,' said Lady Valeria triumphantly. 'Indeed, I am surprised that immodest as you are, you are still able to blush at all. But perhaps it is one of the tricks of your trade.'

'Trade? What do you mean trade?' asked

Frances, passing now from distress to anger. 'I have no *trade* as you put it, Lady Valeria, unless it be gardening. That was all that brought me to this place — not a desire to entrap your brother.'

Her ladyship smiled disbelievingly.

'You will forgive me if I keep my own counsel in this matter,' she said. 'After all, you have told so many lies.'

'Lies! I have not lied to you!' exclaimed Frances.

'And how can you say that,' said Lady Valeria in the nearest thing to a Lyddington roar that she was prepared to muster, 'When your whole life is a lie?'

Frances sighed and looked down. There was a short silence, then she said, 'Lady Valeria, I did practise a deceit upon you . . . and Lord Lyddington, but it was in order to carry on my profession and that was all. I had not even met Lord Lyddington before we came here.'

'Perhaps, perhaps not,' conceded her ladyship grudgingly. 'But whichever way it was, you soon got him into your toils once you were here, didn't you?'

Frances did not know what to say. How could she explain how it had been for her, having few friends, to meet someone who wanted to be a friend, and in whose companionship she felt such happiness, that she could not resist it, even though she knew that she should? At length she managed to say, 'Please, it was not like that . . . '

'O come, do not take me for a fool,' said her ladyship scornfully. 'The only thing that does surprise me is that my brother has been a party to this shabby liaison almost in the very presence of his sister and his guests. No doubt you expect me to ask you for how long this has been going on, but I really feel far too much distaste for the whole matter to make further enquiries. You will, of course, leave immediately.'

Frances drew herself up with all the dignity that she could muster.

'I have every intention of leaving, My Lady,' she said. 'There has been no liaison between myself and your brother, and neither will there be one, but I can quite see that it will be impossible for me to stay. My one concern is for my father.'

'Your father?' Her ladyship looked puzzled for a moment, then her brow cleared and she said, 'Oh, I see. Yet more proof of your deceit. Your father may remain here until he is better. Then I will suggest that he should return home for a little convalescence. No one will blame me if in the meantime I take on another firm of gardeners because I do not want to wait.'

Horrified, Frances took a step closer to the outraged lady.

'Lady Valeria, I know that you believe me to be everything that is false, but please, do not judge my father by my actions.'

'Then he was not party to your deceit?' said her ladyship ironically, raising her brows.

Frances stepped back defeated.

'You are determined to think the worst of me, I can see. Very well then, you must do as you please. But what of Sa — of My Lord?'

'You have had quite enough dealings with *My Lord* — you may leave him to me, now. Fortunately he is out for the day, breaking the news of events to Rance's relatives, so I can be sure that you will be gone without entrapping him any further. I am so anxious for your absence, Miss Sutcliffe, that I have even arranged transport to London for you. No doubt if he wishes to seek you out again, he may find you there in some bawdy house.'

'How dare you!' exclaimed Frances then, losing what little colour she still had.

'Oh, I dare, Miss Sutcliffe,' replied Lady Valeria, stepping closer to her, her voice low and savage. 'I would dare much and a great deal more to rescue my only brother from the most conniving jade it has ever been my misfortune to meet! A pity. As a young man, I rather liked you.'

She turned to go, but as she reached the door, she turned round.

'I am sorry about your servant,' she said.

'Thank you,' replied Frances. 'We shall miss him a great deal.'

Lady Valeria inclined her head, then left the room.

Once she had gone, Frances stood completely at a loss. Much of what Lady Valeria had said had been true on one level, and there was so much that still needed to be said to put things right. How could she explain the real situation to someone who would not listen?

There was an inkstand and paper in her room and, sitting at the table in the window, Frances set down a brief account of her reasons for acting as she had done. She hesitated over writing about her feelings for Sarrell, but quickly added them too, for how else could she explain her willingness to leave the Court, even though she knew herself to be guiltless of trying to entrap the earl?

Having written it all down, she sealed it, wrote Lady Valeria's name carefully on the front, and went downstairs to have a last look at the gardens, where it seemed like a thousand years ago she had once worked so happily. She meant just to have a general look around, but she found herself, like some pilgrim, visiting all the places that had come to mean something to her, because of their association with the earl.

Here was the bench upon which he had been sitting when they had first met. Further on was the wilderness, and there were the bushes into which Lyddington had plunged in order to escape the attentions of Mrs Cranborne and the others. There was the orangery where they had disovered the truth about Masters and Judith Hartington. Last of all, she visited the little temple where she and Lyddington had kissed for the first time. Gently she touched the ivy, and the statue, where his hand might have rested. Then, determinedly, she turned her back and made her way to the house.

Soon afterwards, she and Ruby were climbing into her ladyship's carriage, which was to take them to London on the first part of their journey back to Plymouth. She did not mistake the loan of this splendid piece of transport as being anything other than a means of getting rid of her as quickly as possible. She had been to see her father, but he was still fast asleep, and cravenly, she had decided not to wake him. In another note, briefer than the one she had written to Lady

Valeria, she explained something of her reasons for leaving. She could only trust that her ladyship, having vented her first anger on her primary victim, would allow her, Frances, to give him the full story when he arrived at Plymouth for his convalescence. Her sincere hope was that he would forgive her for losing him this valuable bit of business.

She had expected to leave without any send-off at all. In fact, Briar was there to say goodbye. All the other ladies were well out of sight.

'How did you know I was leaving?' asked Frances.

'I was passing your door and I heard the argument between you and Lady Valeria. No one who disagrees with her hostess to that extent is ever allowed to stay anywhere.'

Frances managed to summon up a little laugh.

'Does everyone know about my disgrace?' she asked.

'Not as yet,' replied Briar. 'I'll do my best to scotch any rumours.'

'Thank you; you're very good,' said Frances hugging her impulsively.

'You always were my best friend,' answered Briar, bringing tears to Frances' eyes at the kindly words. 'Does Lyddington know you are going?'

Frances shook her head.

'Lyddington wants to make me his mistress, but I . . .' She could not go on.

'Are you sure of this?' asked Briar.

'Oh yes,' said Frances drearily. 'He made it perfectly plain. I cannot possibly stay on that basis.'

Briar gripped her hand sympathetically.

'I'll write to you, I promise,' she said, as the coach pulled away. 'If you ask me, when he finds out there'll be hell to pay.'

She waved until the coach turned the corner after the gatehouse and then went inside. Lady Valeria was waiting indoors. The two ladies looked at one another measuringly.

'She has gone,' said Briar, 'and I hope you are satisfied!' Then with something very like a sniff, she marched up to her room.

16

Lyddington had had a very wearing day. He had decided that it should be his responsibility to inform Peter Rance's next of kin of his death. The head gardener was able to tell him that Rance had a sister, one Nellie Baynes, who was married to a farmer who worked land near Dunstable. The farm, he thought, was called Nethercote, or some such name. Armed with this information, Lyddington set off with Ruddles a little before Frances' unpleasant interview with Lady Valeria took place.

He had hoped that his visit to Dunstable would prove to be a brief one, but this turned out not to be the case. The ride there was accomplished quite quickly, but unfortunately the earl was misdirected twice by well-meaning but misinformed persons, and consequently, the day was already well advanced before he reached the Baynes's farm. Naturally that good lady — who had worked in the kitchens at Lyddington Court in her youth — was quite insistent that his lordship accept her hospitality, and Lyddington did not have the heart to refuse her.

She accepted the news of Peter's death calmly, and even with a certain amount of relief.

'I was always afraid of Peter,' she said. 'He could look at you in such a way as to make you feel that there was nothing that he wouldn't do.'

She went on to explain that when Joe Baynes had asked her to marry him, she had been very afraid that any children might be tainted by Peter's madness. Her mother had reassured her: she and Peter were not really brother and sister. Nellie's aunt had been raped by a stranger, and when she had died in childbirth, Nellie's mother had taken the baby — Peter — in as her own.

The earl sketched over the circumstances of Peter's death, and did not mention to Nellie that he had killed Edward. He judged that that was a burden that Mrs Baynes did not have to carry.

By the time they arrived back at Lyddington Court it was very late in the afternoon. They brought with them copious good wishes, and only the fact that they were on horseback saved them from also having to bring several jars of pickled preserves, which deed would have incurred Mrs Bartlett's strong disapproval at their scandalous lack of respect for her catering arrangements.

More than anything else, Lyddington wanted to seek out Frances and discover what she might have to say to his proposition, but as he arrived he was waylaid in the hall by Masters and a very white-looking Judith Hartington.

'Can't it wait?' asked the earl impatiently, dragging his gloves through his hands. 'Devil take me, but I've been out all day.'

'Please, My Lord,' ventured Masters, his eyes anxious. The earl noticed that his agent was holding Miss Hartington's hand. Only the direst of emergencies could have caused them to publicize their attachment in such a way. Lyddington sighed.

'Very well. Let's go to the book-room.'

Once there, they all sat down, Miss Hartington and her swain in upright chairs. They both looked like pupils about to have a severe dressing down from a strict schoolmaster. Lyddington, now resigned to this unwanted delay, sat at the other end of the table in a chair with arms, lounging very much at his ease.

'Now, what is it?' he said.

Masters took a long look at Judith, then a deep breath and said, 'My Lord, we have decided to make our attachment public.'

The earl waited for a moment, then said, 'Yes? And?'

'And . . . we hope that . . . that you will . . .'

'Wish you happy. Hell's teeth, is that why you've dragged me in here? Of course I wish you happy. You don't expect me to forbid the banns, do you? It's none of my business, after all.'

'You will not . . . dismiss me, My Lord?' ventured Masters.

'Why the devil should I? As long as marriage don't interfere with your work. As far as I can see it would probably interfere with it less than sneaking about and meeting at all hours of the day and night.' The young couple were silent. They did not look noticeably more cheerful. Suddenly the earl understood. 'Ah!' he said. 'You haven't spoken to her mother yet, have you?'

'That is what I intend to do, My Lord,' said Masters, pale but resolute. 'With your permission, I will go as soon as possible. But may I have your support?'

'Devil take me, what do you want me to do? Go with you and hold your hand? I've told you I'll not dismiss you, and that holds good, whatever Mrs Whatever-her-name-is may say.'

'Ferrier, My Lord,' interposed Masters helpfully.

'What?'

'I said, her name is Ferrier.'

The earl grunted.

'I'll go further,' he went on, ignoring Masters' intervention. 'I'll support you in any reasonable venture you may have in mind — obtaining your own property, for example. But facing up to your future mother-in-law is one battle you must fight alone.'

Miss Hartington had thus far said nothing. Her only contribution had been to change colour, sway artistically and look adoringly up at Masters. The earl found himself wondering exasperatedly how any man could put up with such a wet goose. Now, she spoke.

'I cannot be silent any longer,' she said in a trembling voice. 'I must . . . confess.'

'Confess?' queried Lyddington wickedly, hoping that there might spill from Miss Hartington's lips a scandalous tale of a secret marriage and a husband already in existence.

'Judith, my dear,' whispered Masters urgently. But his words were not heeded. Resolutely, Miss Hartington stood up and threw back her head.

'My Lord, I . . . I was the one who hit you over the head.'

'Good God!' said the earl. He had been gently rocking back on his chair. Now, he allowed the front two legs to come to the ground with a thump. He could not have been more astonished if she had said that she was running a bordello. He stared at her in fascination. 'What the devil did you use?' he asked her. 'It was deuced hard, whatever it was.'

This was not the question that Judith had expected. Thrown off balance, she glanced at Masters, but getting no help from that direction, she looked back at the earl and said faintly. 'A . . . a brick, My Lord.'

'A brick! So that was what it was! Take good care you don't annoy her once you're married, Masters,' he went on wryly, turning to his astonished agent. 'She strikes a damned hard blow.'

'But . . . but do you not want to know why I struck you, My Lord?' asked Judith, mystified.

'I presume that I was about to intrude upon one of your moonlight trysts,' remarked the earl casually. 'But why the deuce didn't you just step out and tell me?'

Masters tried to interrupt, but now that Judith had found her courage, there was no stopping her.

'I would not let him do so,' she said. 'I was afraid of the consequences.'

'And you weren't afraid of the consequences of killing me with a brick? Now there's a novelty.'

After giving Masters and his future bride further assurances of his forgiveness and support, Lyddington was at last able to make his escape. He went straight up to the room that Frances had occupied the previous night, but found it empty, devoid of any trace of her.

Deciding that she must be with her father, he set off down the passage to Thomas's room, only to be met by his sister coming the other way.

'Valeria, I have had a devilish day, so for the Lord's sake, do or say nothing to delay me, but tell me where young Frankie is.'

Valeria told him.

17

'Damnation, woman, how dare you interfere in my concerns!' bellowed his lordship. 'I spend the best part of the day on a wild goose chase all over Dunstable Downs; I come back only to find myself obliged to sort out Masters' love-life; and then when my business is finally finished, I discover that you have been poking your nose in what don't concern you! In God's name, I insist that you tell me by what right you interfered!'

'By the right of being your closest relation!' responded her ladyship, not quite so loudly but just as angrily. 'I did not want to see you make a fool of yourself.'

'Oh, fool is it? And what sort of a figure do I cut now?' His lordship paced furiously about the small saloon, the skirts of his coat swirling about him. 'By heaven, madam, you treat me like a child who'll forget about things that you don't want him to have if only you can remove them from him while he isn't looking! If I look a fool, it's because you've made me look like one!'

'Don't be absurd.' Her ladyship stood up

and barred his way. 'I swear, Spencer, I don't know why I am even prepared to speak to you at all on this matter, when I think about what an insult you have offered me!'

'Insult? What insult, pray?'

'The parading of your paramour in men's clothing in the presence of your sister and guests. Indeed, Spencer, I should go overseas again if I were you, for the scandal, if it gets out, will follow you wherever you go.'

For a few moments, the earl and his sister stood glaring at each other.

'Paramour? Who told you this?' he asked sharply.

'Well, is it not plain to see? What woman who dresses like that . . . '

'Oh cut line, Valeria,' snapped the earl. 'Anyone would think 'twas I who employed her.'

'How dare you blame me?' said Lady Valeria defensively. 'I employed, as I thought, a respectable man and his company, which included his nephew. I never saw the girl before she came to this place.'

'And neither did I,' retorted Lyddington. 'So as for your assertion that I brought my paramour here . . . '

'Well, if she wasn't then, she was soon after!' interrupted her ladyship savagely.

There was a long silence. The earl took a

deep breath, and looked his sister straight in the eyes.

'Let us get one thing perfectly clear,' he said in a quiet voice that was all the more impressive after all the shouting that had taken place, 'Frankie is not, and never has been, my mistress.'

His sister stared at him. He was undoubtedly completely sincere.

'Then what . . . ' she began.

'Why can't you look beneath the surface?' he went on, his voice rising a little again. 'You accuse me of parading my paramour around, and talk about your guests as if they were so innocent — such ladies! God in Heaven, the antics of such as Felicia Cranborne would — and did — make Frankie blush! But I suppose the fact that your guest smuggled herself into my bed and hoped to entrap me thereby is considered perfectly acceptable to you, dear Sister, because of course she looks the part, doesn't she?'

'Spencer, no!' exclaimed Lady Valeria shocked, her hand going to her cheek.

'Oh yes,' answered the earl savagely, mimicking her gesture. 'Hasn't your experience of gardening taught you that it is what's beneath the surface that's the most important? Felicia Cranborne looks like a lady so she must be one; Frankie dresses in men's clothes — and looks superb in them, you must admit — so she must have loose morals.'

'Spencer, I . . . '

'One thing I would like to know: how did you compel Frankie to go? Threat of exposure of her masquerade to the world? Or perhaps to ruin her father's business by writing a poor account of them to everyone you know? Tell me, Valeria, how low did you sink?'

'I didn't threaten to do any of those things,' said her ladyship, rallying at the injustice of the accusation. 'She agreed to go of her own volition.'

The earl stared at her for a moment, then some of the fight seemed to go out of him.

'I see,' he said, walking to the window. There was a long pause, then Lady Valeria said in quite a different tone, 'Spencer, what were your intentions towards this girl?'

Before he could answer, there was a tap on the door and Briar Storringe entered with a letter in her hand. She had been on her way downstairs, and had found a rather scared-looking housemaid hovering near the door.

'Have you some business with Lady Valeria?' Briar had asked her gently.

'Yes, ma'am,' the housemaid had replied nervously. 'I had to clean the room upstairs after Master Sutcliffe had gone' (here Briar breathed a sigh of relief at hearing Frances being described in such a way) 'and I found this note addressed to Her Ladyship. Then Mrs Robinson, the housekeeper told me to hurry because there was a lot to do, and I put the letter in the pocket of my apron, and . . . and I forgot it, ma'am, and what Her Ladyship will say . . . ' Her voice had faded away anxiously.

'Don't worry about Her Ladyship,' Briar had said reassuringly, as she whisked the letter out of the maid's hands. 'I will give it to her and say that it has just been found.'

'Oh thank you, ma'am,' the housemaid had replied, scuttling away thankfully before Briar could change her mind. Briar smiled to herself. She had been longing for an excuse to get in on this argument — which truth to tell had been a little too loud to ignore — and now she had got one. Once inside, she handed the letter to Lady Valeria.

'This was found addressed to you, ma'am,' she said. 'It had been left in Frances' room.'

The effect was all that she could have wished. The earl swung round, took a step forward, then recalling that the letter was not addressed to him, halted in his tracks, colouring a little. Lady Valeria took the letter and looked at her name written in Frances' neat hand.

'Well, open it for the Lord's sake,' exclaimed Lyddington at last. 'Perhaps we'll find out what other damage you've done.'

Valeria read the first page in silence, then exclaimed as if she could not help herself, 'Six years a boy!'

'Now do you begin to understand?' said Briar beseechingly.

'I suppose I was rather hard on her myself,' remarked Lyddington to Mrs Storringe, his sister by now being engrossed in the rest of the letter. 'My reaction, when I first discovered her sex, was very much the same. But at least I didn't drive her away!' he added, looking aggressively at Lady Valeria, who took no notice, being absorbed in the last page.

'Oh, but I think you did,' contradicted Briar in accusing tones.

'And what the deuce do you mean by that?' demanded the earl, his brows drawing together.

'When you told her that you wanted her to be your mistress, you made it impossible for her to stay.'

'My mistress?' exclaimed Lyddington, amazed. 'God in Heaven, where did you get such a preposterous idea?'

'From Frances herself. She told me that you had asked her to be your mistress.'

'I swear I never did so!' he declared; then coloured as he remembered their last conversation. Could she have misinterpreted what he had said? Was that why she had gone?

'She tells me so here, as well,' said Lady Valeria, speaking for the first time.

'The deuce . . . give me that,' snapped the earl, striding over and snatching the letter from his sister's hands before she could make any protest. He scanned the page, before finding the relevant passage, and he blenched a little.

'Damnation! You're right, she really did think . . . ' He paused for a moment, regained some of his colour, and looked up. 'She loves me.' He grinned bashfully. 'Valeria, she loves me.'

'Which proves she must be deranged,' remarked Lady Valeria to Mrs Storringe. The earl smiled more broadly, but then his face took on an arrested look.

'Where did she go, and when did she set out?'

'For London, this morning at about eleven,' said Briar. 'She is to catch the coach for Plymouth tomorrow morning.'

'Then I must lose no time. What hour is it now?' He glanced at the clock. 'About five o'clock. It should be light until ten, and by then, with any luck, I should be in London.' He rang the bell.

'But Spencer . . . ' began his sister.

'Well, Valeria?' The butler entered, and the earl told him, 'Have Ruddles saddle two horses — we ride for London almost immediately.' When the butler had gone, he went on, 'Surely you accept now that you have been wrong about Frankie in almost every respect?'

'I agree that I have been mistaken in her, but . . . '

'Then do what you can to scotch any scandal. I must be off.' He made for the door.

'But what will you do when you find her?' asked Lady Valeria, urgently.

'Do? I'm blasted well going to marry the wench,' said his lordship forcefully as he left the room.

After Lyddington had gone, Lady Valeria sighed and sat down heavily on one of the sofas as if she had aged a great deal. Briar sat next to her and patted her hand comfortingly. At last Lady Valeria said, 'I shall find all this very difficult to accept, but I know Spencer; if his heart is set on this girl, then he will have her, and I could not bear to be estranged from him.' She took out a handkerchief and dabbed her eyes. 'No doubt you think that because we argue a good deal, there is bad feeling between us, but we have no family but each other, and I am very fond of him.'

'It will be strange for you at first, of course,' replied Briar soothingly. 'But I have known Frances for ten years, and once you know her properly, you will not find her at all difficult to accept, I promise you. And surely, you would not want to accept someone like Felicia Cranborne?'

'Certainly not,' said her ladyship emphatically, thinking of what the earl had told her. 'But Spencer would never be entrapped by her now.'

'Perhaps not — but there are others like her, and even the most quick-witted of men can be caught unawares.' Briar paused, allowing this to sink in. Then she went on, 'In Fran, you have someone who will care for this place and love it as you do. Surely you can see that in her?'

'Yes . . . yes, I can,' admitted her ladyship. 'But how to scotch the scandal, that is the problem. Everyone must know the truth by now.'

'It may not be so,' replied Briar, thinking of the housemaid. 'People are very unobservant you know, even in the most favourable of circumstances. I think you will find that in the confusion of last night, very few people noted exactly who was where, and doing what. If anyone mentions seeing another female figure, you could always say that it was me — ready to help in an emergency, as in campaign days.'

'Or Ruby, the maid from the gatehouse,' suggested her ladyship. 'And Francis Sutcliffe? Where was he last night?'

'In pursuit of Peter Rance, or helping to put the fire out — it doesn't really matter. No one will know for sure.'

'And now — presumably young Sutcliffe has left in order to make things ready for his *uncle's* convalescence,' said her ladyship thoughtfully.

'And Lyddington will go, very courteously, to see how Mr Thomas Sutcliffe is doing, and will meet Miss Sutcliffe there, fall in love, and conduct his courtship in due form.'

There was a short silence.

'That sounds very unlike him,' said Lady Valeria matter-of-factly. They looked at each other and both giggled. Then her ladyship resumed, 'But what of Master Sutcliffe?'

'I think that the poor young man will just . . . fade out of the picture,' said Briar in tones of regret.

'Dead of a fever?'

' . . . or drowned in a river?'

' . . . or trampled by a stampeding bull?'

' . . . or eloped with an heiress?'

The two ladies burst out laughing.

'What splendid conspirators we make, my dear,' said Lady Valeria. 'Shall we plot further over a glass of wine?'

18

It was in fact rather closer to midnight when Lyddington and Ruddles arrived in London. As soon as the earl's first eagerness had run its course, he realized the futility of galloping hell-for-leather after someone who would certainly be unable to travel from London until the following day. He moderated his pace accordingly — to Ruddles' great relief — and they made a stop at Watford in order to have something to eat and change horses.

The earl was well known at the inn where they stopped. Furthermore, it was one which was used by the post, so the horses that they were able to hire were very satisfactory.

On arrival in London, Lyddington made enquiries as to where he might catch the stage for Plymouth and on disovering the name of the inn, he made his way there. The landlord was regretful, but there was no one staying there by the name of Sutcliffe.

'Your young relative might be staying elsewhere and coming on in the morning,' suggested the landlord. 'I can provide Your Lordship with a room if you should want one,' he added hopefully, seeing Lyddington's quality at a glance.

'We'll stay,' said the earl after a moment's thought. 'I'll need a room for myself, and lodging for my groom. He can rouse me in the morning.'

'Very good, M'Lord.'

Once this was settled, Lyddington was left with nothing to do until the morning, a situation that made him feel somewhat frustrated. Forgetting that he was relying on Ruddles to wake him, he packed the groom off to visit some of his relations and resolved, for his own part, to use his time by visiting some of his clubs and looking up old acquaintances.

He therefore repaired to White's and having been absent for several years, found himself being greeted with all the enthusiasm that might have been showered upon a long-lost relation. He was persuaded to recount his adventures, which he did, although it must be said that he kept some of them — particularly some of the most recent ones — to himself. All in all, he had such a convivial evening playing piquet (from which he rose slightly a winner) and drinking deeply, that he did not return to the inn until four in the morning. Strolling happily up to bed, he undressed and in no time at all, he was deeply asleep.

He awoke the following morning and knew immediately that something was wrong. He got out of bed, strode to the window, and pulled back the curtains. The sun was well up. Going back to the bed, he picked up his watch from the bedside table. It was nearly nine o'clock.

'Hell and devil confound it!' he roared. 'Why the deuce was I not wakened?' He opened his bedroom door and put his head out. 'House!' he called at the top of his lungs. 'House, I say!'

A gentleman in the room opposite put a night-cap-clad head out in order to complain about the noise, but seeing the scowl on Lyddington's face — accentuated by his unshaven chin — and observing his height and bearing, he quickly drew back and closed the door.

A servant hastened up the stairs and tapped on Lyddington's door. By this time, he had pulled off his night-shirt and was even now fastening his breeches.

'Why the devil was I not called?' he demanded angrily of the servant. A young lad, he stood staring at the half-naked nobleman with his mouth open, a scared look on his face. 'Did the landlord not tell you to call me?' pursued Lyddington. There was still no reply. 'Oh, never mind,' he said at last in exasperated tones, seeing that he would never get any sense out of him. 'Bring me hot water for shaving and find my groom.' Seeing that the boy showed no signs of moving, he added impatiently, 'Damnation, boy, get a move on! I'm late already!'

On arriving downstairs, he met Ruddles in the taproom.

'There you are, blast you,' said the earl angrily. 'Why the deuce didn't you wake me, you fool? You knew I needed to be up early.'

'You didn't ask me to M'Lord,' replied Ruddles, far too well acquainted with the earl to allow his anger to disconcert him. 'I asked you if I might visit my relations, and when you said I could, I thought you must have changed your mind about setting off again today. I've only just got back; you didn't say nothing about . . . '

'Oh very well, very well,' he said impatiently. Then he turned on the landlord making him jump. 'Why didn't you wake me? You knew I wanted to catch the stage. What the devil were you playing at?'

'Begging Your Lordship's pardon,' said the landlord apprehensively, 'but when you were out so very late, I thought you must've changed your mind. Your Lordship did say as you would ask your groom to wake you.'

He stood anxiously, as Lyddington glared

wrathfully at him, then at Ruddles, and waited for the explosion. It never came. Suddenly, the earl burst out laughing and shook his head.

'What time did the stage leave?' he asked.

'At six, M'Lord.'

The earl stood in thought then at last sat down.

'Well, as we're so late, we might as well have some breakfast,' he said. 'How long will it take the stage to reach Plymouth?'

'About four days, M'Lord,' said the landlord, much relieved at the lightening of the atmosphere.

'Breakfast, then, if you please.' The landlord bowed and left the taproom. Alone with Ruddles, Lyddington went on, 'I've changed my mind. We'll stay in London for a night or two — last night made me realize what I've been missing. Then we'll ride down to Plymouth and pay a visit in form.'

'Very good, M'Lord.' During their ride to London, Lyddington had seen fit to confide in Ruddles some of the story concerning Frances. He had not seemed particularly surprised or shocked, which made the earl wonder whether he had already guessed about Frances' masquerade.

A few minutes later, the landlord re-entered the taproom.

'Will you be drinking ale, M'Lord, or coffee?'

'Ale, if you please. Oh, and Landlord' — reaching into his pocket, he found a shilling — 'the boy who came to my room earlier. I shouted at him, and it wasn't his fault. Give him this, will you?'

* * *

In the event, they stayed in London for five days. The earl had not intended to stay for so long, but once he had made his presence known, he found that there were a number of calls upon his time. By some means his man of business discovered that he was in town and asked for the favour of an interview to discuss various matters. Having obliged him, Lyddington found his mind turning to the family town house in Golden Square. He paid it a brief visit — casting the skeleton staff he kept there into much confusion. Whilst there he inspected it and gave orders that it was to be thoroughly cleaned and prepared for opening, possibly in the near future. This naturally threw the entire staff into a frenzy of speculation.

It also occurred to Lyddington that before approaching Frances with an offer of marriage, he really ought to speak to her father. He therefore spent many hours, a lot of paper and copious oaths attempting to communicate his feelings and intentions. Eventually, with a final 'damn and blast it', he decided that since Frances was of age, and since their acquaintance had taken place under such unconventional circumstances, he might be forgiven for neglecting some of the usual forms.

He did manage to write to his sister very early on, letting her know about his movements. On the morning of their departure from London, he received a prompt reply from her, which gave him considerable amusement, and sent him on his way in a state of great good humour.

The earl and Ruddles at last set out from London nearly a week after they had arrived. They followed the post road, setting off on their own horses (which Ruddles had collected on their first day in the capital). Now that his lordship had decided to take his time, they took the journey in easy stages, stopping overnight in Basingstoke, Yeovil and Exeter.

As Lyddington rode into Plymouth with the intention of seeking Frances out immediately, he was assailed by sudden doubts. He had enjoyed his time in London and all the preparations he had made there, including the setting of his house in order, the discussion of possible settlements with his lawyer and the purchase of a ring, even now reposing in the pocket of his coat.

The journey had also passed pleasantly. In fact, it had been so reminiscent of the many journeys that he and Ruddles had passed in each other's company over the years, that he could almost have fancied himself on the Continent again. Now, however, he began to be anxious.

When they had started on the journey, he had been all impatience to find Frankie as soon as possible, and tell her of his feelings and true intentions. Then, when the journey had been interrupted, he had decided that it was providential. Surely, Frankie would prefer him to declare himself in her own home, rather than in the rush and bustle of an inn? And if, as he suspected, her masquerading days were done, she would certainly prefer him to propose to her when she had accustomed herself once more to female attire. She would also have had a chance to rest and recover from her journey, to settle in, and to forget some of the hurtful things that Lady Valeria had said.

Now, however, his delay seemed to him to be neglectful rather than considerate. Far from forgetting about what had been said, Frankie would more likely have been brooding upon it, and becoming more distressed. What if her distress had been such that instead of coming home, as they had all surmised, she had fled elsewhere?

So preoccupied was he with his thoughts that he allowed Ruddles to lead him to an inn without his even noticing where they were. He dismounted, still in abstraction, but then suddenly pulled himself together.

'Ruddles, I'm going to find her now,' he declared. 'Reserve accommodation for us and see to the horses — I'll hire another from the inn — and with any luck, next time you see me, you'll be able to wish me joy!'

* * *

For Frances and Ruby, in practical terms, the journey from London to Plymouth had been trouble-free and uneventful. They seemed to have picked a week when few people wanted to take that particular route, and for a substantial part of the way, they had the inside of the coach to themselves.

Frances welcomed the privacy. On arriving at the inn in London where they were to stay for the night, they had gone up to the room that they were to share, and there Frances had told Ruby the whole story of what had happened.

When Frances had first confessed to her that she loved the earl, it had not really come as a surprise to Ruby. She had been watching her nursling very carefully, and had become aware of her awakening feelings, almost before Frances herself. A realist, she was not surprised that the earl had made an improper suggestion — after all, was that not what she had feared all these years, and was that not why she had always been so opposed to the idea of Frances dressing as a man?

All her motherly instincts came to the fore, even whilst she nursed a certain perverse satisfaction at being right all along. She had been all for turning round and giving Lady Valeria a piece of her mind, but Frances had managed to prevent that, and after the journey had begun, her sole desire was to get Frances back home, and restore her spirits.

This proved to be harder than she had expected. After that first night in London, Frances had kept her feelings to herself. She had very easily gone back to being Miss Sutcliffe, and to the servants and to any neighbours that she might meet she was the same as ever. But Ruby could see that she lacked sparkle, and always she refused to talk about Lyddington.

Whenever the opportunity arose, she was out in the garden, wandering around, her thoughts clearly miles away. At times Ruby wondered whether she would ever get over this, her first and possibly last, love. And Frances herself was convinced that she never would.

* * *

Having procured an acceptable mount and obtained directions, Lyddington was off at once towards the outskirts of Plymouth. Following the instructions he was given, he soon realized that they must have almost passed the Sutcliffes' house on their way into the town.

Thankfully for his temper, the house was much more easily found than that of Joe and Nellie Baynes, and in a very short time, he was knocking on the door of the white, square-built country house, having first taken his horse round to the stables. Smaller than Lyddington Court, it was aesthetically more pleasing, being much better proportioned, and it was undoubtedly a gentleman's residence.

To Lyddington, it seemed to take an eternity for anyone to answer the door. Before it opened he had already glanced at his watch and realized that it was six o'clock in the evening — a most peculiar time for paying a social call. In addition, all his doubts about his possible reception had returned in full force, so that by the time he was admitted, he was thoroughly on the defensive.

'Lyddington, for Miss Sutcliffe,' he said briefly, having searched in his pocket for visiting cards and failed to find any.

'Certainly, Mr Lyddington, if you will . . . ' began the butler courteously.

'Lord Lyddington, damn your eyes,' snapped the earl. 'And why the devil did it take you so long to answer the door?'

'Please don't swear at my servants,' said a voice that he recognized. Coming from behind the butler was a stately young woman, her blonde hair dressed high upon her head, her gown of blue sprigged with cream rustling as she walked. She made a formal curtsy and Lyddington found himself bowing in response. He had known that she would look very different when properly gowned, but he had not expected the sight of her to take his breath away.

'Wine for His Lordship, please Underwood,' she said to the butler. 'If you would come this way, My Lord.'

The earl followed her for a few steps, then collected himself and bellowed in a voice the like of which this gracious house had never witnessed before, 'Why the deuce did you run away from me, eh? Answer me that!' He seized hold of her arm. Frances whitened a little and shook herself free.

Underwood hesitated, and ventured to say, 'Miss Frances, shall I send for the footman?'

'To throw me out?' asked Lyddington, his brows drawn together. 'Don't be so damn silly. I've only come to make her an offer.'

'Yes, and I know exactly what kind of offer you mean,' retorted Frances, forgetting about Underwood's presence in the agitation of the moment.

'The devil you do,' replied the earl. 'You ran off before I could make myself plain.'

'It was plain enough . . . ' she began, blushing.

'No it bloody well wasn't!' roared the earl, at the end of his patience. 'You should have stayed to listen instead of running off in that brainless way!'

'Why? To be insulted, just as you are insulting me now in my house?' demanded Frances, her bosom heaving in a way that Lyddington would have found downright fascinating had he not been too angry to appreciate it properly. 'What exactly do you want, My Lord?'

'I want to marry you, you silly slut!'

There was a profound silence. Underwood, deciding that he had now heard the juiciest part of the conversation, and reckoning that refreshment was definitely needed, retreated to find some wine.

Frances stared at the earl for a long time, and then said, 'Come . . . come into the saloon please, My Lord.'

The saloon was a bright, airy room which caught the best of the evening sun, and gave the occupant agreeable views of a garden into which the Sutcliffes had put their best endeavours. Unfortunately, neither of the present occupants was in a suitable state of mind to notice such things.

Frances stood with a fast-beating heart. Here was Lyddington offering her everything that she could wish for, yet she was assailed by doubts. What if he were just proposing because he felt guilty? Or maybe Lady Valeria had had a change of heart — perhaps through speaking to Briar or to her father — and had persuaded him that he must offer out of duty? Whatever the reason, his proposal of marriage had hardly been of the stuff of which a girl's dreams are made.

Stealing a look at him, she saw on his face an expression so full of rueful dismay that she began to laugh. The earl, never one to remain angry for long, soon joined in and in no time at all, they had both fallen prey to helpless mirth. The laughter certainly improved the atmosphere considerably, and when it had subsided, Lyddington moved closer to Frances and took her hand.

'That wasn't what I planned to say,' he admitted, still looking down at her hand and absently caressing the back of it with his thumb in a way that Frances found quite pleasurable. 'I've made a terrible botch of it, I'm afraid. I've only proposed twice before: once was to m'sister's governess when I was thirteen — and she very gently refused me, the second time was to Alfreda, and that was very formal. Everything had been arranged beforehand, even down to the lines that I should say. But with you . . . '

'It's all right, Sarrell,' said Frances, thinking that she ought to take her hand from his, but not wanting to because she wanted to relish the opportunity of touching him, perhaps for the last time. 'I knew that you never planned to meet someone like me. There is no need to feel guilty or . . . or obliged to marry me for any reason.'

He looked up, then.

'Guilty? Obliged? Now when have you ever known me to do anything for reasons such as those?' demanded the earl.

Frankie smiled inwardly. He might not

think that he ever did, but his whole life was built on obligation and duty. True, he had been away for many years, but since his return, he had unstintingly made himself available to those who depended upon him for their livelihood. He had not wanted to play host to his sister's guests, but he had done so. And she had seen for herself how regret for hasty words spoken in anger would often cause him to seek out the offended person and compensate them in some way.

She did not say any of these things out loud, but murmured instead, 'You cannot have considered the scandal, My Lord. There is bound to be talk . . . '

'Is there? Why so?'

'Because you would be marrying a girl who had dressed as a man; worked on the land for her living; the daughter of a tradesman . . . '

'Not at all,' replied the earl blandly. Frankie had moved away from him, but he made no attempt to detain her, and instead took a letter out of his pocket. 'I should be marrying the daughter of Thomas Sutcliffe, gentleman, whose young nephew, recently employed on my estate, has gone overseas in search of rare plants, and will, I fear, succumb to some virulent infection in the near future.' He sighed, and shook his head. 'Such an . . . unusual young man, with so many, ah . . . unexpected qualities!'

Frances turned then, confusion written all over her face. The earl waved his letter at her.

'M'sister and Mrs Storringe cooked this up between them. Once I'd decided to stay in town and let you get home before I came to see you, I wrote to Valeria telling her of my plans. She wrote back — she is very regretful of the things she said to you by the way — and told me of the story that she and your ingenious friend have invented between them. Incidentally, all the other ladies have departed now, but your father remains as our guest.' He was silent for a moment. 'By the way, your water garden has now been repaired. I don't suppose we will ever know for sure who did it, but I feel certain in my own mind that it must have been Peter Rance.'

Frances thought back to the moment when the damage to the garden had been discovered. It had been at that time, she now recalled, that she had realized that she was in love with the earl.

'Do you really think that your sister has forgiven me?' she asked him.

'It would appear so.'

'And my father can continue with the commission?'

'Certainly; but without you, I'm afraid. As my wife, I cannot allow you to do more than appear in a supervisory capacity.'

'But, Sarrell, I have not yet agreed . . . '

The earl strode swiftly over to her then, and took hold of her shoulders.

'But dammit all, Frankie, you must agree.' He went on rather diffidently, 'I've no skill at making speeches; well, I suppose I have if it don't matter to me. If you were Felicia Cranborne and I wanted to get you into bed, then I could string together as many pretty words as you please. But I . . . this matters to me, Frankie, more than anything.'

Hardly daring to allow herself to hope, she looked up at him and saw on his swarthy, pock-marked face a look so tender that it almost took her breath away. But even now, she dared not take anything for granted.

'Why . . . why does it matter so much to you — that I marry you?' she asked tentatively.

'Why?' asked the earl in puzzlement. 'Well, haven't I just been telling you? It's because I'm head over ears in love with you, you silly wench!'

She smiled tremulously.

'Well I suppose it's better than slut,' she murmured. Sarrell had the grace to flush a little.

'Forgive me! I told you I was no hand at speeches,' he reminded her.

'I know,' she said smiling. 'But then, that isn't why I . . . I love you.'

With a sigh of relief, he pulled her into his arms and they remained still for a moment, holding tightly to one another, Lyddington's cheek resting on her hair — and thus doing severe damage to its careful styling — and Frankie nestling close to his chest, and feeling that for all her recent journeying, she had only now at this moment really come home.

By mutual consent, they drew apart.

'Well, Miss Sutcliffe? Will you be my wife?' asked the earl, his arrogant tones belied by the gentle laughter in his eyes.

'With all my heart,' replied Frankie. He pulled her close to him again, and this time their lips met in a kiss which for both of them, held so much promise for the future.

'Well,' remarked the earl as soon as he was able. 'The *décolletage* is all that I hoped for, and from this height, I get an excellent view' — and here Frankie blushed — 'but as for these skirts, it is as I feared; I cannot get quite so close to you.'

'Perhaps I should set a new fashion by wearing breeches,' suggested Frankie playfully, caressing his shoulders as she stood in the circle of his arms.

'Perhaps; personally, I am much more consoled by the idea that our wedding night will remedy the matter,' he returned, thus renewing her embarrassment.

Thankfully for Frankie's blushes, Underwood chose this moment to enter with the wine. With a keen instinct for the needs of the occasion, he had waited for as long as he had dared, and had used his initiative with regard to his selection from Mr Sutcliffe's cellar. He put the tray down on the side-board and said with every evidence of satisfaction,

'Champagne, My Lord!'

Other titles in the Ulverscroft Large Print Series:

STRANGER IN THE PLACE

Anne Doughty

Elizabeth Stewart, a Belfast student and only daughter of hardline Protestant parents, sets out on a study visit to the remote west coast of Ireland. Delighted as she is by the beauty of her new surroundings and the small community which welcomes her, she soon discovers she has more to learn than the details of the old country way of life. She comes to reappraise so much that is slighted and dismissed by her family — not least in regard to herself. But it is her relationship with a much older, Catholic man, Patrick Delargy, which compels her to decide what kind of life she really wants.

BLACKBERRY SUMMER

Phyllis Hastings

Debbie converted a wing of the old farmhouse into an Academy for Young Ladies. She hoped this would enable her to make provision for her children's future careers. But she could not foresee the disastrous fire or the regret and guilt she would feel for giving her youngest son to be reared by her twin sister Dolly. Next to the farm, Dolly's wealthy husband Christopher built an imposing mansion in the Gothic style, and planned to run a racing stable, but his schemes were doomed to end in tragedy.

THE SURGEON'S APPRENTICE

Arthur Young

1947: Young Neil Aitken has worked hard to secure a place at Glasgow University to study medicine. Bearing in mind the Dean's warning that it takes more than book-learning to become a doctor, he sets out to discover what that other elusive quality might be. He learns the hard way, from a host of memorable characters ranging from a tyrannical surgeon to the bully on the farm where Neil works in his spare time, and assorted patients who teach him about courage and vulnerability. Neil also meets Sister Annie, the woman who is to influence his life in every way.